I0835791

The Sacred Impostor

The Sacred Impostor

A NOVEL

J R Lankford

Great Reads Books

Published by Great Reads Books
P. O. Box 2112
Bellaire, TX 77402

ISBN 0-9718694-5-6
LCCN 2012930938

Manufactured in the United States of America

To Tenochtitlán
and my beloved brother,
John Porter Rhines

Chapter 1

New York City

On a gray New York afternoon, a limousine glided into Central Park West and cut across on 96th, passing where the old Boston Post Road used to be—where stagecoaches and men on horseback once delivered the New York/Boston mail. Maggie Clarissa Johnson's former employer, Felix Rossi, once told her this story and now that she was about to deliver a personal message to him, she remembered. Maggie hadn't wanted to tell Felix over the phone. She needed to see his face. He didn't even know she was coming to New York.

Signal light blinking, the limo veered from traffic and stopped in front of an exclusive Fifth Avenue address. Maggie gazed at the nine-story stone building she hadn't seen in eleven years—its green awning spanning the wide sidewalk.

Next to her in the limo, Sam Duffy, her fiancée, looked like an Irish-American prince, all 6'2" of his rugged frame ennobled by a Prada suit he'd bought at her request to honor *the missing boy.* That's what everyone in Arona, Italy, where they'd lived, had taken to calling him—the missing boy. They couldn't issue a death certificate with no record of his existence, no birth certificate or passport. With a murder charge possible, her otherwise kind neighbors acted like they'd imagined Jess Johnson.

Sam squeezed her hand and she didn't withdraw, though she wanted to.

Tears again. They happened all the time, now, like steady rain. Her son wasn't missing; he was dead. Her precious Jess, only ten years old. There was no body to bury, no funeral to attend. Sam and Felix left him unprotected and now he was dead. Given who he was, there could be no public memorial. Her mourning clothes themselves were his funeral. They were the only wreath Jess would receive. This black limo and her heart were his hearse.

"Well, here we are, Maggie, my girl," Sam said. "Here we are."

Days ago she would have thrilled at Sam's touch, grateful he was alive and he'd asked her to be his wife; but Maggie had lost track of who she used to be.

She gripped her Bible and stepped onto the building's red carpet. A strolling white-haired couple stopped and gazed at her and Sam. Someone passing on a bike slowed and stared. Then a man in a suit and another and another, until they'd had drawn a minor crowd. Onlookers probably wondered if they'd be on the evening news, getting out of a limo dressed as they were.

Sheer veils falling from her elegant hat's wide brim, Maggie stayed by the limo and let them look. For most of her life, she had been a domestic worker and, for ten years, a frugal stay-at-home mom, but on her way home she'd stopped in Milan. Digging into untouched savings, she told shopkeepers on the famous Via Montenapoleone that money was no object for her mourning clothes. Maggie didn't regard herself as a beauty—5'6" inches, 140 lbs, dark sienna skin, the features of her African ancestors—but she had achieved her shopping goal.

No one could mistake she was in grief for someone magnificent and once alive.

Like Jackie Kennedy, Nancy Reagan, the Queen Mother, Maggie had dressed to symbolize her loss.

The king was dead.

Numbly she peeped from under her hat brim at the building's glass doors, amazed that her eyes saw and her mind still comprehended. Inside this building, she'd begged Felix Rossi to implant an embryo in her womb. She'd always wanted a child—such good luck that she, a simple housemaid from Harlem, worked for a brilliant scientist in need of a surrogate mother. God's will that she was a virgin at the time.

"Wait here, Maggie," Sam said. "Let me make sure that creep who replaced me is gone."

She watched Sam approach the doors he'd once guarded.

He'd been the doorman. She'd been the eighth floor tenants' maid. In secret, he'd been head of security for Theomund Brown who'd lived in the penthouse above them.

As Sam reached for the door, a red-haired woman came through. Maggie stopped breathing. Was it Coral, who'd worked for Brown? Sam stared at the red hair, too, but it wasn't Coral, just a woman with a great dye job.

At Brown's behest, Coral had entertained many of his powerful guests in bed, yet Sam had almost fallen for her, harlot though she was. At the time, Maggie hadn't understood why. Now she did.

Suddenly the building doorman appeared. Maggie didn't recognize him and, apparently, neither did Sam, who came back nodding reassuringly and took her arm. Now that Brown was dead, his people must be gone.

They went inside.

Sam said to the new doorman, "Would you call up to the eighth floor and tell Felix Rossi that Sam Duffy and Maggie Johnson are here?"

"Of course, señor," the man said.

She noticed Sam raised his eyebrows when the doorman said señor.

As they waited, she gazed at their reflection in the floor-to-ceiling mirrors, satisfied that in death, if not in life, they were adequately honoring Jess. Maggie knew the building guards watched through the lobby monitors and, if Theomund Brown were alive, would secretly be telling him that she and Sam were here.

When the elevator came, the doorman entered the eighth floor code then let them on.

As each floor number lit, Maggie's heart sped up. Felix had provided a home for her and Jess in Italy all this time, so they could hide from the world and their pursuer, Mr. Brown.

The elevator slowed.

The doors opened onto Felix's private vestibule, the same two blue and yellow Majolica vases still there in recesses on either side.

Not quite as shiny as in the five years Maggie had cleaned them.

The double doors opened and there was Felix, wearing gray slacks and one of the linen-wool-silk jackets she used to clean for him. This one was a washed blue, well-worn, as he liked them. He looked like royalty. He swept his black hair out of his eyes and stared as if he were seeing an optical illusion.

"Sam? Maggie? What in the world—" He stopped, his gaze on Maggie's mourning clothes. "Why didn't you tell me you were coming?"

She lifted her veils.

"Where's Jess?" Felix's voice rose as he spoke.

Maggie gazed at his moving lips, stepped forward and struck him in the face.

Felix staggered. "Ow! For God's sake, why did you do that?"

Sam grabbed her lace-gloved hand.

Crying again. Last week she watched Jess sail his dinghy on Italy's Lake Maggiore in front of their yellow villa. Today she couldn't stop crying because she'd never see him again. She put her hands to her face and shook her head, thinking this couldn't be happening, felt Sam's arm around her.

Sam said, "Steady yourself, Felix. We didn't want to tell you over the phone and since Maggie wanted to come back to New York—"

"Jess is dead!" Maggie spit out.

Horror on Felix's face. He screamed, "Ah, no!" as if he'd crack open heaven with his voice. Again he backed up, disbelief in his eyes.

The king was dead.

Felix's sister, auburn-haired and womanly; his wife, fragile and pale, were swiftly behind him in the hall, asking what was wrong, begging him to be quiet or he'd wake Ariel, Felix's daughter, whom Maggie had never met.

Sam grabbed Felix by the shoulders and then pulled him close, patting his back. "I'm so sorry, man."

"Let go of me!" Felix gasped. "Jess can't be dead!"

His sister and his wife cried out and went to Felix, comforting him. They forgot about Maggie, standing there sobbing in her mourning clothes, as Felix screamed, "Ah!" like he was dying.

Felix was the one who broke away and came to her. He dropped to his knees and put his face in her stomach, wrapped his arms around her and wailed, "Oh, Maggie! Oh, God!"

She wanted to put out his eyes, this Judas who had left them alone and vulnerable, just like Sam had.

"How? How did he die?" Felix demanded.

"Carlo Morelli threw stones at him," she replied.

"One of the neighbors?" Felix cried. "He's dead because of me! Morelli wouldn't have set foot on the villa's grounds if I'd been there. I should have stayed. I chose my own child instead of the boy I cloned. Maggie, forgive me!" He squeezed her tighter.

At least he wasn't asking her to believe the ridiculous: that Felix, a Harvard-trained physician and Sam, a former detective, couldn't foresee Carlo Morelli's danger to her precious boy.

They'd murdered Jess.

Her son was killed by the action and inaction of three men: Felix and Sam who left them, then Carlo Morelli who threw stones at her son.

"Where is Jess? Where's his body!" Felix demanded.

"He disappeared," Maggie said.

"What?"

"He vanished, just like Jesus."

Felix gripped her arms. "Maggie, what are you saying?"

"Be careful!" came Sam's voice. "Maggie's pregnant again." But Felix seemed not to hear.

A twenty-dollar test had confirmed it and Maggie shuddered at the reminder. She'd thought heaven sent Sam to be her Joseph. If that were true, Jess would still be alive. That the devil sent Sam to pave the way for Jess's death hadn't crossed her mind until six days ago. If so, she was hatching a viper's eggs in the womb that had carried the Son of God.

That's who Felix had cloned using DNA he stole from the Shroud of Turin—the Son of God. Over the years, Felix had come to doubt that, but Maggie knew for sure. After all, she'd raised

Jess. *Get control of yourself.*

She found herself stroking Felix's hair like she used to when he lost courage or faith during her first pregnancy. She listened in detachment as he screamed, "Ah God!" and begged for a pardon she'd never give.

"I said leave her alone!" Sam repeated and angrily pulled Felix away.

Maggie found herself being hugged on both sides by Felix's adored sister Frances and Adeline, his cherished wife, while Sam fumed, "You and me are responsible for this, but nothing, no one, is ever going to hurt Maggie again!"

Red-eyed, Felix got to his feet and for a moment Maggie thought he and Sam would fight, but they didn't. They sighed, apologized, put their arms around each other, and stumbled into the apartment, Sam explaining the inexplicable. Watching them, Maggie longed for the times when, for different reasons, they'd made her the happiest woman on earth.

Jess's death wasn't foreordained. It couldn't have been. God wouldn't roll back the stone that held Jess in the world, reach down, and take him home, breaking her heart for no reason. This could only be Satan's work.

Frances and Adeline helped Maggie inside and closed the door.

"Maggie, I'm so, so sorry," Adeline said. She still looked like an angel with her blonde hair and grey eyes. Her child by Felix was still alive.

Sam's voice was full of devotion. "Maggie. I'm here. I'm here."

As if that mattered, now.

How could she lie beside Sam and love him? How could she possibly bear his child? Raising Jess to manhood had been her life's purpose so he could save the world.

The old Maggie died when Jess did. In her place a new woman had put on the garments of vengeance as in Isaiah and wrapped herself in zeal as in a cloak. *Grief thoughts.*

Jess's voice came back to her in a scene from only weeks ago:

"Chi sono io? Chi sono io?" he'd asked. Who am I?

She'd knelt and hugged him.

He whispered, "Please tell me, Mamma. I feel old enough to know the truth, no matter what it is. Sometimes I think I have always been old." He pulled back and stroked her cheek. "I think you are afraid that I won't love you. Is that it? Do not worry. Even if you are really not my mother, have no fear. When I think of love, I think of you. You are pure, so beautiful ... *Ti voglio bene, Mamma.* Always."

Fresh tears slid down her face.

Gently, Frances and Adeline took off Maggie's couture hat with the veils. Being rich, they probably knew it must be the best hat in Milan. They teased a lace umbrella from her grip. Standing front and back they slid her long jacket off as if she were a priest and they were removing holy garments.

Maggie lingered in this hallway she knew so well, the same Persian carpet runner, the same paintings, the same soft parquet floor. Midway down, a heavy silver crucifix—the most beautiful she'd ever seen—still hung above the ebony prie-dieu on which the Rossi family knelt and prayed. It no longer deceived her. How foolish she'd been to allow her faith to slip into the loosey-goosey Christianity in fashion today when she'd been taught the truth as a child in her Baptist Church. Her eyes had been opened, though. Maggie couldn't see the mark of Satan, but she knew he was here.

"Oh, Maggie," Adeline said and covered her mouth. She rushed off, saying she'd make tea.

In the formal living room she'd once cleaned as a maid, under its nine-foot ceiling, beneath its original Modigliani, Maggie sat on the sofa by the charcoal drapes and let everyone comfort her. She put her head on their shoulders and hugged them back when she was hugged, but in her heart she was waiting for a sign from God.

Chapter 2

Coral Anders approached the building's glass doors, her red hair tossed by the wind, her hips gently swaying under a feathered sleeveless dress. An uncharacteristic New York Indian Summer had delayed October's fall leaves. Regretting she'd have to accustom herself to the sound of cabs honking instead of water lapping against a boat and the smell of garbage in Manhattan on hot afternoons instead of sea water, she reached for the bronze door handle of the Fifth Avenue building where Theomund Brown, her former employer, had lived since she'd known him. In her hand she clasped the newspaper with the headline announcing his death, "American Billionaire Dead In Italy."

An unfamiliar face appeared, a man dressed in the uniform of the building's doormen.

"May I help you, señorita?"

Señorita? She couldn't recall hearing a doorman speak Spanish in New York. "I'm here to see … to locate Luis," she said. "He was Theomund Brown's butler? Brown lived in the penthouse?"

"Sí, el señor Luis. He lives in the penthouse still."

Coral hid her surprise.

"And your name?" the new doorman asked.

"Coral. He knows me. Just call up."

"*Ahorita mismo*, Señorita Coral," the man said and ushered her into the marble lobby. As he disappeared to call upstairs, Coral sank onto the upholstered bench where she'd first flirted with Sam Duffy who'd been the doorman at the time—two centuries ago, or so it felt. Now Sam was in Italy with Maggie and her son.

The new doorman returned. "Señor Luis will see you," he said. He called the penthouse elevator and waited for it to come.

When it did, he punched a code on the keypad and held the door until she entered.

The door closed and in the expensive car's silent ascent, Coral wondered what it meant that Luis, the butler, lived in the penthouse still. Theomund had been dead more than a month.

The car stopped. The doors opened.

There was Luis, transformed. Instead of the nondescript suits he used to wear, he had on boots, black pants, and a traditional Guayabera linen shirt like those she'd seen in Acapulco. He'd abandoned his American hairstyle and slicked his hair back from his face, accenting chiseled features and a frank gaze—not an intimidating one like Theo's had been, but penetrating nonetheless. In his left hand he held a red leather pouch sporting a woven black and white abstract design. She saw the hilt of an ornate silver dagger.

Never before had she thought of Luis as foreign. Now there was no doubt he was an arresting Latino male in his element, as well as his prime.

"Aztec?" she said, pointing at the pouch.

"Mexica to be precise," he said in disdain and offered his hand. "Hello, Coral."

"Hello, Luis," she replied and took his hand, noting his grasp was as cool as ever. "Were you going to stab someone?"

He appraised her with a slow smile that would put no one at ease. "This is an antique I have sought for a long time. It just arrived."

"Oh. Congratulations. Well, I tried to phone, but the number I used for Theo is disconnected. I was hoping you still have my diamond bracelet that broke when I was here. Theo put it in his desk and said he'd have it fixed."

"Yes, it is here. We have other business as well. Come in. I'm glad to see you."

Coral wondered what business he meant.

Head slightly bowed, a man waited at the library door as they approached. He wore a loose white shirt over simple pants. Luis nodded to him and the man left on silent feet shod in what resembled black espadrilles.

Luis entered the library that had belonged to Theomund Brown, sat in his former boss's high-backed chair and, motioning Coral to a leather couch, lifted his booted feet to the surface of the rare American chestnut desk.

Coral knew what to do when in doubt. She flashed a seductive smile. "Well, things have changed, I see."

"I am no longer the butler here."

"That's certainly plain."

She turned away, feigning disinterest in him in favor of the new artwork on the walls. Gone were Theomund's photos of his dad at Africa's Tsumeb mine, the richest ever found. They'd been replaced by what looked to Coral like a replica of an ancient Aztec calendar. Round and studded with gemstones, predominately red ones, she recognized the grinning face of the blond Aztec sun god at its center, its tongue an obsidian knife demanding sacrifice.

There were images of jaguars and eagles that might have come from Aztec temples. In one corner, a post supported a leather saddle, intricately embroidered, studded with silver, its seat cushioned in lamb's wool. Fit for a conquistador, it cost thousands of dollars if it cost a cent. What was going on?

"May I ask what you are now, if not a butler?"

The loose-shirted attendant entered and, bowing, placed a tray before Luis on the desk.

"Gracias," said Luis and lowered his boots to the floor. He stood, poured a drink in a glass, and handed it to Coral. As she took it, Luis said, "I am Theomund Brown's heir."

Her eyes widened. "Didn't Theo have a sister?"

"He gave her money before he died. Theomund would never leave an empire like this to a … I shall be kind and call her a scatterbrain."

Coral didn't miss a beat. She tilted her head, dimpled, blinked, and swept her eyelashes up in an expression that said, *you're just too wonderful for words* as her mind screamed, *Why the hell did you do that, Theo?* The New York County probate records would be her next stop.

Giving no sign of her distress, her lips cooed and she

breathed, "Oooooo. Congratulations, Luis. You're just the man for it, too."

Her target was Luis's vanity, not his manhood, which she'd always doubted. Now she wasn't so sure.

Whenever she came to visit Theo's clients over the years, Luis would coldly inspect her hair and makeup, her nails, her half-naked body. At Theo's bidding, Luis sometimes watched through hidden cameras to assess her performance with the men. Never once had he seemed moved by her or what he saw.

Strange, because even now that she was almost forty, men still became tongue-tied—fell all over themselves—in her presence. Good men, bad men, rich and poor, young and old, American and foreign. That's why Theomund Brown had paid her a quarter million a year, plus bonuses.

Now Brown was dead. She was there when it happened, saw who pushed him to his death, and she wasn't really sorry. All Coral would miss were the salary checks.

"You're curious about the will, I assume." Luis said.

Coral shifted, feeling uneasy. "Well, lover, perhaps you were, but I already know I'm in it."

As soon as the Italian *politzia* cleared her to leave the country, she'd called Brown's lawyers and been assured her inheritance would keep until she arrived—*such as it was*. Disturbing phrase. She'd brought Brown's yacht from Italy on the slow route around the Mediterranean that he'd originally planned—treating herself to three last glorious weeks of freedom on Theo's dime. She'd caught a flight home from Gibraltar, leaving the crew to sail the yacht across the Atlantic to Long Island Sound. She already had an appointment with the lawyers later today to find out what *such as it was* meant.

He laughed. "I too already knew."

It made sense when Coral thought about it. After Sam's betrayal, Brown had relied on Luis more and more. He was smart and frighteningly loyal—probably would have shot someone if Theo ordered him to, but Theo kept the dirty work far afield.

"For your sake," Luis continued, "I hope you have saved some of your money over the years, if you plan to continue with *tu vida de princesita.*"

"My princess life? You never spoke Spanish before, Luis, why now? And you don't know how I live."

"It was never to my advantage to speak my native tongue before and I do know how you live."

"How would that be?"

"Beyond your means."

She decided to moan cutely—like a little girl. It was true. From her quarter million salary she hadn't saved a dime and, except for regular donations to a women's shelter, she'd spent it all on herself, running up massive bills at Bergdorf and Harry Winston's. Sometimes Brown paid them off as a bonus.

"Do you understand finances?" Luis asked, pulling the silver dagger from its pouch. She decided he looked like a Mexican drug lord: romantic and dangerous.

"What do you mean?"

"How much would Theomund have had to leave you if he wanted you to continue living as you do?"

Coral wiggled her eyebrows up. "A lot, I guess. Why do you ask?"

"Let's make it simple. Pretend there is no such thing as inflation, that America rescues itself from economic suicide and the stock market obliges you by resuming its average rise of eleven percent a year. Each month, you take out one twelfth of your previous income."

"Okay, if you say so."

"How much would you need to invest, today, to do this until, let's say, you are eighty-five years old?"

"I'll bite. How much?"

"Roughly two and a half million dollars."

"Is that right? You did that in your head?"

"No, I looked it up."

She sought his eyes. "Why?"

"Of course, the stock market is fitful, inflation exists and you Americans have turned governing into a blood sport. It would be safer to start with more."

Coral unfolded herself from the sofa and stood, brushing at her pale dress, its soft draped top accenting her cleavage. When she put her hands on her hips and swayed over to the desk, the cream-and-brown-feathered skirt drifted, revealing her legs as she walked. Luis stood, smiling at her in an unfriendly way. She knew better than to put herself at a man's mercy without having a hold over him—his mind, his heart, his cock, something.

"Let me guess," she said, placing her hand on an eagle statue on his desk. "Theomund didn't leave me much of anything, but you, *amiguito mio*, want to help me out." She was grateful Theo had made her learn Spanish; glad she had the sense to dress for this visit, just in case.

"Sí, perhaps."

Coral reached over and flicked the fringe on his Aztec knife pouch. It was time to test her instincts about this man. "What are you up to, Luis? Living in some kind of fantasy? Are you Mexican? Mexican-American? Why are you dressed like a gaucho in a museum?"

"The gaucho is South American. I am Mexican."

"What are all these jaguars and eagles on the goddamned wall?"

He caught her waving hand, looked into her eyes, and tightened his grip.

"Show some respect when you talk to me."

"Oh yeah?" Following her instincts, Coral raised her voice. "Who the hell do you think you are?"

"Moctezuma!" Luis growled and slung her arm away. He sat down, thumping his boots up on the desk.

Coral kept her balance. "What?"

"My name is Luis Tepiltzin Moctezuma."

"You're kidding, right?"

"Would you like to see my birth certificate?" Luis picked up the glass and, breathing angrily, threw his head back and drank as she sniggered. "Stop laughing!"

She stopped.

"Moctezuma II had an empress, two queens, several wives as

well as concubines. Cortés secretly slept with one of those wives. I don't mean La Malinche."

Was he crazy? "Who?"

"She was the traitor who helped Cortés by translating for him and revealing Aztec secrets. But for her, Mexico could not have been conquered so quickly. Bad words come from her name—*malinchista*, a disloyal Mexican, and the very worst, *La Chingada* and its many forms."

"What does it mean exactly?"

"It is like your F word, but worse, a great insult. In the Nahuatl language, *chingar* means to rape. Spanish rape of our women was so widespread that the word became our greatest curse. They gave the name to Malinche."

"But not your ancestor?"

"She didn't help Cortés, but she could not avoid his bed. A son resulted. We have kept the name all this time. I have the blood of the conquistadors as well as those they conquered."

Could he know his family history back to the 1500s? Unlikely, but she would humor him. "What does Tepiltzin mean?"

"It is from our original Nahuatl language. It means privileged son."

Slowly Coral sat back down on the couch, her thighs exposed as the feathers parted. "If that's so, why did you hide it all these years? Why would you put up with being Theo's butler?"

"There is virtue in honest servitude. I am born a peón. There is virtue in serving a patrón. I am born of them as well. I am *mestizo*, like most of my countrymen."

"Every Mexican I've ever met takes pride in their Spanish, not their Indian genes."

He sniffed. "That means you have only met the upper caste and know nothing about my people, but yes, that was the real conquest. Spain brainwashed much of Mexico to be ashamed of its own blood."

"You sound like Che Guevara or somebody."

Luis grunted.

"Moctezuma, huh? I think I'll call you Monty."

"You won't."

She saw he meant it. Coral decided not to speak. The next line was his.

They stared at each other.

"Brown changed his will before he left for Italy," Luis said. "He left you a year's salary—$250,000—to give you time to get on your feet."

She held his gaze.

"You weren't here for the reading of the will." He opened a desk drawer, withdrew an envelope, and handed it to her.

From under half-closed lids Luis watched as Coral unfolded the will. This was one of the moments for which he'd carefully planned. He saw her gaze fly down the altered pages until it reached the paragraph concerning her. Originally Coral hadn't been mentioned in the will, but in a last minute change of heart—perhaps sensing his coming death—Theomund Brown had left her five million dollars, which Luis intended to withhold.

Though she read and reread the paragraph, he knew she wouldn't see the change. A master forger had performed it. Now that Luis, instead of Brown, was the source of their fat fees, the lawyers had happily filed the false amended will. Brown's use of corrupt attorneys had backfired on him.

At length she muttered an obscenity and blinked away disappointment. When she raised her eyes to him, he saw an eagle poised to strike, but he was the jaguar, the patrón, and he would win.

She smiled. "You know I'll check this at probate records."

He didn't move as she searched his face. "Of course."

She lowered her eyelids and then wearily raised them. "What are your plans?"

"I am still deciding."

"If you're going to run the business," she said in a cagey voice, "maybe I can help you, like I helped Brown."

Luis couldn't believe it would be this easy. He had supervised all the women Brown employed to entertain men. Coral had not only learned two other languages, she'd familiarized herself with cars, sports, art, clothes, food, wine, and the issues of the day in order to please Brown's clients. She'd also retained or cultivated a disarming coarseness and with her body could satisfy the lust of nearly any man. She was a courtesan, American-style, not an ordinary whore, and the closest thing Brown had to a companion. She could help him immensely. He had world-changing plans. He had to do this perfectly.

He narrowed his eyes. "Stand up, then."

Coral stood.

"Let me see you. Take off your clothes."

With no hint of being mastered, she responded to command, kicked off shoes that were mere expensive straps over gold-painted toes. Then she slid the feathered dress down to the floor, revealing bare breasts and a lace thong, ran her fingers through chestnut hair, reddish brown like a sunset in a storm, her skin like moonbeams. He knew controlling her wouldn't be easy.

"Come here," he said.

Coral glided, eyes down, around the desk and to his chair.

Appraising her, Luis said, "You look older."

She lifted her right breast and left it fall, her left and let it fall. They bounced like a young goddess's breasts.

"How do you keep them like that?" Luis asked, testing their firmness with his hand.

"I take care of myself," she whispered.

"You are still responsive?" He watched her.

Coral looked at him, her eyes pools of lust. "Find out for yourself, Luis."

He looked away. "No, not me. I'll call someone."

Her gaze turned hard. "All those years of examining me like a horse and you never understood?"

Curiosity overcame him. "What did I miss? What is it?"

Coral slipped off her thong, sat on the desk in front of him, and opened her legs. "Do you remember the story of Adam, Luis?"

"I don't play games with religion."

"Before giving him the breath of life, a mind, or feelings, the Bible says the Creator gave Adam skin and bones and muscle, and said it was good."

Luis snorted in contempt.

She moved her hands to her breasts, massaging. "Then He took a rib from Adam and made Eve—flesh of Adam's flesh. They were naked and unashamed, Luis. Who am I to contradict that?"

"Blasphemy," he said.

"Oh, you're a moral pimp?"

Touching nothing but her breasts, Coral continued until she had an orgasm. Luis could see with his own eyes she wasn't faking. He tried not to look impressed.

"All right, you've got the job, but I can't pay you the same. I've got startup expenses. How about $150,000 a year?"

Coral was already getting back into her clothes. Instead of answering she tossed her chestnut hair over her shoulder and walked out of the library. Startled, Luis rose and followed her onto the wide terrace, treading heavily in his boots. Already he'd changed things here. Gone were the potted pines and sedate shrubbery, replaced by birds of paradise, hibiscus, bamboo, and succulent greenery. Marble had been replaced by Terra Cotta tiles and from cages tropical birds called. No longer open to the air, he had turned the terrace into a greenhouse rain forest.

Without asking, she found a chaise and, as he'd seen her do a thousand times before when the place belonged to Brown, flopped down on it, her feathers settling like those of the birds.

"Luis, I won't work for a man until I know him," she said.

He couldn't think of an answer.

"Order us a couple of margaritas or something and let's talk."

"With this insolence you could lose everything," he said.

Coral shrugged and sat up.

He relented. "I'll overlook it once. We'll talk."

The man with black espadrilles reappeared. "Two margaritas on the rocks."

The man bowed. "*Sí, jefe.*"

Coral watched the servant leave. "Who is he?"

"My cousin."

"No kidding? And the new doorman?"

"My uncle."

Coral lay back and gazed at Luis with an inquisitive expression, her body lazy from the pleasure she'd given herself. For a moment Luis envied her—to be so uninhibited, so in tune with the physical. What must it feel like?

"We are strangers to each other," Coral said, "even after all these years."

Pleased with his progress, Luis rested his boot on a stone sculpture of a jaguar. "Not for long."

Chapter 3

Ariel Rossi didn't comply when Maggie said she wanted to be alone. Instead of leaving the solarium, Ariel entered and sat nearby on a Moroccan rug, her legs crossed, a stuffed grey and white toy horse in her lap, rudely staring straight at Maggie. *What impertinence*. Ariel had inherited more than her dark looks from her father, Felix. She had his arrogance, too.

The child was only eight years old, but it was plain she'd been spoiled and had a stubborn streak. That wouldn't have happened if Maggie had been here to help raise her. Sharmina, who'd taken Maggie's place, liked to say *yes* to everything. She wasn't firm enough for a willful child. Neither was Adeline, Ariel's mother, who was apparently still trying to become love incarnate—giving her time and money away, always gentle and mild. How a woman like that could be married to Felix Rossi, Maggie didn't know.

"Sweetheart, I said I'd like to be alone."

Ariel wrinkled her nose, looked down and galloped her stuffed horse across her lap. The horse resembled Twinkle, her Shetland Pony. It was headstrong and spoiled, too.

"No, you don't," Ariel said.

Maggie stiffened. "I do and, if I need to, I'll go back to my own room."

"Stay here, Auntie Maggie."

It wasn't a command, but Maggie didn't like the child's refusal to do as she was asked. Brown supposedly had her kidnapped to lure Felix back to New York and clear the way for Jess's murder. Brown, himself, had been murdered instead. Yet Jess had died anyway. Satan's work—accomplished through Felix, this child, and Sam. Was the kidnapping even real? Ariel showed no signs of trauma that Maggie could see.

Maggie cleared her throat and spoke kindly, just in case. "Did anything unusual happen to you about a month or so ago?"

Ariel frowned. "No."

"Nothing at all? Nothing strange?"

Ariel pulled at her mouth in thought as she galloped her stuffed horse across the costly fabric of her dress. Suddenly she looked up. "I went to Disney World on a big airplane!"

Maggie wanted to roll her eyes, but she restrained herself. However spoiled and self-absorbed Ariel was, she was only eight. Maggie stared at the orchids Felix's sister liked to grow, sun shining on them through the solarium's glass roof and walls. How could flowers still exist? How could the sun?

"Daddy and Mommy sent a woman to my school with a permission slip and we went straight to the airport. I didn't even have to pack any clothes. She bought me new ones. We stayed in Disney World for days! It was such fun! It was just that one time, though. Mommy and Daddy said they wouldn't ever do it again."

Maggie grew still. "Did you talk to your mommy on the phone while you were there?"

Ariel looked up, uncertainty in her eyes. "No. Every time we called, she didn't answer."

Maggie felt numb, felt regret, said nothing.

"Do you miss your little boy?" Ariel asked.

Miss him? Miss him? Maggie wanted to scream in rage. She took deep breaths, her eyes fixed on an orchid's magenta petals—three inner, three outer, a yellow center where the pollen waited. After a while she realized Ariel had risen and come near. With one arm she cradled her horse. With the other she stroked Maggie's hand.

"If you can't find him, maybe he's not dead. Maybe someone took him to Disney World."

Maggie picked Ariel up, put the girl on her lap. They hugged, saying nothing as the sun shone in.

Sam pulled the charcoal Range Rover to the curb, just one car behind the limo he'd been tailing. It contained the daughter of a society woman who'd asked Duffy Detectives to find out if her offspring was screwing the chauffeur. The daughter was nineteen and into body ink, but the tattoos down both arms were *temporary, thank goodness*, he'd been told. The green streaks in her hair would wash out. The chauffeur was twenty-three, Korean and poor, working his way through NYU at night to get his masters in Global Studies. If the girl didn't come to her senses, rinse the ink, the streaks, and start dating an approved boy, she'd be shipped off to a Swiss boarding school. Sam tried to warn the parents that if they banished their daughter to the Alps, the ink might become permanent, but they hadn't listened.

Today the family limo was supposed to have taken her to Bergdorf's. It was on Fifth Avenue, all right, just not in the correct hundred block. The limo was parked near a store that featured "funky street wear."

Sam settled in to wait, glancing now and then into the empty back seat of the Range Rover. Felix bought it years ago while Maggie was pregnant. He'd kept it garaged at his Cliffs Landing cottage and now that she was back, he'd given it to her. She'd almost delivered Jess in this car.

Whenever he was in it, Sam flashed back to that long-ago night—Maggie gasping in the back seat, Felix trying to stop her labor though he had no drugs, Sam in the luggage compartment returning gunfire from Brown's men. He'd carried Maggie from the Rover into the darkness of Central Park, where he'd gotten into the gun battle that put him in coma for the next ten years, eleven months, and fourteen days of his life. He'd saved Maggie and her baby, but he'd awakened a different man—one with uncontrollable appetites and no memory of himself. Sam came out of it just six weeks ago to find he'd raped the only two women he'd ever loved—Coral, who would have freely given herself to him on any day; and trusting, loving Maggie, still virginal somehow, though she'd given birth.

They both forgave him; at least he hoped they had. The trick was forgiving himself—for that and being dumb enough to leave Maggie and Jess alone.

Sam didn't relish driving this car with all its memories, but Maggie had given it to him for his new business and he couldn't refuse. Whatever agenda she set for their married life, Sam knew a wife and baby needed food and a place to sleep.

He watched as the limo rocked slightly on its springs, the daughter and chauffeur inside. Personally, he had no complaints about the Korean kid. He wasn't raping the girl.

Sam sighed, reminding himself to be grateful for getting back up to speed in New York. As soon as he could leave Maggie for a while, he'd started reacquainting himself with his native city. He'd ridden the subway lines from end-to-end and watched the people. He rode the buses that ran more frequently and drove the streets that had more cars, relishing the wind on his face, the taste of food, getting used to the way people dressed and did their hair—so differently from ten years ago. Once again he'd strolled the neighborhoods, regaining his body's strength, smelling everything from tortillas to croissants baking. He loved seeing the women's eyes—round or oval, dark or light—promising to marry a man in the local *iglesia*, screw his brains out for a day, *nella base*, save his soul or damn him, carry his child or murder him in the night. The old Sam would have pursued a few silent invitations, just to see if he'd survive. The new Sam had one woman's happiness on his mind. Two, if he ever saw Coral again.

Other than the Twin Towers no longer dominating the skyline, the most noticeable change Sam Duffy saw in New York City was its demographics. He estimated the city had swollen by a good half million people, maybe more, in the years he'd lain in a coma under guard at Theomund Brown's.

Using the best excuse to talk to strangers in a city full of tourists, he'd asked directions and struck up conversations. Where were they going? What did they do? He listened for accents, drawing on his youth as a sailor, and recognized nationalities. He was surprised to see more Asians, fewer of both Whites and Blacks, and a surprisingly large number of noses that could have come off the walls of Mayan temples; profiles from Aztec pyramids. If he hadn't known better, he would have thought he was in Texas or another border state.

Last he knew, New York didn't have a single good Mexican restaurant because few of Mexican descent lived here. Now they'd found their way to the big apple and sliced out parts of it for themselves, especially in the Coronado neighborhood of Queens.

On the trains Sam learned that the Puerto Rican Day Parade was no longer the sole big Latino event—boys who manned cameras for the parade's cable access show aiming them at girls' butts. Few faces, just butts, guaranteeing high ratings for cable access coverage of the parade. New York now had big celebrations of Cinco de Mayo, the Day of the Dead, and Mexican independence day, Grito de Dolores, as well. That meant *charro* suits and *china poblana*, the long red and green skirts. A few dozen Mexican hometown associations had sprung up. He heard a new term, Puebla York. It referred to *Poblano*s who came from the state of Puebla and kept the old traditions. Neza York stood for newer immigrants from the crowded settlements surrounding Mexico City. Neza Yorkers often looked down their noses at the more numerous Puebla Yorkers, he was told.

New York had changed and Sam loved it.

Two weeks ago, on the chance it was still there, he'd looked up the Irish bar called Molly Malone's, knowing his old buddies would fill in the gaps of his knowledge. He'd been thrilled to see the green shamrock still hung outside and to find Pat, the bartender, still behind his bar. Sam's previously dark brown hair had gone platinum, but Pat was still a bulky, copper-haired Irish sod. He looked like he'd have a heart attack when Sam opened the door.

"Sam, lad? Sam? My God, boy, you're alive!"

His shout had brought a stampede across the sawdust-covered floor from the dart room in back to Molly Malone's main room, the wood-trimmed green walls still studded with Guinness signs and Irish memorabilia. They were firefighters and policemen, legal hacks, bail bondsmen, cabbies, doormen, and guards.

Charlie, his old rival, said, "I knew they couldn't kill you, boy.

Your head's too thick to break." He'd clasped Sam in his arms.

They drank McSorley's half the night and shook the walls of Molly Malone's with a rousing, stomping, cheering version of "Finnegan's Wake," in honor of Sam:

Tim revives! See how he rises!
Timothy rising from the bed.
Whirl your whisky around like blazes,
Thanum an Dail! Do you think I'm dead?

They filled Sam in on what had happened in the years he was asleep and asked about the *smoking hot babe* he'd brought there, named Coral. Sam replied that he and Maggie were getting married.

When he told his cronies he was starting a business, Duffy Detectives, they hooked him up with a friend who had a friend who had offices to rent. They spread the word in the hotels, skyscrapers, cabs, and courtrooms of New York and sent Sam his first clients.

He'd been busy ever since, which helped ease the pain of remembering Jess. They'd known each other only a few days, but Jess was the most wonderful kid Sam ever hoped to meet. He'd still be numb with grief if his own child weren't on the way.

In the Range Rover, he made a note in his casebook: *11:30 A.M. Followed limo to 5th Avenue store.* He paused, thinking of his youth, and wrote: *No evidence of sex.* Then he remembered the mother was paying for the truth.

Just then the limo's back door opened and the daughter and chauffeur got out, looking at each other like there was no one else on Fifth Avenue. The Sam who headed Theomund Brown's security would have turned them in. For the Sam who was in love and full of remorse, things were complicated. Their absorption in each other made him realize what else had changed in his city. Famously nonchalant before, New Yorkers seemed more aware of each other since the Twin Towers came down.

His cell rang and he answered on speakerphone, watching the

couple start for the funky street wear store, holding hands.

"Yeah."

"Is this Sam Duffy?" It was a woman's voice. She had a mixed New York/Southern accent like Maggie's.

"Who's asking?"

"It's me, Sam, Sharmina. Maggie's friend?"

Sam forgot about the couple. "What's the matter? Where is she?"

"She's all right. That's not why I'm calling."

Sam let out his breath. "Oh, okay. What, does she need me to pick up something?"

"No …"

The pause was too long. Sam went on alert again. "Something's the matter. Tell me."

"I'm breaking her confidence."

"Break it."

"Have you noticed anything different about Maggie?"

"Yeah, a pregnant woman in grief for a lost child … among other things."

"I can't do this. I shouldn't have called."

"Yes, you should. Where are you?" Sam turned on the ignition, checking traffic as he talked, ready to pull out and get where Sharmina was.

"Don't come here," she said, "but, Sam, do you have any idea where your fiancée is?"

"Where?"

As Sharmina spoke, Sam wrote the address in the notebook below the entry about no sex.

On Luis's balcony, Coral downed the remains of her second margarita and rolled onto her stomach on the chaise, her feet crossed behind her in the air.

"And that's how I met Theo. You know the rest, Luis, because you were the one driving the Rolls the night he bought out that restaurant so I could be that actor's dessert."

"Yes, I remember." He'd switched from margaritas to a dark Mexican beer. "Your last name is Anders. Is that Norwegian?"

"Yep. Short for Andersdatter, daughter of Anders. He died trying to reach my mother the day I was born. He had a heart attack running to the hospital. He passed his bad luck on to me."

Luis went to her and lifted her chin. "You could have been a model, a rich man's wife. Why didn't you try for something like that? You are not an ordinary woman."

"I did want to dance."

"Why didn't you stick with it?" he asked. "Why did you let Brown take you away from it?"

"Too busty," she said. "Too big an ass. Ever see a photo of Margot Fonteyn? No boobs. No hips."

"Oh, too bad."

"Doesn't bother me. I dance every day."

"Aha! So this is why you still have a perfect body. You could have been a movie star," Luis said.

Coral rolled her eyes. "It's hard to see yourself as a movie star, honey, when you've been fucked since you were eight."

He stepped back. "*¡Eso es terrible!* You were violated."

"Tell me about it," she said.

"Who did it?"

"The man my mother married."

"*¡Muy terrible!* And when it happened again, right here only weeks ago?"

Coral rolled over and stroked her stomach as if she were in pain. "Turns out I wasn't the only one Sam Duffy had his way with. He helped himself to a virgin, too."

"A virgin? *¡Es un criminal!* Who?"

"The clone's mother. Sam said she was still a virgin somehow. Go figure."

She could hear Luis snort in disbelief. "You have forgiven him?"

Coral sighed. "It wasn't his fault."

"Ah, yes, the amnesia."

"It was Theo's men who shot Sam while he was guarding

Maggie, as you know very well." Coral rolled her eyes. "What he sees in that woman, I'll never know. Maybe he felt sorry for her. It was such a stupid thing—carrying a clone like that. I'd sure never do it. Anyway, Sam's brain was all screwed up when he came out of that coma. He had no idea what he was doing. Yeah, I forgive him. Why not? He's okay now."

Luis gripped the silver knife he'd been carrying about. "Was Sam Duffy there in Italy when Theomund died? Did he have anything to do with it?"

She looked into his eyes. "Sam wasn't there. He had nothing to do with it." *That much was true.* "Theo fell to his death over a cliff." Coral made sure she didn't lower her eyes.

"This is the truth?"

"Yes. Satisfied?"

He nodded.

She felt no pangs of guilt. Brown, a world-class creep, had been murdered by a decent man. It just wasn't Sam.

"Okay, your turn," she said.

"What do you want to know?" he asked grudgingly.

Coral gazed at the ornate knife in the Mexica pouch. "Are you gay?"

Luis smashed his beer bottle against the brick wall of the penthouse, making the colorful birds screech and flap their wings.

"*Cabrona! Pinche retardada!*"

Coral held her breath as she took the measure of the man she'd just enraged. She was glad she had. Now she could judge—would he try to beat her if she worked for him, let others beat her?

Luis raised his finger. It shook as he spoke. "I am a believer! I am a man of faith. I am a follower of Juan Diego to whom Mary appeared on Tepeyac in 1531 and imprinted an image of herself on his cloak. I was born on the feast day of Our Lady of Guadalupe, December 12, and I devote my life to her!"

Luis trembled like a cornered stallion.

Coral rose, understanding him at last. Slowly she reached out and put her arms about his neck so he could rest his head on her shoulder. For a moment he allowed it and she could feel his shaking body.

Then he stepped back and slapped his palms hard against his chest. "This body is the temple in which my soul resides. I will never defile it before Our Lady!"

She thought if he weren't so angry, Luis would cry. "I am not gay, I am celibate. That is how I will remain."

"You've always been celibate?"

She saw the steel in him return and now understood its source. "Always!"

Reaching into a cooler, she handed him another beer and saw the servant had quietly swept the broken bottle away.

"Tell me about you, Luis," Coral said, sitting down. He was as elegant as the jaguar statues and just as dangerous as the real thing, she surmised. Inside he was a spurned child—his latent homosexuality rejected by his machismo mother country.

He glared at her. "America is becoming a Latino country."

"Yes, in a way. Hispanic culture is in fashion."

He sneered. "You mean Latino culture! It is not a fashion. It is a growing tide that will sweep away the reign of the gringos."

Coral had long wondered the same, but she decided to laugh.

Luis stalked toward her. "By 2125 there will be more Latinos than gringos here."

She frowned.

"We come across the border, day-by-day, and don't return. In your hospitals we have our babies, three for every one of yours. More and more of us don't bother to speak English. There is no need. Our twin Latino capitals, San Antonio and Los Angeles, will be like Miami. The gringo who doesn't speak Spanish will soon be extinct there. He'll have to move or live on welfare without a job."

Coral decided to draw him out. "I doubt if Texans will ever let that happen."

"They won't be able to prevent it. Enjoy yourself while you can. Even by 2050, you whites will be a minority here. We are already reshaping your world. Do you know that the states with the largest electoral votes—Texas, California, New York, Illinois—are where Latinos live? Soon, we alone will decide who the President is."

"Is that right? I've been to San Antonio, Luis. I've met Mexican-Americans. Most of them don't bother to vote. They're barely eking out an existence, not trying to take over anything, much less the country. The most prosperous ones want to stop illegal immigration as much as everybody else."

"Mexican Americans are eight-five percent of the Latino population in this country and that number will only grow."

Coral glared. "In that case, we're safe. How do you plan to pull this off?" She stretched her arm toward the door. "With *peones* like your cousin, there? In what time frame, Luis? *Mañana*?"

She noted that he didn't slap her face.

"You talk like a fool." Luis smiled. "Those who cross the border illegally are national heroes. Day-by-day their sacrifice reclaims what was once ours: Texas, Nuevo México, Sonora, Alta California."

"The whole Southwest, in other words?"

"Yes, some of our families have been in America three hundred years, but more of us for only three months, three days. Do you know what it is called?"

"No, Luis, I don't."

"*La Reconquista.*"

"The reconquest?"

"Yes, day-by-day, of what was ours."

"Let me get this straight. You think the drug lords are trying to conquer the USA?"

"No! Not them. They have no souls."

"Who then?"

"Me and many like me."

She sat down. "Jesus Christ! You really do think you're Che Guevara or Zapata or something. What's the matter with you, Luis? You were never like this before."

He sat across from her. "I was always like this. I did not show it."

"So, in other words you're saying the day will come when most of us get our asses kicked by Mexican-Americans, instead of by the folks who're kicking us now? I mean, *ya ni modo*."

He bristled. "*Ya ni modo* is not a phrase my parents allowed in our home. They taught us not to be resigned, that problems and failure aren't inevitable."

"No ya ni modo? Okay, then Mexican-Americans are going to be assertive about pushing people around."

"No! This is the way of the gringo, stomping across the world. The Mexica are compassionate, we value family."

"Oh? Is that why most of Mexico is dirt poor and a handful so rich they couldn't spend it if they tried?"

"Lucky for America because of all the cheap labor. Anyway, this country is becoming the same."

She grimaced. "There's a big difference between USA poor and Mexico poor."

"Mexico has problems, but it is my country. You are gringa and cannot understand."

She sighed. "You're not making sense, you know, Luis—conquering those who conquered your conquerors? You're talking for only half of your genes. What about the other half? What about your Aztec—excuse me—Mexica ancestors? Who speaks for them?"

"I do!" he growled. "You will find no monument to a conquistador in Mexico City, though we speak their language and their blood runs through our veins."

In his heroic stance Coral could almost see Moctezuma before the Spaniards came, see Cortés on his horse, see Cuauhtémoc making a last, lost stand against the Spaniards when Moctezuma died. The contradictions in his genes had produced a striking man.

"After tonight, you will not speak to me again in this way. Work for me if you choose, go or come as you choose, but you will not speak to me like this. I am not a child to be chastised by a gringa, to be told by a woman that I do not understand. You will treat me with respect. This is my truth, take it or leave it. It is of no consequence what you think. The day is eventually coming, whether you believe it or not. I intend to hasten that day."

"I'm sorry, I didn't mean—"

"Be quiet, *mujer blanca*."

Coral stood there thinking as Luis gazed imperiously at her, his head back when he drank his beer.

She was remembering the last time she saw Sam—standing on a beach in Italy, waving to her as Brown's yacht moored. Having once been a sailor, Sam had tracked the yacht's location from its satellite service. He said Maggie made him come to apologize, but he would have done it on his own, anyway. Sam had stayed on deck because he'd promised to meet Coral only in public. A woman running with her poodle, two teenagers on a jet ski, saw what happened when he told Coral he was sorry for raping her during his trauma-induced personality change. In a lounge chair on the yacht, Coral lost control and tried to beat him and his personality to death with her fists. All he did was grab her hands and keep saying he was sorry. Then he got off the boat and went back to Maggie, the woman he loved.

Luis said, "You have heard about the wedding?"

"What wedding?"

"Sam Duffy and Maggie Johnson. They are back in New York to get married."

Coral blinked and stared at Luis. He had struck her, all right, just not with his hand. "How do you know?"

"For twenty years, Theomund had this building bugged. Felix Rossi has removed them, but not before I heard about this. Her son is dead, the so-called Christ clone."

"Dead, but how?"

"Some stupid local man."

"That's awful."

"Yes, because tomorrow, His Eminence Evaristo Cardinal Salati will arrive here from Rome. I could have used the boy as a bargaining chip."

"Luis, you'd use a child?"

"I wouldn't hurt him, but I would have handed the boy over."

Coral blinked. "Why?"

"God is not so foolish as to allow one person to prevent a whole people from being saved. Now I must find something else to interest Salati since the clone is dead. Tomorrow he will be my guest. I want you, and only you, to entertain him."

"He was Theo's man in the Vatican, right?"

"Yes. I want him to be my man, now. First, I want you to find out if His Eminence believes God decreed celibacy upon the clergy."

She said, "Priests mostly want their asses whipped, you know, before they sin."

"I have good Spanish whips."

Coral laughed.

"She is carrying his child."

Coral stopped laughing. "What?"

"She is pregnant with Sam Duffy's child," Luis said, resting his hand on Coral's shoulder, "Maggie Johnson, the abomination."

Unexpectedly, Coral felt crestfallen and thought *ya ni modo*, though she didn't say it. "Why do you call her that?"

"The Black Virgin? The Secret Madonna? Mother of the cloned Jesus Christ? This woman and her boy were an affront to the Virgin of Guadalupe. Not anymore, *gracias a Dios*. Will you help me?"

She sighed deeply, thinking of Sam's child in Maggie's womb. If Coral ever had a chance with Sam, it was over, now.

"Why not? Why the hell not? You're right, Luis, I've helped bastards stomp on others my whole life. How can you be any worse? It's a deal. Except you'll pay me my quarter mil, understand?"

He nodded.

"I'll help your Latino tide sweep the rot away. Why the hell not?"

Coral saw admiration in his eyes.

"I have always liked you," he said.

She gave Luis a brotherly hug, feeling sorry for him. He was nuts, but he was rich and she kind of liked that he thought he was Zapata. Maybe one day she'd learn why he was so crazy and try to help him, if he kept his word.

He responded in a whisper. "In my prayers, Coral, I beseech Our Lady of Guadalupe for this alone: in my lifetime, La Reconquista." His voice broke. "That aside, you can trust me. I will pay you and do you no harm. Just don't betray me."

Coral picked up a beer and clinked his, trying not to think about the coming wedding. "I won't, Luis. The Reconquista it is, sweetheart."

Chapter 4

Tell me more, Sharmina. I need to know," Sam said, pulling into traffic and heading north toward East Harlem's El Barrio, a traditionally Puerto Rican neighborhood, separated from the rest of Harlem by Fifth Avenue and Mt. Morris Park. Sam had learned both neighborhoods were in transition. On the west side wealthy Blacks, and on the east side wealthy Whites or Asians, were picking off the best nineteenth century brownstones, restoring Harlem's former glory one house, one storefront at a time.

Meanwhile in El Barrio an influx of Mexican immigrants struggled for the unrestored leftovers.

Sam listened to Sharmina explain that Maggie had stopped seeing her doctor and made an appointment with a midwife there. Having branched out from her Mexican clientele, the woman had a good reputation at Maggie's church. In addition to being a *partera*, she was also a *curandera*, a folk healer. When she wasn't delivering babies, she ran a *yerbería*, dispensing candles and herbal cures. That's where Maggie was.

"Thanks, Sharmina," Sam said and hung up.

In his youth as a merchant seaman he'd had cause to visit many such establishments and had come to value the world's folk herbalists. He'd never guessed Maggie would go to one, but to Sam it wasn't alarming. Only Sharmina's worry was, and the fact that Maggie hadn't told him.

He sped up, passing the 116th and Lexington subway stop. Keeping an eye out for cop cars, he sped east on the main strip, Luis Múñoz Marín Boulevard. Puerto Rican *cuchifrito* meat joints went by in a blur, blasting the salsa music invented here. At Third Avenue he knew the music changed to mariachi but he was going too fast to hear it. Sam had reached Little Puebla, full of Mexican taquerías and stores selling cowboy boots. Hurriedly he parked in front of a glass-fronted shop with a sign over its door, Yerbería Guadalupe. He got out and assessed it. On the left window was a crude painting of *La Mano Poderosa*—the powerful hand—supporting the Holy Family in heaven. On the right the Virgen de Guadalupe stood on her crescent moon, an angel beneath it. The yerbería advertised its wares in hand lettering: *Sexopronto, Aguas Espirituales; Libros Místicos; Lectura de Cartas* and more. His potency could be enhanced while Maggie had her Tarot cards read. Harmless enough.

Inside, wooden shelves full of creams, oils, and jars of herbs lined the room. Statues of saints, of Aztec emperors, colored candles in tall glass jars were there as well. Dried herbs hung in bundles from the ceiling beside skeleton figures for the Day of the Dead, a mural of the last supper near them on a wall. Another wall featured labeled portraits of great curanderos of the past, the folk saints Don Pedrito Jaramillo, El Niño Fidencio and Teresita Urrea, Mexico's counterpart to Mother Theresa—all said to have performed miracle cures.

To his relief, he saw Maggie in a corner, she and her curandera huddled over a table, a black candle burning as the curandera prayed. To Sam it made an unexpectedly somber sight: the curandera, the black candle meant to ward off evil, Maggie in her mourning clothes.

He cleared his throat and they looked up, Maggie's green eyes surprised. Her hand quickly covered a plastic bag full of herbs. In her closed expression, he was startled to see a woman he didn't know. He shrugged it off. This was Maggie.

"Maggie Clarissa Johnson, now what might you be hiding?"

The two women glanced at each other then Maggie said, "Sam, where did you come from?"

"I asked Sharmina where you were." *Not quite true, but close enough.* "What are those herbs for?"

"I've been having headaches, is all."

He walked over and kissed her forehead, sensing she'd lied. "Well, then, we can't be having that."

With keen interest, he reached out to shake the curandera's

hand. "I'm the guilty father and soon-to-be husband."

The woman smiled, black hair cascading around an attractive face. She wore a dark linen dress and white sweater. A blue-robed Virgin of Guadalupe sat on the table beside her, a red rosary draping from its crown.

"I am Doña Teresita."

"Good name," Sam replied.

The herbs disappeared into Maggie's purse and Sam tried to make sense of what he was seeing. He reached down and rubbed her stomach.

"And how is our baby?"

He gazed into the curandera's eyes, searching for any hint she was a black curandera who might cast spells of *envidia, mal de ojo, salacion, maleficio.* Couldn't be, he thought, if Maggie was here.

"I am happy to meet you, Señor Duffy. The child is fine."

"Well, I guess we'll be going until next time," Maggie said.

Sam patted her shoulder, turned and examined framed documents on the wall. "I suppose you've delivered many babies, Doña Teresita?"

"All over Harlem and in many other places," she replied. "I'm licensed." She pointed to a certificate from the State of New York. "A safe and loving home delivery is my motto."

"And how long have you been in Harlem?"

"Many years."

"Well, I guess we'd better be going," Maggie repeated.

"Yes, my girl," he said and took her arm, helping her up.

Outside, he opened the Range Rover's door for her and when she got in, pretended to remember something. "Stay here a minute. I'd like to thank Teresita myself and leave a nice tip so she takes good care of you."

"That's not necessary," Maggie said.

Sam touched Maggie's chin and went back into the Yerbería Guadalupe where the curandera seemed to be waiting for him.

He laughed. "Don't tell me you're an *espiritista,* too. A medium?"

Doña Teresita held out her hand. In it was another plastic bag of herbs.

"A little bit," she said. "Here, take this. When she is not looking, replace the bag in the señora's purse with it."

Sam didn't take the bag. He walked close enough to speak in a whisper. "Now why in the world would I do that, Doña Teresita?"

Though he was a man she didn't know, a tall man who outweighed her, Teresita didn't look afraid. "You are not the person your wife described, señor. Not at all. I see your spirit."

Sam's heart sank. What had Maggie said? Bad things Teresita now thought untrue or good things she now doubted?

"What's in this bag?"

"Only green tea. It will not hurt her."

Sam glared at the woman. "Then what's in the bag she has?"

"Mostly thyme."

"Thyme? You mean thyme, like a seasoning?"

"Yes. A woman newly pregnant who drinks a tea of it for three days will lose her baby. Too bad American women have abandoned the wisdom of their great grandmothers. They let a Supreme Court run their lives."

Sam thought he hadn't heard right. He'd almost died saving Maggie. He'd given up Coral who, in terms of sex, was his female mirror. Could Maggie ignore all that and abort his baby? He closed his eyes, remembering the rape, his heart stopping. She hadn't forgiven him.

"She asked you for an herb like this?"

"She is troubled, overwhelmed by sorrow."

Sam turned away from Teresita and glanced at the statue of the Virgin of Guadalupe, Mexico's Christian version of its Aztec mother goddess Tonantzin. Maggie had a brown Madonna statue of her own, Our Lady of Rocamadour, from France. He hadn't seen it since Jess died. Yes, he'd assaulted her, she'd lost a son, but would Maggie abort a child?

He searched Teresita's face. "What you say can't be true. Maggie is a deeply religious woman and I—"

Teresita shook her head and touched his shoulder. "The señora is in the grip of feelings she cannot fight. She is not the same woman you may have known."

"But how could she think—"

"If she talks to you or someone else, if she makes love, it may help. You must try. It is important. She is not thinking. Only feeling. Remember this and it may help you, Señor Duffy. Good luck."

Doña Teresita gave Sam the plastic bag and walked away.

Sam fingered the herbs. Would a Catholic midwife engage in abortion? Then he remembered. Under the guise of the conquistador's Catholic religion, Mexico had retained much of its ancient belief. A Virgin of Guadalupe Catholic and a Roman Catholic weren't the same.

He noticed a bookshelf and scanned the reassuring titles: *Obstetrics: Normal and Problem Pregnancies*, *Varney's Midwifery Fourth Edition*, *Holistic Midwifery*, books in Susun Weed's *Wise Woman Herbal Series*, Jethro Kloss's classic, *Back to Eden*, next to books about the green medicine or *remedios caseros* practiced in curanderismo, including the famous *Codex Badiano* of the Aztecs.

Sam decided to discard both bags and replace the herbs in Maggie's purse with loose tea from a grocery store.

He stepped outside to Luis Múñoz Marín Boulevard and saw his precious Maggie sitting where he left her, lost in memory or thought, listening to the strains of mariachi music through the open window, her black veil moving in the breeze.

As she walked up to her building, Coral's doorman said, "Good evening, Miss Anders. Did you enjoy your trip?"

"Hi, Chris. Yeah I did."

They stood for a moment, Chris holding the door, Coral absently staring at the gold trim on his collar. Then it struck her where she'd last seen that collar. Behind the wheel of a brown Porsche of the same milky brown color as one that went missing from the building's garage—on the same day the car disappeared. A coincidence?

"You stole that Porsche, Chris, didn't you?" she said, glad of being diverted from her problems for a moment. She eyed him with mixed disapproval and admiration.

"What? I did not!" He looked around.

"You stole that Porsche that poor Mrs. Lee's husband gave her before he died."

The doorman flushed, giving himself away. "Don't let people hear you say that. You're wrong, Miss Anders."

"I am, am I?"

"Yes, but even if I did, she wasn't going to drive it from a walker."

Coral laughed. "You dog."

"How … how was your trip, Miss Anders?" he repeated.

She paused and looked into the air. "You know, my last stop was Gibraltar. I took the cable car there just to look across the straits at sunset when the wind turns west. You can actually see a cloud of dust from Africa rise up to catch the light."

She retrieved her keys. "Yeah, it was a great trip." She turned to him and whispered. "But the real question, Chris, is: will you return that Porsche?"

Chris turned scarlet. "Miss Anders, I don't know why you think I took—"

"Blushing is a bad trait in a thief, Chris. That's what you are and I know it." She grinned. "I'd turn you in if you weren't so cute and useful to me." She put a finger on his chest. "Steal anything from me or my friends here, though, and I'll turn state's evidence on you in a minute."

"Miss Anders, you must know how I admire you. I would never, ever, ever—"

Smiling, Coral went to the east elevators, calling. "See that you don't."

She got off on the 17th floor and went to her apartment.

"Home at last," she said, entering the foyer. It had polished floor tiles, gold baseboards, and a black table with yellow tulips against the foyer wall below a stunning editorial painting of the ballet dancers, Fonteyn and Nureyev.

She went toward the main room. On the right was a kitchen

in slate, chrome, and polished wood, on the left a powder room. Two steps more and she was in the spacious living room, deep burgundy carpet beneath her feet. One side had wallpaper with a sophisticated gold, green, and mahogany stripe. On it hung more portraits of dancers: Bill "Bojangles" Robinson, Fred Astaire and Ginger Rogers, Baryshnikov. A baby grand filled an alcove.

This place was hers and hers alone. No man had ever been here, not Sam, not any of her clients.

"Hi, Kathryn," she said to a portrait of a woman dressed in the style of the 1930s. The brass tag on the picture frame identified her as Kathryn Dunham, founder of the anthropological dance movement.

Preoccupied, Coral scanned a group of small labeled frames: Chagall's FireBird in blue and red, Albert Arthur Allen's photograph, "The Chorus Line" which consisted of seven nude ladies facing left—taken in France in the 1930s.

This was her sanctuary, free of men. Not even Theo had seen it.

She went to her master bedroom suite. It had black furniture, gold lamps, and a sumptuous yellow satin comforter on the bed, the head piled with different-sized pillows.

She changed into leggings and a big white shirt. In the living room she stared at her spectacular view of the Hudson River, framed by the lights of the Jersey shore beyond.

Remembering her brief days of freedom, Coral let out a bitter sigh. She'd left from Rapallo on Italy's north Mediterranean shore and, bypassing nearby but overly fashionable Portofino, had the crew take Brown's yacht south to the island of Sardinia. She bypassed lovely but bustling Cagliari on the island's southern tip and instead headed for the Costa Verde where the boat anchored off Scivu so she could swim ashore naked at dawn and walk the long stretch of golden sand, seeing no one. She'd passed up most of the French Riviera, too, and had the yacht drop anchor near Perpignan, where Sam had caught up to her. At the station Dali designed, she took the little yellow train, *Le petit train jeune*, up to Font Romeu in the Pyrenees for skiing after he left. While she toured Cathare ruins and photographed flamingoes in salt marshes, they'd loaded a case of the Muscat de Rivesaltes she fell in love with onto the ship.

Days of sheer bliss, of autonomy, but they were over.

She couldn't believe Brown hadn't provided for her in his will like he'd promised. Now her hoped-for independence was gone, the days of sweet freedom an illusion. It was either work for Luis and help with his crazy schemes or be forced to accept a sugar daddy—or, worse, a sugar granddaddy, given the competition nowadays. Beautiful girls from good homes didn't seem to mind being whores so much anymore.

"You're a fucking bastard, Theo," she said to the Jersey skyline. "I hope you're in hell."

Coral turned to another door near the bedroom. She opened it and flicked on lights in her private studio, went to the barre and started doing plies and relevés.

Here, no one could buy her. No one could force her to be witty or sexy—make her smile if she wanted to frown. In this apartment she was true to herself.

Here, she was Coral Anders, the dancer.

Chapter 5

In Felix's kitchen, Maggie put the teapot on to boil and removed the herbs from her purse, thinking of the first moment that she stepped back into the 131st Street Baptist Church. Doña Teresita had been there in the lobby in front of the double doors. The light that streamed in through the glass windows highlighted her black hair and intense eyes. She'd been dressed in black.

Maggie had immediately felt drawn to this Latina woman who didn't seem at all out of place in their church.

"*Saludos, madre querida,*" Teresita finally said. *Greetings dear mother*, as Maggie later understood. At the time Maggie thought she'd said *Hail Holy Mother* and she'd stepped back, fearing she shouldn't have returned to her old church, like Sam warned.

Teresita reached into her purse, drew out a midwife business card, handed it to Maggie and said, "Come to see me if you like." Somehow she'd known Maggie was pregnant.

That night Maggie had dreamed of Doña Teresita—a strange dream, full of dried roses. The next day, she went to Teresita's yerbería. Soon Maggie found herself pouring out her fears to the woman with intense eyes. It was in the yerbería that Maggie faced what she'd been thinking all along—she couldn't give birth to Sam's misbegotten child.

She heard footsteps and looked up. Sam stood at Felix's kitchen door. Why hadn't he gone back to work after he picked her up at Teresita's? She'd have to tell Sharmina not to give her whereabouts to Sam again.

"Maggie—" he began.

She looked away, her mind flashing back to Italy and the morning she'd told Jess who he really was. His reply had staggered her. Jess said his genes weren't from the DNA Felix had stolen from the Turin shroud. He'd come because Maggie called him—

she and Felix. He said he could come no other way. Jess told her his sole mission was their personal happiness. He hadn't come to save the world.

Overcome by guilt and remorse, Maggie had fled the lakeshore into the house. She'd found Sam in her bedroom, uninvited, sprawled out naked on her bed. Every day Maggie still had to block out the memory of what he did to her.

Felix later said Sam's condition had a medical name: trauma-induced paraphylias. If it was anybody's fault, Felix said, it was Theomund Brown's. His men shot Sam the night Jess was born. For ten years, they'd all thought Sam was dead. She wished he was.

She turned to him. "Did you know it's been less than two months since Felix brought you to Italy, Sam? Less than two months since we found out you were still alive?"

Sam reached for her, but she pulled away.

"Look what's happened since. The day you came to our villa was the day Senora Morelli died. Three days later, you … you attacked me. Three weeks more and Carlo Morelli killed Jess for not saving his wife." Sam looked guilt-ridden. "Only bad things have happened since we got back together, Sam."

He stood there, wringing his hands, his mouth open but not saying words. Maggie ran to the guest room and locked the door, her breath as rapid as her heartbeat. She listened for Sam's footsteps, for angry knocks. They didn't come. Relieved, she went to a suitcase, opened it, and drew out the statue she hadn't looked at for so long: the Notre Dame de Rocamadour from twelfth Century France—a Black Madonna.

Her nose was wide like Maggie's. She and her child wore golden crowns. Jess had loved it. Maggie put it on the dresser and knelt to pray.

"My womb was virgin, too. I had a son, like you. What did you do after Jesus was torn apart?"

She touched the wooden child.

"I guess it was wrong of me to think I was a second Madonna. I must have sinned real, real bad. I must have offended the Holy

Ghost. That's why God let Satan visit me. That's why He took my Jess, sweet Jess!"

Maggie put her hands over her eyes. She knew she had descended into the valley of the shadow of death and was lost, so lost.

"I know it's wrong," she said. "Vengeance is mine, sayeth the Lord but Holy Mother, look what's happened to me!"

Maggie gripped her stomach, staring at the wooden child.

"So I've got to fix this! I can't let Sam's evil seed keep growing in me where my sweet Jess was. I'm not asking you to forgive me. I know I'll never be forgiven for what I've already done. I'm just explaining. That's all."

Maggie waited for a sign—anything to say she might be wrong. Feeling nothing, she put the statue away.

She went back into the kitchen and found Sam standing over a cup and saucer—trying to be helpful, she supposed, but it was way too late for that.

"I went ahead and made your tea for you," he said.

Maggie frowned, noticing the plastic bag Doña Teresita gave her. "You used the herbs from the plastic bag?"

"Yes." He held out the cup.

She took it and stirred the tea, watching Sam. How could he look so concerned, look so human when he wasn't? She carried the cup into Felix's guest room.

Sam followed.

"You don't have to stay with me," she called. "I know you have to work."

"I want to be with you."

Maggie snorted. Sam's lust must be acting up. Very convenient for him not to have to share her with Jess, a child who wasn't his.

She sat on the bedside, found Sam's gaze, put on Isaiah's cloak of vengeance, and drank the curandera's tea straight down. From the taste, it must be a mild kind of thyme. Three days of this, three times a day, and she wouldn't be pregnant anymore. The curandera had said not to drink the tea longer. If it didn't work, come back. She'd try something else, but thyme usually worked.

To Maggie's surprise, Sam walked over and crushed her in his arms. She wanted to tell him his child would soon be a bloody clot. *How could she think such things?* Then she remembered. Jess was dead.

Sam took the cup and kissed her forehead, nose, and mouth and she let him. "Maggie, don't you know I love you?"

She plastered on a smile. "Of course you do, Sam. We're getting married, aren't we?" She'd been too grief-stricken for the last two weeks to do much besides cry. Stronger now, she'd lie until the deed was done.

He groaned. "Maggie, I want you to sit down and listen to me."

She sat, indifferent.

He took her hands. "I read an article about the stages of grief. Sweetheart, I think you're between the denial/anger parts. The point is—" He searched her face. "Don't trust your feelings right now. I'm having a hard time myself, but men and women don't seem to grieve the same. You need to talk to someone, Maggie. You really do."

She glared at him. "I told you I'm not seeing any shrink. What can they tell me? My son is dead and I'm sad? I already know that."

"You need to talk, Maggie. I haven't pushed you, but now I see I was wrong. I'm here. I'll listen. Won't you try to tell me what you're feeling?"

Maggie closed her eyes. It didn't matter what she told him. In three days her pregnancy would be over.

"I just want to take a nap, Sam, if that's all right."

She pulled away and undressed down to her slip, got under the covers, seeing the same vision. Her gun. The one her daddy gave her in Macon, Georgia when she was twelve. A group of white men had attacked her in the woods, but her dad came just in time. Afterward he bought the gun, taught her how to shoot it, and said, "Kill em, baby, if they come for you. God don't mean for you to be abused."

Maggie had never carried the gun. She'd relied on prayer. The gun was still where she'd hidden it thirty years ago, in a sock at the bottom of a box of keepsakes in a trunk. Felix had let them store it in the basement where the building's nine wealthy tenants kept the things they didn't use.

Uninvited as usual, Sam stripped to his shorts and got in bed beside her. "Maggie, let me help. What are you feeling?"

At his touch she cried, "You left me and Jess alone!"

"I shouldn't have, but Maggie, you told me to."

"How could you trust my judgment at a time like that when I'd been under such stress? Aren't you supposed to be the man who outwitted Theomund Brown?"

Sam rubbed his forehead. "I guess that's the downside of loving a guy who knows how to shut up and deliver. You asked me to go and apologize to Coral, so I did. I shouldn't have. I accept that much of the blame for Jess's death. As for the other part, Maggie believe me, there isn't a moment I don't wish I could undo hurting two women who loved and trusted me. I go to church now all the time, like you always told me, but not to confession because what priest could absolve me of that?"

Maggie grunted. So he hadn't even considered joining her 131st Street Baptist Church. Lucifer must prefer Catholic churches already full of boy-molesting men in skirts.

"You think Coral loved you?" she said. "Do prostitutes love?"

"I didn't mean to hurt you!"

She shut her eyes to keep from seeing him. She covered her ears to keep from hearing. "Why did Felix leave, too?"

Sam took her hands from her ears. "You know why! Brown had his daughter kidnapped. Stop tormenting yourself. Please, Maggie, let me take you to see someone who can help."

At that, Maggie dug her nails into his flesh.

Sam stared as blood seeped from his arm.

She felt glad to have hurt him.

"Oh, my girl," he whispered. "I'd give anything, do anything, to take away your pain."

How could he look so sincere?

She tilted her chin up. “If you think you’re the only man who’s ever loved me, Sam Duffy, you’re wrong. Adamo did, Carlo Morelli’s brother. Adamo used to propose to me every five minutes, you know.”

“Do you wish you’d chosen him instead of me?”

Maggie wouldn’t tell Sam that Adamo had been the town drunk, if a cheerful one. He’d sobered up to try to help her, but he’d probably gone back to drink by now.

“You don’t have to answer,” Sam said. “Adamo couldn’t miss how wonderful you are.”

How could he look so earnest?

“It’s Jess who was wonderful! You weren’t there all those years so you don’t really know. He could do anything, read and understand anything. I'm not smart like that. We thought he was a little backward at first. It turned out he wasn't. He just didn't need to read because he already … Oh, God!” She took deep breaths. “He already knew everything—in his heart. Everything! And—”

“Go on, Maggie. What else?”

She looked out the window. “He was such a good sailor. The way he handled that little Mirror Dinghy Felix gave him, he could have been in the Olympics, he was so good.”

“Yes, he was. He was smart.”

“More than smart. He spoke Hebrew. The rabbi taught him.” She counted on her fingers. “Jess spoke Hebrew and Italian and English and he said … he finally said he wasn't just Jesus Christ reincarnated.” She made big gestures with her hands. “ He said he was all the names—*all* the names—we hear whispered in our sleep and …”

She closed her eyes and imagined her beautiful son, his bronze skin, his sausage curls, the carefree ease with which he moved, how he always said he loved everyone.

After a while she realized Sam was stroking her arm and it felt comforting. She wondered how it could.

“Grief experts say to make love,” he said.

He drew closer and kissed her, but it made her cringe.

"You're just gonna take what you want, again? That's all you know how to do is force women, Sam?"

"Don't say that."

Maggie sobbed and beat her thighs. "How can Jess be dead, Sam?"

He grabbed her hands and she arched her back in agony. "How? How can my son be dead?"

They heard Felix playing piano for Ariel.

Maggie felt trapped by these two men who never put her first, as if she were still the maid. She leapt from bed, covering herself with a sheet, but she couldn't think where to go. Listening to Felix's piano, she gazed at the patterns the sunshine made on the wall—long, sensuous curves like a jaguar.

"Maggie, come talk to me."

She saw the longing on his face. *Yes, he'd saved them from Brown, but that was only a trick until the real assassin came.*

Maggie slipped on a robe and smiled. "I need another cup of tea."

When she returned from the kitchen, Sam had transformed the guest room. Felix's prie-dieu from the hall was there beside lit candles, the silver crucifix above it.

She froze. "Sam, what in the world?"

He looked disappointed. "Put the tea down." His voice was menacing.

"What?"

He picked up a Bible. "Just put the tea down."

Maggie wanted to run. Instead, she put down the tea and defiantly met his gaze.

He held out the Bible. "Take this in your hand."

"What are you doing, Sam?"

He raised his voice. "Take this Bible!"

Maggie flinched, but said, "I don't pray on command, yours or anybody's."

All six-foot-two of Sam seemed to bear down accusingly on her. "Why not, Maggie?"

She blinked and took the Bible, deciding to play his silly game.

"Do you still believe this is God's book?"

Maggie scanned his still-handsome face. Was Satan testing her through Sam? "What kind of question is that, Mr. Duffy? Of course I do!"

Sam took her wrist and walked her to the prie-dieu. "Kneel down, Maggie."

She glared at him. "Why?"

"Just do it! I won't take no for an answer."

Angrily, she knelt.

"With this Bible in your hand, on your knees before God's cross, I want you to swear—"

"Swear what? What?"

"Put your right hand on that Bible and look up to the cross."

"Samuel Duffy, what do you think you're—?"

He thundered, "Put your right hand on that dad-blasted Bible and look up to the cross!"

Maggie did, frightened now.

"Say, 'God, I promise not to throw away our baby."

Shocked, she tried to rise, but Sam's hands were on her shoulders.

"Say it! Say, 'God, I promise not to kill Sam's baby.'"

Now she wept, knowing Sharmina or the curandera had betrayed her. "I can't, I can't—"

"Do it, Maggie."

The door flew open. It was Felix. He swept his hair back as if he'd lost all patience. "Just what are you two doing in here? Sam, what are you doing to Maggie?"

Sam lowered his voice, "Felix, if you want to take another breath, close that fucking door and mind your business!"

Scrutinizing Maggie, Felix asked her, "Are you all right?" Maggie wasn't, but she nodded. Felix stormed out and slammed the door.

Tears again, the Bible in her hands, candles burning around her, Jesus on the cross above her head.

"Say it," Sam insisted. "Say I swear."

"I swear."

"To God."

"To God."

"That I won't murder our baby."

"That I won't," she looked up at Sam's angry eyes, "murder our baby."

"On the soul of my son, Jess, I promise."

"On the soul … oh, Sam I can't."

"Say it! Say it!" he demanded.

"On the soul of my son, Jess, I promise."

"Amen."

"Amen."

Breathing hard, Sam stared at her, ran a hand across his chin, as if he didn't know what to think of himself. Finally he nodded.

"I had to do that." He walked around the room, snuffing out candles. "You're not yourself, Maggie. I couldn't let you kill our baby."

Maggie rose from the prie-dieu and put the Bible gently down. She ran to the dressing room and the bathroom beyond, locking the door. Stripping off her clothes, she gazed at her stomach in the mirror.

On the Bible, on her knees she'd promised God?

Would God hold her to it? She'd been forced. Maggie closed her eyes, knowing she could have refused. Sam wouldn't have hurt her, just yelled and stomped around.

In truth every word she'd vowed seemed right. She'd felt complete as she spoke, like she did while carrying Jess—but this baby was no Jess.

She stroked her stomach and whispered, "All right, then. All right, in there. God must mean for you to be born. Somebody else has got to raise you, but I'll bring you into the world."

Maggie turned on the water, thinking of how she and Sam had gone apartment hunting yesterday. His idea, not hers. She'd only meant to play along until she wasn't pregnant anymore. She stepped in the shower, realizing everything had changed.

If she was going to have a baby, she couldn't deny it legitimacy. Every child had that right. She'd have to marry Sam after all. By accident she'd found a receipt for his big wedding night surprise: a Rolls Royce to The Plaza and inside a Central Park suite, red roses, champagne. Sam could afford it because they weren't having a reception and the church and the minister were free. He'd promised her a designer wedding gown. How and when was a secret.

She wet her hair, remembering Doña Teresita's words when Maggie confided the hate she felt.

"Your feelings are from the earth," Doña Teresita said. "They are those of the mother jaguar that hunts the ones who slew her cub."

If she understood so well, why had Teresita told Sam about the tea? Or was it Sharmina?

She pictured Sam in the bedroom, congratulating himself on outwitting her. If he thought he'd won, he was wrong. He could force her to bear his child, but he would never have her.

Soaping in the shower, she looked down on her breasts, already more swollen, more tender. If she had a decent man, she'd go to him now, but all she had was Sam who'd wrecked her life.

Chapter 6

In the guest room in which she hoped to later entertain him, Coral finished dressing for the arrival of Salati. The room had exquisite eighteenth century Chippendale furnishings, a mirrored ceiling and wall, and a huge bed. Theo had furnished it and Luis had so far made no changes. He'd said the room was hard to improve. Men could watch themselves lie with beautiful women in surroundings fit for royalty.

She inspected her clinging gown in the mirrors, walking back and forth to see how her hips moved. A shimmer of silver like her heeled slippers, it was so thin that in the right light Salati could not only see her legs but also inspect the outlines of her crotch. She stroked her breasts to see the effect through the sheer fabric and decided to repeat this for Salati's enjoyment. Her hair was a mass of curls. Her silver earrings dangled, mobiles of elegant ear art, fashion forward to say the least. She'd had them made, like the scent formulated for her in his Paris atelier by a besotted perfumer, one of the famous French *noses*, as they were called.

She decided not to wear lipstick. Her eyebrows, complexion and face were more than good, and naked lips made an intriguing contrast to her stunning outfit. Coral had one decision left: what to withhold from Salati. Perhaps she wouldn't let him kiss her mouth or her breasts, wouldn't undress—or allow him to—when they made love. Perhaps no oral sex, either giving or receiving, or no turning on lights, or looking into her eyes. It was part of her art. Withhold something from each man. Whore like mad on the rest. Now and then be unavailable. It drove them crazy.

At the door she took a last glimpse in the mirrors and stepped out, nervous in spite of her considerable experience with clergy. She needed Luis to be pleased with her accomplishments tonight.

To her right was another bedroom, to her left the kitchen and, beside it, the servants' suite. Beyond the kitchen were the dining room, the library, the opulent master suite, and a spacious room Theo had referred to as the salon. Celebrities and world leaders once surveyed Central Park through its glass wall.

Coral had the sense that Luis was busily changing things, but she couldn't tell for sure because most of the doors now had locks operated by keycard. She'd tried, but the only private door her card opened was the room she'd just left.

Theomund had been security conscious, but Luis's precautions bordered on paranoia. What was he afraid of? She also wondered what role Salati would play in La Reconquista, assuming he knew about it. Perhaps he didn't and was visiting without an agenda. He'd had hidden financial dealings with Theo, once the richest man in the world, and now Luis had taken Theo's place.

Wandering past locked doors in the penthouse, she reached the lobby. Theo had made it a museum for his collection of precious stones. She found Luis waiting, his Mexican Guayabera shirt replaced by an Italian suit as good as any Theo ever owned. Luis stood when she entered.

"*Dios mio!*" he exclaimed, admiration in his voice, but no desire.

She turned around for him.

"Fantástica," he said.

"You're fantástico yourself."

Luis smiled and motioned to the elevator. "He is coming."

Shortly the doors opened and there was His Eminence Evaristo Cardinal Salati, dressed in a black priest's suit. He had the soulful eyes and long lashes of a 1920s movie star and the profile of a Roman statue. He was lean and beautifully shaped. The Pope might be the head of the church, but, given his looks and power, Salati must be its prince. Two equally slender and beautiful dogs got off the elevator with him—so well behaved they weren't on a leash. Man and dogs outshone the gems and crystals backlit on the foyer walls.

Luis stepped forward. "Your Eminence, I am honored by your presence."

Coral curtsied and said, "Your Eminence."

"I am also honored," Salati replied. For a moment Salati's gaze lingered on Luis in his expensive suit. "I remember you, Luis. You look so different now; though I know you were less butler than right hand man to Theomund. I'm beginning to think it was wise of him to leave things to you. Please call me Evaristo and I will call you Luis and if you, charming lady, will tell me your name—"

"Coral. We haven't met."

He smiled through beautiful teeth. "I am very aware of that."

They had drinks on the terrace then Luis's servant called them in to an authentic Mexican meal featuring delicate fish steamed in banana leaves, the lights of New York blinking on through the glass wall. As they ate, and drank memorable wines, Coral wondered what other grand destinies were being woven in New York tonight. Methodically, Luis steered the conversation to the politics and economics of Mexico.

Coral was able to contribute some history. She knew Vicente Fox became the president in 2000. Elected to the standard six-year term, he'd brought democracy to Mexico by defeating the centrist PRI, Institutional Revolutionary Party, which had been in power since 1929. However, it was democracy Mexican style, which meant corruption hadn't ended.

Luis explained to Salati, "Before Vicente Fox, the PRI had always won in national elections, whatever the actual vote count, because of influence peddling and bribery controlled from the top by the all-powerful current president."

"How does that old joke go?" Coral said, 'What time is it?' the President asks. 'Whatever time you say it is, Mr. President,' comes the reply."

Luis and Salati laughed.

"Vicente promised to end all this," Luis added. "He did begin, he really did. Now there are three to four candidates per party, not just the one the President wants. But, sure enough, in the 2006 election, Fox's handpicked man, Felipe Calderón, won. In exit polls Mexicans said they had voted for his opponent. We can only guess the outcome of the 2012 election, but I hear the PRI intends to regain power. Have Mexican politics really changed?"

Coral had done some research. Yes, Fox had stabilized the economy, but in the process he and his successor Calderón increased the population of Mexico's millionaires from twenty-four to in excess of a stunning 170,000, including Carlos Slim, who surpassed Bill Gates as the richest man in the world, now that Theo was dead. Yet extreme urban poverty rates—those living on less than a dollar a day—remained stuck at twelve percent and in rural areas at around twenty percent.

"I guess what the U.S. defines as the poverty level would be outright wealth to much of Mexico," she said.

"Yes, that is correct, Coral," Luis said, his voice solemn. "There is hope in the PRD party, in power in Mexico City since 1997, but if the PRI comes back, "the perfect dictatorship" may return."

Salati nodded. "That is what the Peruvian writer Vargas Llosa called Mexico's one-party rule. It is as if, once brutally subjugated by Spain and, unfortunately, by the Catholic Church, the country has remained so, psychologically. Even during prosperity Mexico's government, in league with the elite, keeps its boot on the people's neck."

Luis spoke passionately about the 1982 and 1995 peso devaluations that had plunged Mexico into bankruptcy and destroyed the small middle class.

Salati listened closely, his beautiful dogs eating leftovers from his hand. "Yet, in spite of all this," Salati said, "Mexicans love their country. Most don't speak about its flaws like you do, Luis. It is their mother and, though she is crippled, she is beautiful to them. Immigrants dream of returning to her and this is no surprise. I have seen Mexico's extravagant beauty as well as her horrors. They exist together, a single mystifying truth."

Luis sat back, as if he didn't know what to make of Salati's remarks. Perhaps they didn't fit in with La Reconquista.

Salati, said, "Excuse me if you will. I must make a call to your west coast. It will take a little while."

Alone on the terrace, Luis beamed at Coral. "You know more about Mexico than I thought."

She sensed an opening. "Where is your family, Luis?"

He paused in thought then rose and pulled out her chair. "Perhaps knowing will help you in your work. Come with me." His cousin appeared and Luis instructed him to attend to Salati if he returned before they did.

Coral followed Luis down the terrace to the curtained glass wall of the salon—a locked room. With a key, he opened the sliding door and led her in. Coral gasped when she saw dark shapes.

"Don't be afraid, *hermosa*," Luis said. "Stay there."

She liked that he called her by the Spanish word for beautiful one. Moments later when dim lights came on, Coral saw the outlines of people in the room.

"Don't be afraid," he said.

She smelled incense and heard music, a haunting pipe, a simple drum accompanied by rippling sounds, like dry bean pods blown in a breeze. She heard bamboo wind chimes. The music made her think of flowing water. There was chanting, as if from ancient ceremonies in villages far away. The sound was beautiful, but who were these people?

Luis turned a spotlight on and Coral saw that they were statues—a boy kneeling, a lovely woman, life-sized, her hair dangling over a young girl asleep on the ground. On the woman's shoulders rested the strong hands of two standing men, one younger, one older. The latter looked off toward the horizon in despair.

Rocks and cactus lay around them. Fresh-cut marigolds encircled them and lined a path to a three-tiered altar like those she'd seen in Mexico for *Los Días de los Muertos*, the Days of the Dead. A group photo was on the wall and above it white *papel picado*, tissue paper cut with intricate designs. There were candles and costumed skeleton figures—a doll, a tobacco pipe, a fan, roller skates, a man's gold ring.

"Who are they?" Coral asked as the haunting music drifted through the room.

"My family," Luis said. He approached the statues and put his hand on the man's back as if he were greeting him. "I brought them from my old apartment."

"Your family?"

He touched them one by one. "Juan Pablo is my father. Aileen-Reynoso is my mother. Cyntia Cualli is my young sister. Eduardo Itzli is my elder brother. Roberto Mazatl is my young brother."

She didn't know what to say. Who had statues of their relatives in the living room? "Goodness. You and your siblings all have Nahuatl middle names."

"Yes, my parents fought against *malinchismo*, the racism the Spaniards created: pure *gachupines* and *criollos* at the top, the many castes of mestizos in the middle, *indios* at the bottom. They gave us all both Spanish and Mexica names because that is who we are." Standing among the statues, Luis seemed cut off from the world.

"Where are they, Luis?"

"Somewhere on the Tohono O'odham Indian Reservation in Arizona."

"They are living with the Indians?"

"No."

She gazed at the altar with the white papel picado. "Why are they on an Arizona Indian reservation?"

He looked away. "They are dead."

"Dead?"

"Their remains are somewhere in a big, empty desert."

"What happened to them?"

"A coyote happened, a human one. In traditional Mexican culture the coyote played a vital role. He disrespected authority when those in power went overboard. We call the ones who smuggle illegal immigrants across the border coyotes. Once they weren't bad people, but the drug cartels became involved in the smuggling. Many coyotes can't be trusted now."

"You think a coyote killed them?"

"I think the sun killed them." He walked over to another Aztec calendar and touched the sun god's obsidian tongue. "When the coyote stole their money and abandoned them, Tonatiuh took them in sacrifice to help forestall the end of the world."

In reply to Coral's stare he added, "It is one of our myths."

"Oh, Luis, why did they ever try that? Why didn't they wait, if necessary, and come legally like you did?"

For a long time he didn't speak. "In your work, you will help me rid Mexico of the corrupt coyotes who fed my family to the sun."

Coral had a sudden hunch. "Luis, did you hire the coyote?"

Instead of replying, he went to the statue of his mother and put his hand on her head. Luis's pain radiated to Coral. He looked up, a plea in his eyes. It was true. Coral nodded. She would keep his secret.

He switched the lights out and turned the music off, led her out and locked the door.

When they returned, Salati was back on the terrace and as Luis's cousin served dessert the subject of illegal immigration came up.

Luis leaned forward, his expression determined. Now Coral knew why he'd ignored Salati's haughty reminder that Luis was once the butler here. Luis had goals, and they were personal. He'd killed his family. In penance, he meant to save all the poor of Mexico—not a bad use for a humongous fortune, after all.

"Evaristo," he said, "what is your opinion? How does Holy Mother Church regard the wandering and the lost who flee from poverty?"

Salati looked questioningly at Coral.

"She was Theomund's confidante," Luis said.

Coral thought, *That wasn't always true, but it sounds good.*

"I can speak freely in any case," Salati said, "because the Pontiff has an unflinching policy of openness to immigrants, even illegal ones. He has urged immunity for ours from Albania and North Africa, even in the face of protest by the rest of Italy. The Pope said, 'The illegal immigrant comes before us like that stranger in whom Jesus asks to be recognized.' He has urged dioceses around the world to be helpful."

"I am glad to hear that," Luis said. "I'd like to talk about this more."

Salati yawned, his thick lashes closing.

Immediately Luis changed the subject. "Perhaps in the morning. You've had a long trip."

Salati stood. "Yes, I'd like to rest."

Luis clasped his hands. "Of course. Coral will show you to your room."

Coral doubted if Luis realized how much Salati had drunk and how often he had seemed transfixed by Luis's passionate conversation. If she didn't miss her guess, she might have an impossible assignment tonight.

Chapter 7

Coral wiggled her eyebrows up at Luis as she left, making him smile. She led Evaristo Salati past the locked doors to the main guest suite, his dogs following.

Inside, Salati excused himself and went to the bathroom. When he returned, he took off his jacket and sat in a luxurious chair, watching with a pleasant, slightly drunken smile as Coral turned down his bed. As she did, she made subtly seductive motions then sat on the rug by his chair.

Salati smiled and it was as if the silent screen star Rudolph Valentino had returned. "I see you are aware of your extravagant beauty," he said.

She feigned a blush. "You're not bad, yourself."

"And you believe I'm not strict about my vow of celibacy."

Coral arched an inquisitive eyebrow.

"Luis believes the same. You are his present to me for the night, lucky me."

She took his hand. "I'm curious. Why in the world would someone like you decide to be a priest, Evaristo?"

Salati sighed. "Being attractive and being devout seem mutually exclusive to you?"

Stroking his hand, Coral slipped a strap off her shoulder.

"Oblige me, lovely one, and don't take off your clothes though I am sure I would be transfixed by the sight. Tonight I'd prefer to pretend that things are as they ought to be—that I, a priest, don't experience lust, though I do."

He reached down and stroked one of the dogs. They had large sensitive ears that were pink on the inside and stood straight up, like Egyptian cats she'd seen statues of in museums. Their coats were sable, but so pale they looked ghostly.

"My darlings," he said to them with passion. They both sat up.

"What are they?" she asked, warily. *And what do you plan to do with them?*

"Sicilian Hounds."

It still amazed her how rich and powerful men gave no thought to revealing themselves to women they didn't know. It must be this environment. Theo had created an extravagant den for exclusive rogues who would never turn each other in.

"Dogs aren't exactly my thing," she said, eyeing them.

Evaristo smiled. "Not even when they sing?"

He opened his mouth and began a Gregorian chant. Both dogs lifted their throats and howled along, almost in tune.

Coral watched, delighted, half-wishing he'd strip off his collar, open his pants, and act like the alluring man he was. Then she decided she was excessively depraved, thinking of sex in the face of this angelic-looking man who was singing religious music with his dogs.

When he stopped, she whispered, "Is there nothing I can do for you?"

"Yes," he said. "Continue to be beautiful. Continue to love because I can not."

"I know priests who do," she said and pursed her lips seductively.

For an instant he gazed longingly at her mouth, then he said, "So do I."

She decided to venture her guess about him. "It's not really a woman you want, is it?"

He only stared at her and smiled.

She decided he was like Luis, caught between his penis and his God—so much so that he wouldn't allow himself release. She began to feel intensely sorry for the handsome Cardinal Salati, who began to sing another quiet chant with his dogs.

Coral felt embarrassed. She tiptoed to the door, waved goodbye, and stepped out. Talk about priestly abstinence. She'd never actually seen it.

She found Luis still on the terrace. He handed her a beer and she sat beside him.

"So, what happened?" he asked.

Would Luis think she'd failed? She decided to make a joke of it. She swigged the beer and said, "People are sick."

Luis turned, "What did he do to you?"

"Not a goddamned thing. He made me keep my clothes on, then he sang Gregorian chant while his dogs howled along."

"That was it?"

She wiggled her eyebrows up. "Yeah. Sheesh!"

Quietly they looked at each other and smiled. Chuckles turned to laughter, which Salati couldn't hear because his room was soundproofed—all the rooms. Luis's laughter reinforced hers. She had to put her beer down as Luis staggered, his shoulders shaking, overcome. In peels of mirth, he bent at the waist. Coral slid from the lounge chair and rolled across the terra cotta tiles in her silver dress, convulsed in laughter.

"Oh God, he's really celibate?" Luis choked. "I wish I could have seen him singing with the dogs."

Coral gasped, "No, you don't; no you don't. You would have laughed and he never would have spoken to you again! No more Reconquista."

Luis sank to his knees in his Italian suit, holding his sides. "You are right!"

"I don't think he really wanted me back there anyway. I think he wanted you!"

Luis paused to glare at her then laughed more.

"People are so damned sick. Why didn't he just screw, instead of having canine three-part harmony?" Coral wanted to keep Luis amused, rather than have him analyze her usefulness with Salati. "People are sick. They always have been and they always will be."

With effort she regained control, kicked off her shoes and stretched out, her elbows on the tiles, yoga-style. "But, you know, maybe not. The ancient Egyptians said the first people weren't made of clay, but of cum. That would explain it. They believed God masturbated and created life."

Luis was still laughing.

She slapped his arm, not sure why he found Evaristo so funny.

The two of them were exactly alike. "Stop it or I'll puke!" she said.

He lay on the tiles beside her and stared at the night. "Sometimes I wish I'd been born in ancient Greece."

"Or better yet, ancient China," she said, understanding Luis's wish. She sensed another chance to deepen the growing bond between them.

"Why?"

"Love between males wasn't illegal then. No Chinese God said it was wrong. There is a story that Emperor Ai's lover, Dong Xian, fell asleep on the imperial robes. Rather than wake him, the Emperor cut off the costly robe's sleeves."

Luis gazed at her a long time. "When was that?"

"About 6 B.C. or so."

"Now that you mention it," Luis added, "Alexander the Great had a male lover named Hephaistion. It didn't keep him from conquering the world."

"Apparently not."

"They didn't know it was wrong."

"Wrong?" Coral sat up. "How can you be sure what's right and wrong?"

He rose and went to the terrace edge, Central Park below. "I do not fly in the face of God."

"Luis, why are humans the only creatures who give ourselves grief for being us? There have always been males who mated with males and females with females. Why don't we conclude it's normal human behavior?"

"The Holy Bible says it's not."

Coral stood and put her arm around Luis. "Personally, I think the lions are going to hell. They're a lot worse than us. They're polygamous and the males sometimes kill the cubs. Did you know chimpanzees are bisexual? All of them? They fuck whatever lets them. Females sell sex to whoever brings the most fruit. I think the chimps are going to hell."

Luis turned. "So God's law doesn't' exist. Only nature? That means a beautiful woman like you should be ready for sex with every man she passes on the street. They all want you."

Coral looked up at the sky. No stars. She wished she weren't in the city. "God sure thought women would have a lot of sex partners, that's for sure. Otherwise, why did he make two kinds of sperm? The kind that swim for the egg and the kamikazes whose only job is to block or attack another man's swimmers?"

"This is true?" Luis seemed amazed.

"Sex is my business, remember? It's called sperm competition. Want another fact? You know testosterone is the sex hormone, right? I can't remember the units, but do you know how women and men compare?"

"How?"

"It's a range. The *low* end for men is almost three times more than the *high* end for women'. So explain to me Luis why God, if he meant for us to be monogamous, gave men as much as from three to twenty times more testosterone than any woman? Another thing, her testosterone only peaks for a couple of days when there's an egg and she needs to fertilize it. The rest of the time, sex is *not* on her mind. What's that poor guy supposed to do?"

"But you are highly sexed."

"Yeah, and I'm grateful for it, but I'm still nowhere near a man's sex drive. Anyway, I'm talking averages, which is what should count when society starts making rules. Human beings are promiscuous, bisexual, and if necessary, we masturbate and rape, just like chimpanzees."

Luis sat on a striped love seat. Coral joined him. She curled up and put her head against his chest.

"But you were upset when Sam's raging testosterone made him violate you, hermosa."

Coral held back tears. She fell asleep while Luis stroked her hair.

Next morning she woke in the other guest room, still wearing her silver gown. As she showered and dressed for a second day of charming Salati, she wondered if she and Luis were really closer and if the new keycard he'd left would open more doors today.

She took a slow stroll out to the terrace to find a table beautifully set for three and Luis inspecting it. He'd conjured up real *gorditas infladas*—puffed breads—and scrambled eggs with black beans, onions, and jalapenos, as well as a tropical fruit salad.

Salati arrived and pulled out her chair. As they politely wolfed down the delicious food, she stroked his leg under the table with her toe. He returned a friendly, disinterested smile. She had no power over him. Worse, Luis still didn't trust her. She'd tested the keycard and it didn't open more doors.

Gazing back and forth at these two men who'd vowed their celibacy, she had an idea, a bold idea. She lowered her head into her hand, stroked her neck with the free one and said, "Excuse me, fellas, but I'm hot." Panting through parted lips, she lowered her robe off her shoulders and let her head drop back.

"Touch my breast, Luis. Pretty please?" she said, peering at him from under her lids.

He looked so shocked; she would have burst out laughing if money weren't at stake.

Sounding amused, Salati said, "Perhaps I should leave."

"No, touch the other one," she moaned.

She saw Salati's eyes register comprehension, saw him look at Luis. It seemed forever that nothing happened then Evaristo said, "I think, in courtesy, we must do as she asks, Luis."

Coral wanted to cheer. She'd been right.

She saw Luis flush scarlet, felt Evaristo's cool palm, and closed her eyes. A moment later, she felt Luis's hesitant touch. She moaned louder, to keep them from thinking too hard.

"That's it," she whispered, "that's it."

Salati said. "She is a passionate woman."

"Yes," Luis said. "An asset to me."

She felt their hands touch, followed by a sharp increase in heat. Coral stopped moaning, her purpose accomplished.

Quickly Luis jerked his hand away. She heard his chair scrape as if he'd stood and then, "Excuse me for a moment."

At the sound of departing footsteps, Coral opened her eyes

and grinned at Salati. "You can stop now," she said, closing her robe.

He didn't look the least embarrassed. Instead, he took a slice of bacon from his plate, whistled, and fed his dogs from the palm that had caressed her.

"Coral, you are an interesting woman," he said.

Luis returned, cleared his throat, and began to explain his plan.

"The drug gangs of Mexico kill innocent people every day. There are literally wars on the border now. However hard the Mexican president tries, I see nothing that will change this. Even a bad economy here is better than no hope there. Meanwhile, terrorists may be slipping across America's southern border." Luis gestured. "But what if someone managed to steal the coyote trade from the drug gangs and in their stead put men more like eagles, pledged to safely escort their kinsmen across the border, and to keep out those who don't belong?"

"Interesting," Salati said, his expression neutral.

"If such a thing happened," Luis continued, "where could the eagles fly for safety with their Christian charges? Who would take in these Mexican Catholics, who will one day form the majority population of the USA?"

Salati put down his fork. "It's surprising to hear a wholly charitable request come from this address."

Luis set his jaw. "I am not Theomund Brown."

"That is apparent. Let's speak plainly. I know you are aware of many of my dealings with Brown. He phoned me not long before his death. He said he'd located the boy."

"If you mean the supposed cloned Christ," Luis snorted. "He is dead."

"You are sure?"

Luis rose from the breakfast table and returned with an Italian gossip rag called *Chi Mai*, published more than a month ago in Milan. He handed it to Salati, who read it. "His name was Jess Johnson?" Salati asked.

Luis nodded.

"How tragic," Salati said. "In recent days many at the Vatican saw the error of their fears. They began praying this boy had survived so we could bring him to Rome. If there's a chance he really has the genes of Jesus Christ, imagine the power he might possess. At worst, he'd be an ordinary boy, but at best? Someone to speak with, learn from, study, and if possible, direct. If this happened, there need be no schism in the Catholic Church because of him. He would be one of us."

Coral had assumed Salati wanted the clone dead. She'd guessed as much from Theo's actions—sending Sam to Italy when he had amnesia, then going himself—keeping in touch with Salati all the while."

"He's dead," Luis repeated.

"What a shame," Salati replied. "In exchange for that boy, I might very well have been inclined to transmit a private message to every Catholic Church, school, convent, and seminary in America where the Virgin of Guadalupe is enshrined. I might have been willing to say *the Holy Father wishes you to assist the new eagles who will come.* What will you call this organization, Luis?"

"Mexica Eterna."

Salati stood. "I might have instructed that they assist Mexica Eterna, this group that will protect the lives and money of immigrants, keep terrorists from crossing the border and, I take it, hasten La Reconquista?"

Luis's mouth fell open. "How did you know?"

"It is an old but interesting concept. La Reconquista, if it happened, could indeed bring faith to godless America once again. A Latino and therefore Catholic majority in the American southwest in this century, and sweeping the entire country in the next? This might be of interest to future Popes."

"And if I could hasten this?" Luis asked.

"You are doing so?"

"I'm making plans."

"Plans are mere conjecture and you tell me the boy is dead." Salati rose. "Would you phone down to my driver and tell him to be ready?"

Luis snapped his fingers. His servant appeared and made the call.

"Evaristo, if there is something else you want—"

Coral thought Salati gazed longingly at the accidentally touched hand.

"I'm sure there is," Salati said. "You are in control of Theomund Brown's vast resources, so I'm sure there is."

"Anything," Luis said, holding himself upright to look the patrón. "Just name it."

"Thank you for your hospitality. On my next trip, we will talk again." He stroked Coral's cheek and said to Luis. "I hope to see this interesting woman then as well."

Chapter 8

Maggie stood between the drapes at Felix's twelve-foot living room windows, watching for Sam. Since his success with the forced Bible swearing, Sam had taken to issuing orders when he couldn't get her to agree. At least, that's how his insistence that they go out today seemed.

He pulled up in the Range Rover.

She was relieved to see Sharmina wave from the back seat. Whatever the purpose of this mysterious pre-dawn trip, at least Sam wasn't spiriting her off to a secret love nest. She had to marry him for the baby's sake, but he could forget a wedding night.

Downstairs she saw the building guard who knew her secret. He left the lobby. She was glad she didn't have to say hello to him in front of Sam. In despair yesterday she'd gone to the basement, opened her trunk, and found the gun her daddy gave her. She'd held it, remembering the woods in Macon, Georgia. In her mind, one of the white men after her was Sam.

Later, Maggie took it to the guard she knew best and asked him to keep it for her. She told herself she wasn't afraid to use it. She just needed a sign from God.

Sam, waiting by the car, saw her long-sleeved, black turtleneck dress, black pillbox hat and veil. He said, "Well, now, Maggie."

She'd ignored his hint not to wear widow's weeds today.

"You look … wonderful, my girl."

"I'm still in mourning, Sam."

With him at the wheel beside her and Sharmina in the back, they rode onto I-95, the New England Throughway, heading north.

Irritated, Maggie looked back at Sharmina.

"Shar, do you know what the big secret is about this trip?"

Sharmina's eyes grew round, which meant she did. "No, ma'am."

"Oh, Shar. Please don't call me that. We're friends."

"Yes, ma'am."

Sharmina had been treating her like a returning potentate. Maggie hadn't found a way to get things back to normal yet.

"Well, it's not that much of a surprise, Shar. Where could we be going except to some kind of swimming pool?" Sam had repeatedly insisted they wear bathing suits under their clothes. To shut him up, she put on a one-piece black suit, but she had no intention of swimming anywhere.

"'Where else except a pool?' she asks," Sam said, smiling.

"Where else?" Sharmina repeated.

Maggie stared out of the windshield and let them have their game. A week after the incident with Doña Teresita, Sam visited the curandera again and now wanted her to deliver his child. He'd concluded Teresita wasn't just a talented *partera*, but also a woman of unusual understanding. Afterward, Teresita sent Maggie a gift: Heidi Murkoff's *What to Expect When You're Expecting*. Indifferent, Maggie kept it, intending to hide her feelings until after the wedding. If he wanted the baby, it was his. If not, she'd give it away.

An hour after they'd left Fifth Avenue, the sun rose on Long Island Sound. Its gauzy beauty threatened to crack Maggie's control. How many sunrises had she watched in Italy with Jess? She fought the urge to insist Sam turn around and take her to the airport so she could fly back to Lake Maggiore, in case Jess was waiting there. Adamo had offered to help her and Jess disappear. Sam's arrival intervened. If Adamo had succeeded, Jess would have lived.

Maggie thought about the road. Being on I-95 always reminded her it intertwined with US 1, the old Boston Post Road, backbone of the famous Underground Railroad long ago. In places actual tunnels had been dug beneath this road by which mail was delivered and slaves escaped.

Wondering if ancestors of hers had stolen north along it, she dozed and woke just as they entered Boston, a city with which she felt kinship because of its role in freeing the slaves. Ignoring their questions, Sam drove the winding cobbled streets to Faneuil Hall, the 250-year-old brick market building with a white cupola on top. Once it hosted historic town meetings in which revolutionaries and abolitionists made famous speeches, but now it was the center of a vast shopping/dining area where they stopped for breakfast. Returning to the car, they reached a large old building just east of the Boston Common at exactly 10:00 A.M.

"Here we are," Sam said.

Perplexed, Maggie replied, "Filene's Basement? But that's a department store, Sam."

"Yes, my girl, and the biggest bridal event in the country."

So this was Sam's wedding gown surprise. In the one city that to her meant freedom, he was conspiring to take hers away.

"This is where my mother bought her wedding dress and every woman in my family. Designer gowns for almost nothing, one day a year." He got out and came around, opening her and Sharmina's doors. "They call it 'the running of the brides'."

Maggie had never discussed finances with Sam. He didn't know she had no need for a discount gown.

He opened his wallet and counted out ten hundred dollar bills. "Courtesy of Duffy Detectives, Maggie."

She took the money, planning to go in and find the ugliest wedding gown. Black, if they had one.

"I'll tell you the secret my mother told her friends," Sam continued. "Don't arrive at the sale at 8:00 A.M. That's when the crowd is like a beast. In two minutes, they snatch all the gowns off the rack and hoard them like plunder, trading them back and forth, tit for tat. By 10 A.M., their lust is slaked and the gowns are back on the racks."

Sharmina dispensed with protocol. "Time's a wasting if this is just one day!" She grabbed Maggie's arm and hustled her across the parking lot into the building, down a flight of stairs, and into a massive room hung with signs saying *Bridal Event.* It was crammed with what seemed miles of wedding gowns, women trying them on over their bathing suits.

Sharmina rushed to the nearest rack and reached for tags, gleefully shouting out prices. "$250, $500, $750! Every one a steal. Maggie, you've got it made in the shade, honey; I mean ma'am. He gave you a whole thousand dollars. You've got a good man there."

"I do, do I?"

"Do you want sleeveless, short sleeves, long sleeves? It's all here. Quick, lift up your arms. Get out of that dress." She took Maggie's purse, yanked her hat off and pulled her dress over her head, leaving her standing in her black bathing suit. "Do you want strapless?"

"Long sleeves." Maggie saw a dreadful gown and smiled.

Suddenly Sharmina seized a hanger which, at the same moment, must have been grabbed from the other side because a tug of war ensued as an invisible voice called, "Let go!"

"I saw it first!" Sharmina jerked, causing the rack to sway. Before Maggie could move, they were buried in an avalanche of wedding gowns. She struggled to a sitting position as Sharmina's head emerged, followed by her hand holding the hanger, gown attached.

"Look at this!" Sharmina rose, pulled the plastic off and swirled the gown.

Maggie's eyes softened. Sharmina held the dress of Maggie's dreams—ivory white, a sculpted waist, a beaded bodice—so lovely it would make any bride pretty on her wedding day.

"It's a Vera Wang!"

"I'm a size 8," Maggie whispered, staring at it

"Size 10, but wedding gowns run small."

Maggie stepped into the ivory gown, its bodice and pointed cuffs studded with pearls and beads. Sharmina hooked what felt like dozens of pearl buttons then unfolded a cathedral length train.

"It fits!" Sharmina exclaimed in glee, opening her purse, to pull out a large hand mirror and hold it up.

Maggie gasped. All her life she'd pictured looking like this.

The dress hid her figure's flaws and played up the assets. She turned at the waist and the dress moved with her. It was perfect, except she'd never imagined stepping from mourning clothes into her wedding gown to marry an enemy of hers.

Rain again. Silent tears. Pouring.

Women nearby stopped searching for their gowns to watch her cry. She knew they wondered what could cause tears on such a day—buying a beautiful wedding gown on sale. One woman whispered to Sharmina, who responded, "Her little boy died."

Sympathetic moans and sighs.

Sharmina kneeled and took Maggie's hands.

"What are you doing?" Maggie whispered, "Get up, Sharmina."

"Don't cry, ma'am. I know your heart is broke but God's sent you another one."

Maggie tried to pull her up. Sharmina shouldn't be kneeling to her, especially in public. She heard murmurs all around, heard someone ask if she was a princess.

"Praise God for his miracles," Sharmina said.

"Get up, Shar."

Shar rose.

"Don't ever kneel like that to me. What's the matter with you?"

Raising her eyebrows significantly, Sharmina gazed at Maggie's stomach. "It's okay, I know."

"What do you know?"

"Which is why I can't be your bridesmaid!" Sharmina wailed. "We always said we'd be each other's bridesmaids if we ever found a man we could stand. I can't do it, Maggie—I mean, ma'am."

Around them, women looked aghast. How could a woman's best friend abandon her on her wedding day?

Panicked, Maggie gathered up their things. Making her way through racks of white, and the aisles full of brides in their bathing suits, she went in search of a dressing room, Sharmina in tow.

"Here, sit down. Tell me what's wrong," Maggie, said when she found a room.

Sharmina wiped her eyes with a tissue and confessed, "It don't seem right that God would let you be married without me, but in your position you need someone better than me, somebody really—you know—pure."

Maggie bent and hugged her. "Nothing on this earth is purer than love and I know you love me, Shar. I love you, too."

Sharmina slid to her knees and clasped her hands. "Oh, heavenly mother! Guide me!"

Horrified, Maggie frowned. "No, no! Get up, Shar! I'm not a heavenly mother. I'm just me."

"Thank you for forgiving my faults! How many times will I get to stand up for the pregnant mother of God?"

"What did you say?" Maggie helped her to her feet.

"It's okay, I know about the clone," Sharmina reassured her. "It was kind of obvious. Jess dies. You're pregnant again. I hope this one takes, ma'am. I really do."

Maggie felt hot and dizzy. "You've got this all wrong. You can't go around thinking, much less saying—"

"I know, but you should be treated with respect. One of the reasons I call you *ma'am* is to remind Felix and Sam to treat you nice! Felix acts like you're still his maid. You're not! I am! I know he's partly putting on a show, I guess. Sam acts like you belong to him, when you're really so much more."

Speechless, Maggie shook her head.

"I know it's partly because they don't want people to learn about the clone unless they can be trusted, of course. Even so, not everybody gets to carry a sacred clone."

Maggie found her voice. "Clone?"

"The one you're carrying," Sharmina whispered. "I know Felix is trying it again—to clone Christ. It's okay. I know."

She grabbed Sharmina's hands. "Felix didn't do a thing. There is no clone. I'm carrying Sam's child. That's the truth! Have I ever lied to you?"

"Only when you were pregnant with Jess, but I understood. You had to protect him."

Maggie groaned. "Okay, okay, but I'm not lying now! It's just my baby, Sam's and mine. Do you believe me?"

"No, but I know why you want me to."

For a few seconds Maggie heard only the rustle of gowns coming off and on in the dressing rooms around them. Then she remembered Sam's Bible-swearing trick.

"Get me out of this dress. We're going to church," she said.

Sharmina undid the Vera Wang gown's many small buttons as fast as she could. In another part of Filene's Basement, they bought Sharmina's bridesmaid dress. Pink and strapless, it was marked down to $150. They paid for their purchases and went to find Sam, who was careful not to look at the gowns as they put them in the car. Four hours later they were back in New York. Maggie asked Sam to drive straight to the 131st Street Baptist Church and wait.

Ignoring his questions, she and Sharmina got out beneath the church's neon cross, climbed the brick steps, and entered. The nave temporarily empty, they kneeled in the front row, their heads down.

Sharmina pointed to a barely visible film on the hymnal ledge. "Who's on dusting duty this week?"

"I don't know. First, let's pray together. Let's speak from our hearts."

"Dear God," Sharmina began, "make me rich as the Pharaohs. If you can't do that, make me wise as Solomon and Einstein."

They were quiet.

"Sharmina, I don't mean to interfere with your relationship with God, but do you honestly one hundred percent believe that will happen? I'm not saying it can't. I'm just wondering if you totally believe it because when he did miracles Jesus almost always said, 'your faith has healed you.'"

Silence.

"Dear God, make me good as I can be."

Maggie bowed her head and mumbled, "Me, too."

They looked at each other.

"In Jesus' name, Amen," Maggie said. She retrieved a Bible. "Now, Shar, I want you to hold this Bible. I'll put my hand on it, so you'll know for sure that I'm telling the truth when I say—"

They heard a sound at the double doors and looked over their shoulders. In the silence of the church, her second home, Maggie heard a man's voice humming, "O Sole Mio."

"*Mia cara.*"

The double doors opened. She saw the silhouette of a man. He came forward and Maggie recognized his beautiful black mustache. He wore Italian shoes, an Italian suit, an Italian tie—not from Milan's designers, but from a village like the one where she'd lived with Jess.

"Mia cara?" he said.

"Adamo?" She couldn't believe her eyes. "Adamo Morelli?"

Holding onto her, Sharmina whispered, "Who's this creep?"

Maggie gaped at the man in the aisle. This *creep* was Adamo, formerly Arona's town drunk. He had been her friend until the tragedies that stole the ones they loved—Adamo's sister-in-law and Maggie's son. She saw tears on Adamo's face.

He called her by her assumed name. "Hetta I am here."

In disbelief, Maggie went to him. Italian style, they kissed each other's cheeks.

"Adamo, where in the world did you come from?"

"From the basement, mia cara. I have been waiting for you. They said you would come. I didn't know where you lived." He looked around. "But, luckily, you told me over and over again about the 131st Street Baptist Church. At the airport I told the taxi the name, and presto, I am here."

She couldn't believe it.

"But why, Adamo? Why have you come?"

He took her hands. "To keep from making another mistake. Look how many years I thought I loved my brother's wife. I was wrong." Adamo kneeled, kissed her hands, and then spread his arms wide. "Marry me, Hetta. It is me you love—me and Arona and the sunny villa where you lived with Jess. I woke up yesterday and knew I cannot live without you. Return with me today to Lake Maggiore and to love."

For a moment she wanted to do just that, leave here with

Adamo and return to Italy where she'd been happy for so long. She couldn't. She was carrying Sam's child and Jess was dead. She couldn't return to Lake Maggiore where he'd died. Besides, she didn't love Adamo. He must have been drinking, anyway.

"My name's not really Hetta, Adamo. I had to use a different name over there. It's Maggie. Maggie Johnson."

He wrinkled his brow then beamed a smile at her. "By any name, you are the rose of my heart. Too long have I lingered in my brother's shadow, thinking I loved the woman who was his wife. *Sono così stupido*. All the while I had a true love of my own. I did not see it until you went away. I have come to take you back."

Sharmina's upset voice interrupted. "Well, you're just too late! She's spoken for and she's getting married in a couple of days."

Alarm in his eyes, Adamo searched her face. "Tell me this is not true."

Maggie had enough of people kneeling to her. "Please get up, Adamo. Do you remember Sam? He was there at the end?"

Adamo nodded, breathing as if his heart had started to beat too fast. She watched his face become the mask of comedy he wore to hide woe like the Pagliacci he'd always been—a sad clown. He flew dramatically to his feet.

"Tell me where Sam is! I will kill him!"

Maggie couldn't tell Adamo how often she'd thought the same. "I … I'm pregnant," she said.

Adamo slapped the side of his face and paced back and forth, muttering Italian words that weren't polite.

"The child is his?" Adamo asked.

Maggie nodded.

He stopped and demanded, "Do you love him?"

Sadly, Maggie looked into his eyes. "Nowadays, Adamo, I don't think of anything but Jess and Sam."

On cue, Sam appeared at the door. For Adamo's sake she hoped Sam hadn't overheard much and that he didn't remember who Adamo was. While Sharmina folded her arms and smirked at Adamo, Sam came forward. To Shar, Sam was Joseph and Maggie was Mary, which meant Adamo could only be a snake in the garden they were about to occupy.

Sam made a big to-do of kissing her cheek and Maggie said, "You remember Adamo Morelli?"

Sam didn't offer his hand, which meant he'd heard. "Surprised to see you in New York, fella."

Adamo cocked an eyebrow. "I am a surprising person, Mr. Duffy."

Maggie tried to ease between them, but Sam prevented her.

"What's your business here?" Sam asked.

Indifferently, Adamo shrugged. "I think I will live here. Right now I am looking up old friends."

"You mean my future wife. Maggie and I are getting married."

Adamo turned his palms up in a gesture of doubt. "So I hear."

"You hear correctly. Please don't see my wife unless I'm around."

Maggie thought if Sharmina grinned any wider her teeth would hurt.

"Thanks for coming, Adamo," Maggie said "And thank you for being my friend." She glared at Sam, pushed past him and shook Adamo's hand.

Smiling, Adamo said, "This church is just as nice as you described, mia cara. I think I will join."

"Mia cara?" Sam put his face inches from Adamo's. "Stay away from my wife!"

With Sharmina glancing back to scowl at Adamo, Sam walked Maggie out to the car.

Chapter 9

It was standing room only in the 131st Street Baptist Church. Every pew, every aisle but the main one was full of people. Men wore their Sunday suits, the women had on extravagant hats with flowers and feathers and ribbons. In her wedding gown, Maggie stood next to Sharmina, peeping in amazement through the church's inner double doors. To get inside, six ushers had to clear a path because half of Harlem was out on the street beneath the church's neon cross.

Sharmina whispered, "If they had a hat contest today, Mag, we'd lose!"

"Where did they all come from?" Maggie whispered.

Sharmina bent to adjust Maggie's train as the minister's son and daughter—the ring bearer and flower girl—fidgeted. "Well, I suppose they heard about the wedding," she said. "Most of Harlem knows who you are and we're all so proud of you, ma'am."

Sharmina rose and lifted Maggie's veil to refresh her lipstick.

"And just why are they proud of me?" In the confusion of Adamo's return, Maggie had forgotten to swear on the Bible to prove she wasn't carrying another clone.

Sharmina lowered the veil, tugged at Maggie's long white sleeves with the pearls and beads at the cuff, made sure they were straight, adjusted her neckline. "What a question! You're the only one who doesn't think it's important to carry a clone of Jesus."

Aghast, Maggie searched her face. "Oh, my goodness. You didn't tell anyone that, did you? I told you this is Sam's baby."

"Well, no, not exactly. They just know you *were* the mother of the clone of Christ, even if you're not right now."

"But everybody thinks Jess died at birth, don't they? Felix put it in the papers. They don't know he lived ten years. They don't know he was wonderful—" She stopped, determined to face death down—this animal that had stalked the village of her life and picked off those she adored: her father, defeated by the loss of his farm; her mother, defeated by the loss of him; Jess, defeated by his willingness to die. She'd had enough. She'd marry Sam because she had to, but he'd never put his hands on her, wedding night or not.

She just hadn't expected this would turn into a circus.

Maggie slumped onto the same wood bench where her parents had sat when they first came to New York from Macon, Georgia thirty years ago, their land stolen, her father broken. The 131st Street Baptist Church gave them refuge. It took care of Maggie when her parents died. Even with this commotion, her wedding couldn't happen anywhere else. Because of Sam, she'd had to promise to raise the child a Catholic, but that didn't matter since she didn't plan to raise it all. Her eyes watered. If this marriage were real, she'd want her parents here.

"Now none of that," Sharmina said and lifted Maggie's veil again to dab at her eyes, "You're messing up your makeup. Besides, you know as well as I do that black folk don't believe what newspapers say."

"But how does everyone in Harlem even know I'm here, Sharmina? I was supposed to have died too, remember?"

Sharmina looked guilty. "Well, it could have been the minister's wife, or the deacon's wife. It could have been anybody that started spreading the word that you're alive and back in Harlem and getting married to the man who saved you. Some of them think your son was crucified and now you're marrying your Joseph, just like Mary did."

Maggie shook her head in dismay.

The organ music for the processional began. She'd said she couldn't bear to hear trumpets, much less "Here Comes the Bride." Could the choir sing, "Wade in the Water?" Sharmina had countermanded, insisting this was a wedding, not a wake. Maggie finally decided she would walk down the aisle to the, "Our Father."

"There, there," Sharmina said, comforting her. "One last look?"

She reached inside her pink purse and pulled out the large hand mirror. Maggie saw herself in her wedding gown a final time—black veil traded for white. If she cared about Sam, she'd feel guilt for his effort to match the splendor of her mourning clothes—driving all the way to Filene's Basement's main store. He was fiercely proud of paying for the wedding by himself. Determined to marry the mother of his child, and probably atone for raping her, he chalked her cool behavior up to grief.

"I guess I'm ready," Maggie said.

Sharmina wiggled her waist. "I know I am. Here comes the bride and Foxy Mama in pink."

The deaconess in charge of the wedding tiptoed over. "It's time." She opened the wooden doors and beamed at Maggie.

First the flower girl went and then the ring bearer. Sharmina stepped into the doorway and disappeared. When the organ began to play the, "Our Father," Maggie heard rustling and creaking as the packed church turned to see the bride all dressed in white.

It didn't feel right to be doing this without Jess, but when the deaconess motioned, Maggie stepped through the doorway and the church fell silent.

They'd laid a white satin runner down the red carpet. It ended at the altar where Sam waited next to Charlie, his best man and buddy from Molly Malone's, both of them in tuxedos. When Sam saw her in her gown, he pushed out his Irish chest and wept. It was only the second time she'd seen Sam cry and, if she cared, it would have touched her.

She wished this were a real wedding and her father were alive to lean on, wished Jess were here, her flower of the lily and the rose. She heard a hiccup and at the far back pew saw Adamo. He hadn't gone back to Italy. He looked drunk again. Maggie felt sorry for him.

Our Father who art in heaven, the soloist began, *hallo-wed be thy name.*

As in any wedding, the entire congregation stood when she started down the aisle. The minister. The guests. The choir and the wedding party. So many had come for the bride and so few for the groom, that they hadn't assigned sides. Felix stood next to his wife, Adeline, who had dressed simply so as not to outshine Maggie on her day. But Adeline couldn't help looking like an angel as she stood there in the church. Next to her, Frances, Felix's sister, wore a beige suit and an approving smile. All of Sam's cronies from Molly Malone's waved when they saw her, as did Pat the bartender. They were dots of white in this crowd of black faces, all staring as Maggie slowly came down the aisle.

Soon the men's deep voices joined the soloist, as did the tambourine and the drums. Maggie's church erupted in thrilling song as people started clapping and the church began to shake:

O-oh, O-our Father...Our Father ... which art in he-e-eaven ... Our Father ... hallo-wed be-ee ... Our Father ... thy holy name.

The music swept over Maggie. She swayed to it a little in her wedding gown, shook her head a little in the habit of her congregation, as she faced down death to take marriage vows. Sam willed her down the aisle with his eyes. *Come on, Maggie, you're doing it. Be brave, I'm here.* Yeah, right.

Halfway down, to Maggie's unease, some of the clapping congregation began falling to their knees as she passed. A woman touched her dress. A girl touched her hand. When someone tore a petal from her flowers and kissed it, she stepped back, afraid.

Sam started down the altar steps to protect his soon-to-be wife, but she caught his gaze and shook her head. Maggie was alone when she lost her son. She had no father to give her away. Alone she would make this walk.

Thy kingdom come ... thy kingdom come ... Thy w-i-ill be do-one ... Our Father ... on eeeearth ... Our Father... as it is in heaven sang Maggie's church, falling to its knees though Jess wasn't there, her flower of the lily and the rose.

Hallo-wed be ... hallo-wed be ... thy holy name... thy holy name.

When Maggie reached the altar she was so full of warring

emotions she thought she would faint, but there was Sam, holding her. There was Sharmina, taking the flowers. The deaconess stepped forward and vigorously fanned Maggie, saying, "Hold on child; hold on."

The ceremony would start with her traditions and end with his. Maggie heard prayers but didn't understand them. She only knew she stood next to Sam and Jess wasn't there. Still she smiled. The choir sang. By rote she repeated the minister's words. She heard the Irish vow Sam said to her:

> "By the power that Christ brought from heaven, mayst thou love me. As the sun follows its course, mayst thou follow me. As light to the eye, as bread to the hungry, as joy to the heart, may thy presence be with me, oh one that I love, 'til death comes to part us asunder."

When the minister declared them man and wife and Sam had kissed her, a guest soloist stood and sweetly sang the, "Irish Wedding Song," as they'd planned.

> "Here they stand, hand in hand
> They've exchanged wedding bands"
> Today is the day of all their dreams and their plans
> And all of their loved ones are here to say
> Oh, God bless this couple who marry today

Arm in arm they left the church, to the sound of Irish pipes, the six ushers trying to keep the applauding onlookers back.

"Bless us, Mother," someone called.

At the bottom of the steps she threw her flowers, and Sharmina, the blabbermouth, eagerly caught them. There would be no reception because Jess wasn't there.

Maggie had planned to tell Sam they were through at the hotel, but his smitten expression made her want to go back inside, take off this dress, and bunk at Sharmina's place tonight, but the stairs were blocked.

Startling her, an old man broke through the crowd and kissed the hem of her dress.

"Pops, let her alone!" Sam ordered. He moved the man away and while Sharmina sheepishly waved goodbye, hustled his new wife into the waiting Rolls Royce.

"What the hell was that all about?" Sam said when the door closed. He gripped her hand then kissed it. "You look gorgeous in that gown, but I thought they'd tear you to pieces."

Maggie couldn't tell him about the divorce here in the Rolls. The driver would hear. She'd have to tell him at the hotel, after all. "You ever been at a whole black church service before, Sam?"

"Can't say that I have."

She looked away, thinking of Jess, and the gospels they once sang at their villa on Lake Maggiore.

"Don't bother to try to tell me that happens all the time, Maggie. Who in the world do they think you are?"

She took off her veil, sat back and sighed. "You know they know I was Jess's mother, Sam."

Sam slapped the seat. "We never should have come back to New York!"

"Yes, we should." Maggie looked around and pretended surprise, "Sam you rented a Rolls! Oh, you shouldn't have."

"The boys at Molly Malone's arranged it. It's their wedding gift. I know I've said this before, Maggie, but one of these days I might actually stomp Felix Rossi to death for what he's done to you." He gazed out of the window. "Look at this mess."

"It's over, Sam." Maggie scanned the full sidewalk as the Rolls slowly began to move. "It's all over. Jess is gone."

Sam fingered her beaded cuff. "I know how you feel, but trust me. Your life is just beginning. You look beautiful, by the way. Just beautiful. Shall I tell you where we're going, Maggie, my girl?"

"Tell me." She already knew.

"The Plaza. It took everything we've got, but don't worry, I'll make more."

He had started a business, put a down payment on a town home, and laid out his last dime for this wedding, refusing Felix's help. At night when she was asleep he slipped out to handle his detective cases. She'd let him knock himself out. Sam didn't know how unnecessary it all was.

"The Plaza? My goodness," she said.

As the limo pulled away, Sam embraced her. She didn't fight him because what she saw through the side window was more disturbing—a woman with clasped hands stretched toward the car, hollering hallelujahs.

Chapter 10

There were a good four dozen men in the penthouse that night, all related to Luis: cousins upon cousins, uncles, grand uncles, nephews, once or twice or thrice removed. Luis took them in groups to the salon where the statues were. The men seemed moved when they returned. Until today they'd been farm workers with sun-etched skin, day laborers with calloused hands, gardeners and office workers, small business owners and policemen and students. They were the men of Luis's *familia* who had come from far and near. It was plain to Coral that Luis trusted them with his life.

Yet there was something distinctly different about this company of Mexican men. She could see their family closeness yet their behavior often seemed ritualized, at times almost formal, compared to equivalent gatherings of American men.

It didn't surprise her that when she walked by, they turned sullen stares on her. A few of their lips smiled, but not their eyes. It was the mask she'd noticed Mexicans often showed the world—a personal wall between them and a stranger until they knew how you fit into the scheme of things. Were you above or below them, friend or foe, ill mannered or not? Until they knew, Mexicans presented an inscrutable wall on which barbs appeared if you offended them. Or maybe she just imagined it.

On her visits to Mexico, she learned that affronts to *honor* and *respeto* were easy to avoid if you behaved as your grandmother taught you. Overlook no one. Ask permission. Criticize no one. Address men as señor, older ones as don, women as señorita unless they tell you they are married, and if so, señora or doña. Insult no one's wife. Challenge no one's masculinity or, in Mexico, violence could result.

A single act of human decency could bring the walls crashing down, making you *gente buena.* At least, that's what she understood. She didn't really know Mexican men. Most of her time south of the border was spent with Americans connected to Brown.

As for women like her, there were multiple names—none good. That's why Coral for the most part stayed away from the men, unsure of what Luis had told them. That way, she couldn't transgress against respeto. From her room she watched them on the terrace, seeing Luis assert his dominance over them. With expansive speech, repeated *saludos* and gustatory largesse—evidenced by jacketed waiters who moved about with food, drink, and fine cigars—Luis was establishing himself as the Moctezuma family's new *el patriarca*, the source of *nepotismo*, their guardian and guarantor, their arranger of intercessions, giver of educations and mortgages and business loans.

Yet one man seemed to withhold obeisance. Coral noticed him when he arrived. He was taller than the rest, dignified, fit, barrel-chested, with strong hands and legs. He conveyed both keenness and strength. He seemed serene, reserved, and yet dangerous. Not that Coral thought Luis wasn't—she knew he was, just not palpably so.

When Luis put his arm on the man's back and began to talk, she cracked the sliding door enough to hear.

"Everyone knows Francisco Miguel," Luis said, raising his voice.

"Hey Francisco," someone called in Spanish. "*¿Sigues secuestrando gente?* Still kidnapping people?"

He was a kidnapper?

In the good-natured laughter that ensued, Francisco gave a tolerant smile.

Luis said, "I have an announcement."

At this, the men fell silent and gathered round.

"Fate has decreed a wonderful destiny to the Moctezuma family and from tonight we will extend it to *La Raza* itself, the Mexican race—to the mestizos and indios who languish in poverty in our country. In my actions, I will do as Zapata would, had he been rich, but I need your help."

As they murmured, he raised his glass.

"From this night," Luis said, "no longer will I hear you say, *Yo no soy digno*, I'm not worthy. You are worthy. You are my family. ¡Salud!"

"¡Salud!" They roared.

"From this night, no longer will I hear you say to the outside world, *mande usted*—as you command."

At first they hesitated, as if to see who knew the correct response to this. When someone replied, "Sí, señor," the rest followed suit.

"From this night," Luis continued, "you will always know your place—*siempre sabrán su lugar.*"

This time there was silence. Luis had spoken one of the catch phrases of Mexican servility. Handed down from the conquistadores to modern-day elites it implied there'd be no resistance to their starvations and their deaths. It was not a phrase for those who risked their lives venturing north to earn enough cash to keep their families from starving.

"Here is your place," Luis shouted, "*¡La cima!*—the top."

"¡A la cima! they cried.

"*¡Primero la familia!*" Luis replied. "Viva Mexico!"

"*¡Cabrones!*"

Amid murmurs of approval, Luis lifted Francisco's arm. "*Ahora hablaré con Francisco.* He and I will discuss business tonight."

That seemed to be the cue for everyone to leave. One by one they exchanged *abrazos*, the formal embrace, and said goodnight. In one day, Luis to his extended family had become el señor. Some called him Don Luis as they departed.

Moments later, she heard his knock at her door.

"Come in," she called.

He entered, carrying a box. "You were listening?"

"I was listening." She went to him and impishly curtsied low then she rose and hugged Luis. "You were great."

He smiled. "Now it is your turn. Put this on."

She took the box and opened it.

"Go ahead. I want to see. Put it on."

He waited while she donned an off-the shoulder blouse of white organza. It left her midriff exposed. Its long sheer sleeves descended in puffs down her arms. She stepped into a black organza skirt. Cut low to hug her hips, it flared out in sculpted ruffles, which trailed behind her on the floor. The box held a white camellia, which she pinned in her hair.

Luis reached in his pocket and held jewelry out, saying, "Coral for Coral."

She took a beaded coral necklace and matching earrings from his hand, put them on, and posed in front of the mirrors. "Just call me señorita, tonight."

"You have never been more beautiful."

"Thank you, Luis."

"You know today is the wedding?"

She looked away. "Yes. What's my assignment tonight?"

"Entertain Francisco Miguel. He will form my flock of eagles and drive away bad coyotes. He will neutralize the drug cartel's smugglers."

"Tell me something about him."

"We grew up together. When I went off to college, Francisco went to the Military Riding School, which gave him a job in the stables and promised to make him an equestrian. Instead, Francisco learned first hand how corrupt much of the Mexican military and police are. When he left the Riding School, he formed a kidnapping ring, Los Jinetes, The Horsemen."

Coral turned. "A kidnapping ring?"

"It was one of Mexico City's most successful, famous for using accomplices in the victim's life—a hairdresser, a disgruntled employee—to gain access and information. Francisco and his men would snatch the person without using any guns then, after the ransom arrived, return the victim well fed and without a scratch. There was no physical threat, only the prospect of not seeing the victim again for a long, long time. Everyone said that if they had to be kidnapped, let it please be by Los Jinetes."

Luis could have been describing a hometown baseball team. “A humane kidnapper,” she said. “How nice.”

“He wasn’t nice to those who harmed their kidnap victims. Francisco’s name still strikes fear into the gangs. While I was in New York, making money from Theomund Brown, Francisco formed strong ties inside Mexico’s power structure. He paid off politicians and worked with the police, sharing the ransom money. They were glad to be bribed by someone moral like him. Francisco is the ideal person to run Mexica Eterna.

Out on the terrace, Francisco Miguel looked able to do just that. She sensed that—however much Luis admired him—Francisco had killed and would again, yet still there was serenity on his face, as if he were unconnected to his sins. He exuded manliness in his expensive olive shirt and gold ring. On his wrist she saw a luxurious watch, a Tourbillion by Roger Dubuis. Francisco wasn’t broke.

Coral lingered at the terrace door until Francisco gazed at her. He was a man in control of his face, but when their eyes met she saw he was impressed.

Slowly she walked toward him then at the last moment deliberately turned and ordered a drink from a waiter.

Luis said, “Francisco, this is Coral. She works for me.”

She and Francisco nodded coolly to each other then the three of them began to talk, but during the entire conversation Francisco didn't address her.

She didn't know if he meant it as an affront, or a sign of respect, but since Luis didn't seem concerned, neither was she. Coral knew her role. She was Luis's extra pair of eyes and ears. She would seduce on command and report what she learned in bed. In Francisco's case she wasn't sure her opinion would matter to Luis unless Francisco had a hidden side.

Coral listened as they talked about the smugglers who trafficked in central Mexican towns. Two and three times a day, they stuffed dozens into trailers then headed north. It was harder now with the U.S. upset about illegal immigrants and with drug gangs horning in on the trade, but vigilance was still fairly spotty and the border was long. Often they were forced to pay to use the tunnel system the drug gangs dug under the border. Some came by sea and landed on a California beach. Too often their human cargo made it across the border only to find themselves crammed into a slum apartment's back room and held for ransom. To free them, relatives had to fork over double or triple the agreed price. Every year scores died of heat exhaustion in the desert, or drowned crossing the Rio Grande or in the Pacific, or suffocated in trailers.

Luis and Francisco talked of formidable obstacles: extreme violence now in the lucrative coyote trade, USA gringos pressuring politicians for a crackdown on illegals who cut their fences along the border and let their cattle out, gringos complaining of the refuse that littered their farms and ranches when immigrants slipped across the border and left behind what had sustained them. Hospitals in small border towns, unable to turn away the sick, going broke responding to immigrants' medical needs. There were complaints about the cost of bilingual education. Also growing were protests from immigrants themselves—of theft, beatings, rape, or forced prostitution. Mexican-style kidnappings, once unheard of in the USA, were now more common in border states because of the drug cartels. Yet the bad economy hadn't stopped the tide of Mexicans into North America, only slowed it. As jobs improved, it would pick up again.

Coral shuddered as she listened. Then she made a mistake. "I think I'd just stay put," she said. She paused and bit her lip, realizing she'd forgotten about the statues in the salon—their relatives who had died.

Francisco looked at her with contempt. What a careless thing she'd said. No gente buena for her.

Luis drained his glass. "Unfortunately, mi hermosa, much of Mexico is so poor there is no other choice. It is either go north, or watch your family die of malnutrition, disease, or violence after resorting to crime. And the U.S. businessmen who employ them cheaply would have it no other way."

He stood and so did she.

"Discúlpa." Apologies, she said.

Luis nodded. "It is late. Francisco, Coral will show you to your room."

Her black skirt rustling, she walked ahead, trying to erase her mistake by speaking in Spanish. She stepped aside and let Francisco enter the luxurious bedroom with the mirrors. Once alone, she'd get him to talk.

"Por favor, perdóname no debi haber hecho ese comentario," she apologized when the doors closed. Please forgive me. I should not have made that comment.

She walked gracefully across the room and stopped boldly before Francisco, hands on hips, her eyes flashing. She'd been with Mexican men before and knew their passionate temperament. Machismo wasn't just about *dignidad*; it was sex.

He fingered the beads around her neck and, holding her gaze, said, "Ni modo."

Apparently Francisco hadn't been taught not to say *ni modo.* She smiled.

"Tú solamente eres una putita gringa." You are only a gringa whore.

Though it was absolutely true, his words stung fiercely.

She spat at Francisco Miguel, standing there tall, handsome and confident, prepared to take on the dangerous coyotes, much less her.

Her spit landed on his shirt. He looked at it and laughed. *"Cusca!"* Slut.

"Chilito," she countered. Little dick.

He smiled knowingly. "Incorrecto."

He was playing a game but Coral was trembling, thinking of a wedding night happening somewhere else while she faced down a man who had killed. Why didn't Luis see it? Then it occurred to her that Luis might know precisely how brutal this cousin of his was. As if confirming her thoughts, Francisco put his hands on her face, looked into her eyes then ripped off the organza blouse."

"Oho! Qué grandes," he said, fondling her.

"Come mi panocha," she retorted.

Her vulgarity hit its mark because Francisco, roaring with laughter, picked her up, tossed her into bed, and finding her naked beneath her skirt, immediately began to do what she'd asked.

———

In their suite at The Plaza, Maggie stood by pink drapes at triple living room windows watching Sam close the door as the room service waiter left. She still wore her wedding gown. Maggie had been in grand places before—the Rossi's homes, La Scala in Milan, but she'd never stayed in a hotel room with potted ferns, a white marble fireplace trimmed in gold, and such elegant furniture—Louis-the-somethingth, she was sure.

A chandelier hung above her. Perfume from flowers filled the air.

Sam walked toward her, his hand extended. "Milady, your table is ready."

Nervous, she smiled. She should leave.

He led her to a chair at the little table set for them—beautiful linen, silver and crystal, two tall candles, roses in a cut glass bowl. Maggie gazed at the flowers' delicate veins, layered circles of dark crimson velvet petals enclosing the heart of each rose. Sam poured champagne when she sat on the fancy chair.

"A pregnant woman can't drink," she said.

"Not even a sip? It's Cristal, the best champagne in the world for the best woman in the world."

She shook her head, rehearsing how to tell him it was over. *Sam, we're through. I want a divorce after the baby comes. I hate you, Sam.* "Not even a sip," she said.

He handed Maggie her water glass and began again. "'As light to the eye, as bread to the hungry, as joy to the heart may we be to each other, my girl."

She said nothing.

"Straight down?"

She nodded. "Straight down."

They drank. He lifted their silver plate covers. Steak and

potatoes for him. For her, okra, corn, smothered chicken, dumplings. He knew how much she'd missed southern cooking during her years in Italy. He'd had The Plaza make this feast for her.

Maggie decided to tell him after dinner.

As they ate, soft music played. She refused drunken pear dessert. Then Sam stood, came around, and before she could speak, lifted her in his arms—he was still in his tux.

"Wait," she said. "Sam I … I"

He started toward the bedroom. At the threshold he paused. "Blimey, I forgot!" He put her down. "Don't move. It's a surprise."

Maggie watched him dash to a console and fiddle inside. The music stopped. Something else began. She recognized the opening strains of the love song from *Madama Butterfly* and stood frozen as memories of Italy crowded back—how Sam had betrayed her, like Cio Cio San, the heroine of this, her favorite opera, had been betrayed. How Jess had died in her arms, her flower of the lily and the rose. That's what Cio Cio San called her own son in the opera.

Sam returned, beaming with pride. "Antonella told me this is your favorite opera."

Antonella, her housekeeper back in Italy, had despised Sam at first then grudgingly accepted him.

"Oh, she did?"

The music peeled off layers of her soul, leaving pain so intense Maggie wanted to fall through the floor and keep falling until she was beneath the earth.

"Sweetheart, what is it?" Sam said.

The music echoed in her ears like a massive gong, shattering her.

"Maggie, what is it?"

Blindly she stumbled toward her purse, a beaded thing Sharmina found at Filene's basement.

"What do you need? I'll get it for you."

She snapped it open, reached inside and found the pearl-handled gun her daddy gave her. She'd retrieved it from the guard in case Sam lost control and she needed to point a weapon to get out of here. The gun was sized to fit a woman's hand. Maggie grasped it as Cio Cio San sang:

> "Love me, please
> A little love,
> A child-like love,
> A love to suit a child like me."

She pointed the gun at Sam.

"What's this, Maggie? A joke?"

She cocked the gun.

"God! Maggie, what are you doing?" He backed toward the marble fireplace.

For years and years, Maggie had imagined her wedding night, a wonderful husband at her side. Sam thought he'd done everything to make this moment right, but the music revealed the lie. This opera had accompanied her deepest sorrows, the two worst injuries to her heart and he was responsible for them both.

> "Give me your dear hands and let me kiss them.
> My Butterfly! —"

"I'm killing you, Sam. Killing you, killing you!"

"Why, Maggie, why?"

"As if you don't know!"

Swiftly she reached into a chair, grabbed a satin cushion, and as Sam yelled, "No! No!" she put the cushion to the muzzle and fired.

The blast made her hand jump. She saw fire and smoke and then Sam jerked and almost toppled off his feet. He grabbed his arm and looked dumbfounded as blood seeped from his tux, through his fingers, and onto the floor.

"You stupid woman, why did you do that?" He looked incredulous.

Maggie knew he was watching her hands to take the weapon.

She retreated to the pink drapes and brought her arms to her body where he couldn't reach the gun.

"What haven't you done, Sam?" she cried, struggling for breath. "First you were unfaithful—"

"What! When?

"With Coral, your female mirror!"

"But … but you and I weren't together. We weren't even engaged yet."

"You're right. I was pregnant with Jess. You were only trying to get in my pants and I hadn't let you."

Sam eased closer, holding his shoulder.

"Stay there, Sam. I'm not letting you take this gun."

He stopped.

"I guess you've talked yourself out of feeling bad about things," she said, "but since I've been involved with you, Sam—" She raised her voice. "I've had a broken heart, been raped, now my son is dead and you're responsible for it all!"

"So you're going to kill me, are you?"

Maggie pointed at his heart. "Yes, yes, yes!"

"Do it, then."

"What?"

"I always knew that's how I'd die—over a woman, or by a woman's hand."

He began walking back and forth as if he wasn't bleeding and she wasn't holding a gun. He asked, "Do you have to kill me first?"

"What?"

"I always thought it would happen after sex."

Maggie's vision whirled. She trembled in rage, fought tears, tasted bile. "I'll die before I ever—"

Sam picked that moment to vault across the floor and knock the gun from her hand. As Maggie shrieked, he grabbed it, emptied the bullets into his hand, opened a window, and threw them out, Maggie clawing at him to get them back.

He turned and pulled her to him. "What now? A knife?"

Maggie wailed, hearing the beautiful, soaring music that was bringing back the past.

"Come, oh come.
Away from your troubled breast
All pangs of fear."

Sam swept her off her feet and carried her to the king-sized canopied bed strewn with rose petals.

"Before you make decisions about killing and dying, Maggie, I'm going to teach you how to love. If you want to cut my throat later, fine. For now, you're my wife."

He left, went to the bathroom and returned shirtless, dabbing his arm with a thick, bloody Turkish towel. "The bullet went through," he said.

Sobbing, Maggie looked away.

"And I see my wife is greatly relieved."

He laid her on her stomach and, with Maggie wriggling to get away, began unbuttoning her wedding gown. Soon it was on the plush carpet along with her shoes and stockings and earrings. Her white lace underwear followed. He turned her over and she lay naked on the rose petals, weeping as Sam gazed into her eyes.

"Maggie, darling girl. You're so wrong about yourself. Those green eyes aren't your only good feature."

She said nothing and he sighed.

"If you killed me I wouldn't blame you. I'm forever yours, either way. Why won't you be mine?"

She couldn't talk. All she could feel was hate so strong, Maggie thought she'd pass out.

He bent to her stomach and put his lips there. She cringed as he kissed the skin his baby was inside. His lips moved to her breasts to kiss the nipples that would give milk to his child. His lips moved to her face and he whispered, "Hit me if you want. Hit me, Maggie, if it will take away your pain."

She balled her fist, but couldn't move.

"Well, if you don't hit me, I'm going to make mad, passionate love to you, so I give you fair warning. We're having physical contact tonight, either from your fists or the nicer parts."

Maggie stared at Sam's chest half covered in curly hair—some of it going gray now that he was getting older. He still had a powerful physique, one that many women had loved. Yet it was her fate to be here with him—Jess dead, Sam alive.

If he made love to her, he'd fall asleep. Then a knife could as easily replace the gun.

She listened to Cio Cio San's love song end as the man who would betray her sang,

Ah! Vien! Sei mia!
Ah! Come! Be Mine!

Maggie felt numb, said nothing.

In their suite at The Plaza, she let Sam caress her until her skin burned. She let him put his penis between her breasts, put his tongue between her legs to bring her to the peak of desire. After a while it seemed to Maggie that they lay on a bed of fire, molten lava running through her veins.

She'd never even imagined sex like this. It was like a Tantric ritual in which the object wasn't to climax, but to use the body to fuse two souls. Sam's sweat was in her pores, she could taste him. He held his hand above her skin and she felt it without being touched. She grew thirsty and he poured her water. She cried and he tasted her tears.

At last her rage bubbled over. Maggie jerked Sam's belt from a nearby chair and before she knew it lashed his back. He lay face down and didn't move, said nothing. She hit him again, raising a welt. On his back, on his legs, she hit him and hit him until one stinging lash reopened the gunshot wound.

When she saw it, Maggie dropped the belt.

"You left us! You killed Jess when you left us. You forced yourself on me!"

There was blood on the sheets like there should be on a wedding night; except it didn't come from her, it came from Sam.

He sat up. "You said you forgave me. I should have known you never could. I'm such a fool. I guess I do everything wrong." He let out a sob. Why was he doing that? Because it had worked once before?

Of their own volition her arms opened, betraying her. Of their own volition her lips found his. They started making love.

When it finally came, her orgasm was so intense Maggie felt herself losing consciousness in Sam's arms. She fought to remember what she'd planned to do to Sam—stab him, poison him, something like that. She hoped the morning was soon enough to start hating him again. Sam was holding her so close that, for tonight, she didn't care.

In the night Francisco and Coral tested their command of Spanish sexual obscenities, Mexican style. They didn't really sleep. Until dawn, she felt no reality but their connection.

At one point, Francisco carried her naked onto the terrace, saying he wanted to see her in the moonlight. He recited a poem by someone named Elías Nandino, "You were born in me, to blood bounded—in a growing root, cosmic knot. ..." All she felt was desire for him—a hunger she'd had only briefly with one other man and that was Sam.

When she awoke late in the day and found him gone, her distress was physical, primal. Their long night alone felt like a reunion, as if they'd had their hands on each other before. Repeatedly they'd talked and dozed, woke and screwed. When she asked why he ended Los Jinetes, Francisco said he grew tired of seeing terror in people's eyes. Besides, he'd had a dream about Santa Muerte, Mexico City's unofficial patron saint for the poor who turned to crime to survive. He'd dreamed if he didn't stop the kidnappings, Saint Death would come for him, her skeletal face smiling from within her lace-trimmed satin cloak, head crowned by a tiara, bony bejeweled hands offering him mercy from her scythe.

At lunch the next day, Coral reported to Luis her fears about Francisco and that, whether or not he'd ever murdered anyone, she found him a killer of women, in a fascinating way. She wasn't surprised to feel a blush on her cheeks, given what had occurred last night. It had been hard to withhold anything from Francisco, but she managed, if barely. As punishment for his first sexual assault, delightful though it was, she'd allowed his mouth on no part of her, only his hands. Her own mouth she'd used freely.

Luis had on another of his Guayabera shirts, simply being Mexican again—being the religiously devout Luis Tepiltzin Moctezuma, not el señor or el patriarca or el patrón. She admitted to herself that in the past few days she'd come to like Luis enormously and value his good will. She even admired his dreams and impossible goals. Coral hoped they wouldn't end badly as they did for his hero, Emiliano Zapata, shot down in the dust. She briefly wondered if Luis had anything to do with the modern day Zapastistas, still seeking "land and liberty" in the Mexican state of Chiapas. She decided that, with all his money, Luis probably did or would.

She also liked Luis's familia, a band of courageous men who escaped the pitiless slums and villages of their mother country for a land more merciful in theory but, in practice, sometimes just as bad. Did they hate Mexico in response? No, they loved it and sent all their money to their families still living there. The government counted on it.

Hearing of her success, Luis bowed his head over their lunch table and, unexpectedly, said a prayer of thanks to the Virgin of Guadalupe. Then he rose, saying he'd be back.

He returned holding a large envelope, and trailed his fingers through Coral's hair as he sat down. "Francisco finds you captivating, hermosa." He reached into the envelope and handed her an airline ticket. It was roundtrip New York to Mexico City, first class. The dates were open.

"Francisco Miguel invites you to join him. You may come back to New York if and when you choose."

She gazed up from the ticket at Luis. "No strings?"

He looked suddenly grim. "From Francisco? No."

Coral swallowed, knowing she was about to learn what she'd gotten herself into. "From you?"

"None from me. If you enjoy Francisco and really want to stay with him, then do it, hermosa. A beautiful Spanish woman named Adriana said he was wonderful company last year. A mesmerizing African model named Abeni thought he was captivating the year before. Both complained that Francisco paid attention to other women while they lived with him. But, actually, he didn't send either of them away. They both left voluntarily. Francisco would have supported either one the rest of her life, I am sure. I just think he wouldn't have visited her bed as much, after a while."

Coral heard and understood Luis plainly. Her body and her heart didn't. She sensed Francisco Miguel was a life event waiting for her, one not to be missed. Perhaps she could handle him, tame him. Every molecule of her being wanted to try, though life should have taught her better than to imagine such foolish things.

"Go with Francisco," Luis said. "Be with Francisco. For my purposes, not his."

"What purposes, Luis?"

"If you do as I say, I will secure your future."

Coral took a deep breath and reigned in her feelings for Francisco. However much she yearned for him, she'd waited years to hear words like, *I will secure your future.* She'd expected them from Theo, or to be remembered in his will, but he'd kissed her off with $250,000, not even enough to get her out of debt. If Theo could do that, trusting her future to Francisco was flatly insane.

Coral batted her eyelids at Luis and cooed out her reply. "How much security did you have in mind?"

"Five million dollars."

She extended her hand across the lunch table. "Luis Tepiltzin Moctezuma, you have a deal."

Instead of taking her hand, he sat back, steepling his fingers like Theo used to, "From now on, you are to be with only three men and only when I say so, Coral. Francisco Miguel, Evaristo Salati, and Sam Duffy."

"Sam Duffy? Huh? I don't get it."

He reached into the envelope and removed photographs. The first was of a wedding couple in a tux and a gown. They were getting in a Rolls. Around it, some people were kneeling.

One by one, Coral examined the photos of Maggie and Sam on their wedding day. “Well, at least he looks happy,” she said.

Luis said, “Why are people kneeling?”

“What do you mean?”

“Why are some people kneeling?”

“I guess it's Maggie. She did carry that Jesus clone, you know.”

“Why are they kneeling if the clone is dead?”

Coral tossed the picture aside. “Like I said, people are strange, Luis. I mean really. They'll believe anything.”

Luis sneered, making Coral think of the jaguar statue he liked to put his boot on. She felt a little afraid of him and wondered how she could forget Luis was no one to play with. Once or twice he'd carried out some pretty unethical orders for Brown.

She remembered the five million dollars. “Let me see if I get this. You think Maggie's not carrying Sam's child, but another clone?”

“Perhaps, but for our purposes, Coral, does it matter whether her infant is an impostor? It was always inconceivable that she could really give birth to a sacred child.”

Coral shot him a look, remembering her own stolen childhood. “I'm sure your Virgin of Guadalupe thinks all children are sacred, Luis.”

“I won't harm the baby, only use him for a greater good. He will help restore my people to the land that's really theirs and end their tears.”

“Yeah, I know, Luis. Land and liberty. La Reconquista. Yeah, I know. You're just lucky most Americans never heard of La Reconquista or know that Mexico's secret government policy is to send their poor to us.” Coral rose from the table and paced. “What if the baby isn't a boy?”

Luis sighed. “If it's a girl, we are lost, but I think it is a boy. I have a gut feeling this is going to work.”

“Where exactly do I come in with this sacred impostor of yours, Luis?”

Luis's hands moved expressively. “Sam Duffy will have the

child when it is born. Francisco will take the child. Salati will receive the child."

She stared at him.

"You, hermosa, are the link I have forged between them."

"Hell's bells. You're way ahead of me and everybody else, too, aren't you?"

Luis smiled. "One day I will teach you how to speak respectfully."

Coral stood behind Luis's chair, put her arms around him, and looked over the terrace into Central Park. In this city she'd met Theo who'd turned her into a whore then left her virtually penniless. Here she'd met, and lost, Sam Duffy who'd almost killed her, if unintentionally. Last night she'd met Francisco Miguel, whom she now yearned for. Though Coral was impatient to board any plane that would take her to him, she knew their passion wouldn't last.

She snuggled her face against the top of Luis's head. "I need the five mil on deposit in my name. Deposit the money, Luis, give instructions I agree with to the bank, and we're on."

Chapter 11

In the past eight months, Coral had lost count of the times she'd gazed on the Valley of Mexico as her flight descended into Benito Juarez airport. To her relief, she didn't see the brown haze that on most days gave Mexico City some of the worst air in the world. At 7400 feet above sea level and surrounded on three sides by soaring mountains, the pollution from cars usually remained trapped in the valley, burning eyes and searing throats.

Today an afternoon *monzón* rain had washed the sky. This time of year, there would be no *tolvaneras*, dust storms from the dry bed of Lake Texcoco to the east, drained to prevent flooding. It and deforestation had caused an ecological disaster in this valley, which housed the largest city in the world and the oldest in the western hemisphere.

As the plane began its final approach, Ciudad de México gradually dominated Coral's view. Once the Aztec capital, Tenochtitlán, the city's historic and modern buildings, the grand avenues she'd come to love, the teeming slums she'd never seen, now sprawled in all directions. On her first visit, its unexpected vastness had inspired awe in her, much like the first time she'd entered Paris at night and drove along the Ile de Cite in the dark, not knowing that the massive, lighted edifice which gradually crowded out the sky was Notre Dame.

The Mexico City Metropolitan Area seemed endless. To her, it ought not to exist in the western hemisphere. Its inhabitants, called *chilangos*—fifty percent of whom had no running water—should have razed the place in riots and caused the intellectual, cultural, and financial elite to flee. The city had extreme wealth, extreme poverty, crime, pollution and corruption, but there was no organized social unrest in the Federal District of Mexico and its surroundings, where a fifth of the country's people lived.

The city was a pulsating enigma, existing simultaneously in the present and the past—full of splendor and squalor, hope, fatalism, secrecy, passion—like she and Francisco were.

Only the lure of five million dollars had restrained Coral's emotions enough to carry out Luis's plan. Back in New York, she intentionally didn't answer the phone when Francisco called—delayed or overlooked replying to his messages. When they did talk, he would say, "¡Alo! Coral, soy yo Francisco," and she would reply, "¡Ah! Francisco. ¿Como estás, como te va?," as if she didn't have time.

It was a carrot-stick ruse, designed to gain mastery over him. Only when Coral was here did she drop the pretense—until now, that is.

When the plane landed and taxied to a stop, Coral rose quickly, ignoring the wealthy businessmen ogling her in first class. She slung on the jacket to her couture pantsuit, white and printed with green and purple flowers. It was as florid as the gardens here. In her ears, on her fingers, on both wrists, she wore the gold and diamond jewelry by which Francisco had staked his claim on her.

When the door to Aeroméxico Flight 403 opened, letting in heat and the indescribable city smell—flowers, dust, coffee, fumes, unplaceable other things—she was first off the plane. There was Francisco, on the tarmac walking toward her, breaching every security and customs procedure in the book. No one dared prevent him from going where he chose.

As she walked to him, he stopped, shaking the wrist with the gold, alligator-banded Tourbillion. He said, "Buenos dias, Coral," and she replied, "*Qué dice mi chico?*" What say you, my dear boy? As always, he put his hand behind her waist and jerked her to him, forcing the deplaning passengers to part around them as they kissed in Benito Juarez airport.

Between visits, Coral dreamed of their greeting kiss—her mouth still the only part of her not taboo to his lips. It had taken nerve to pull it off, but she did, aided by the *marianismo* that goes with the machismo of Mexican men. Francisco obsessed about putting his mouth on her, but accepted that he could not. Their kiss ignited a desire too intense for any more waiting. Sometimes Francisco would take her into the terminal and push on office doors until he found one empty or chase a frightened clerk away so he could make love to her right there in the airport. He was *atrevido,* and Mexico responded to those who pushed. But usually they made it to the car where they had feverish sex as his chauffeur drove them through the vibrant streets.

This time she forced herself to break off their embrace, or try. Francisco hung on, saying, "Coral, por favor, no" and in reply she whispered, "*Sueltame,*" let me go. He resisted until she had to slap at his hands and shout, "*Qué me sueltes te digo,*" let me go.

A few foreigners took notice, but the Mexicans around them were no more perturbed by a passionate lover's spat than by the extreme wealth and poverty of their capital city. It had always been like that with lovers and cities.

Inflamed, Francisco put on black sunglasses which made him look even more romantically dangerous, grabbed her arm and hustled her into the terminal, brushing off with a glare the official who sheepishly asked for her passport. He pushed her into a room where they'd once made love, backed her to the wall, unzipped her pants and put his hand down them.

"Now we are going to fuck, *mi putita preciosa.*"

She knew he was trying to rouse her anger, thinking its outlet would be sex. His hand felt wonderful, but instead of her usual vulgar retort, she pushed at Francisco and snarled, "Only if I am dead first!"

He persisted as she fought, grabbing as if searching for the *on* switch.

Though she was desperate to kiss him and feel his hands on her, Coral screamed, "¡Sueltame!" until frantic knocks on the door forced him to step away, looking hurt and confused. That's when Coral did what she'd never done. She opened her palm and slapped Francisco's face.

She held her breath. An American man might leave you for that. A Mexican man, if he didn't kill you, might become your slave.

Francisco Miguel just stared at her. He growled, "*¡No moleste!*" to whoever was knocking.

Coral turned to the wall, covered her face, and began to cry.

After a while she heard, "Preciosa, forgive me. How can I make it up to you?"

He put his hands on her shoulders and in mock anger she shrugged them off and left the room. Francisco followed, telling his driver to collect her bags. In the arrivals area, one of his *cómplices*, now called bodyguards to suit Francisco's new status, elbowed a path through the crowds for them. She'd gotten used to being accompanied by armed men in Mexico. Kidnappings happened all the time here and, unlike Francisco's old Los Jinetes, the new gangs were merciless.

Out at the curb, another cómplice opened the door to Francisco's Bentley.

She got in the back seat. As he climbed in behind her, she moved against the far window and looked out at the airport where she knew she'd never feel Francisco's ardent welcome kiss again. He was too proud to risk public rejection.

More importantly, the unanswered slap meant their relationship had changed. No longer equals, he was the lover now, she the beloved. In reality, she had an agenda. She was the huntress and he the prey.

They wove through traffic on Blvr. Puerto Aereo, two more of his *gente* in a Hummer behind them, Coral intent on what she had to do.

Francisco stroked her shoulder. "You want to go *a la casa, chulada?*"

She shrugged and said, "I don't feel gorgeous when you handle me like that." It was a lie. It thrilled her.

Lowering the divider, Francisco rapped on the back seat. "¡A la casa, rapido!"

Horn honking, the driver took their usual route onto Fray Servando Avenue, passing the reflecting skyscrapers, the monuments, parks, and fabulous churches. In or near most of them, she and Francisco had made love—in the ruins of the

Templo Mayor where Luis's ancestor, Moctezuma II had worshipped; in a pedicab near the Basilica of Our Lady of Guadalupe who had consoled the conquered Aztecs; near a Diego Rivera mural in a corner of the National Palace Cortés built; in more than one fashionable Zona Rosa restaurant, in flower-filled boats, on park benches, in street markets all over town. Typical of lovers here, they'd christened Mexico City with their passion. Since they met, it seemed to Coral she was either engaged in hot-blooded sex with Francisco, or completely out of his reach.

Sometimes she imagined they were the twin volcanoes, Popocatepetl, Smoking Mountain, and Ixtaccihuatl, White Lady, at the southern end of the valley—smoldering lovers the Aztecs said couldn't bear to be out of each other's sight. Francisco once sang a serenade to her about them.

Soon they merged onto Avenue Chapultepec and entered Lomas De Chapultepec, the exclusive neighborhood where Francisco lived. Also here was Los Pinos, home to the Mexican president—convenient because, through his Mexica Eterna organization and Francisco, Luis was bribing half the government and the police.

The Bentley pulled up to Francisco's hacienda. The man at the guardhouse saw them and opened the black-filigreed gate. Coral got out of the Bentley and walked through, ignoring Francisco's call. "Wait, preciosa."

She crossed the pink cobbled courtyard, which had covered parking for seven cars. One level below were the estate's gas station, electricity generator, car repair shop, and thirty-six-car garage, its laundry, plus a gymnasium and a shooting range.

At the front door, which had a bell atop it like the Alamo, Coral took off her jacket and dropped it on the ground. By the atrium fountain just inside, she kicked off her shoes. In the foyer with its candelabra, and paintings in dark, heavy frames, she stepped out of her slacks and pulled off her knit shirt. Coral padded through the formal dining room, opened a door, and stepped onto a terrace bigger than many public squares. It was surrounded by high walls, up which vines and flowers climbed. It had trees and shrubs and fountains and graceful wrought iron furniture. At one end were a Jacuzzi and a pool. Peeling off her underwear, she ran across the cobblestones and jumped in, diving beneath the cool water. When she came up for air, she saw Francisco and, behind him, a maid picking up her things.

Luis had spent twelve million dollars to buy this estate, the local headquarters of Mexica Eterna. Every day vans and trucks left here going north, driven by the eagles Francisco had given wing—each full of people carrying forged passports and identity cards, made in the estate's print shop. Every day, men left to confront the coyotes who wouldn't join with Francisco in conducting an honorable smuggling trade. There'd been deaths, she heard.

Luis's eagles needed one thing more and Luis said Francisco wouldn't willingly provide it. Her job was to persuade him. She swam to the edge of the pool near where he stood, a big, flawless, colorless, ideal-cut, solitaire dangling between her breasts on a gold chain.

"How goes it?" she said, acting the part of Luis's courier—*it* being the goings-on at the estate.

"What's the matter with you, Coral?" Francisco gazed in helpless frustration on her body. "*¡Carajo!* What have I done?"

She lifted her hands and looked at her fingers. On them were a tube of gold, the pavé diamond-studded gold Cartier tiger with emerald eyes and onyx nose, and a diamond orchid, inlaid with gemstones. She liked that Francisco overdid it when it came to jewelry.

"I don't see an engagement ring." She was pulling out the stops.

Francisco grabbed his hair. They'd had this conversation before. He paced along the pool, making frustrated gestures. "What will it take for you to understand? I cannot marry you, Coral. This is Mexico. I have relatives. I have a mother. I cannot marry a woman like you."

"What if I get pregnant?"

He sighed. "I will love our babies. I will feed and house them and give them an education. I cannot marry their mother."

She lay back, floating, kicking her legs, open, close, glad he'd told the truth when a lie would be so easy. "Yeah, a woman like me. A putita. Yeah, Mexico's into virgins when it comes to wives. You used to sacrifice them on altars, right?"

Francisco stopped pacing. "I will never leave you. I will give you anything you want."

Coral swam to where he stood. She saw him stare as the breasts he'd never kissed rose from the water. "Take me there, Francisco."

"Where?"

"Where they used to sacrifice the virgins."

"You don't understand our history. If needed, those of high rank volunteered. Many gave their children. It was a religious rite, an honor."

She glared at him. "They slaughtered thousands, Francisco, and you know it."

He looked ashamed.

"Take me to the pyramids tonight."

"You mean to Teotihuacán? The Mexica didn't build that. It was already centuries old in their time. They called it the City of the Gods."

"Take me there."

"It is not wise to be on a country road at night. There are bandits."

"You mean narcos."

"Yes. There are men who want to kill me now."

"It's a toll road, honey, I looked it up."

"Yes, all right, but it is still dangerous."

"No pokey-pokey in the holey then, Francisco. Suit yourself."

Francisco put his sunglasses back on and stammered at the naked woman he suddenly couldn't possess, "You—you have a filthy mouth."

"Yeah, but you love it," Coral said.

She spent the rest of the day locked in her private suite, soaking in its marble tub, dozing behind the curtains of its four-poster bed, watching soccer on TV. At 10:00 P.M. sharp, the Hummer stood in the courtyard, loaded with what they'd need—two Jeeps at the ready as were four of Francisco's men, holding shotguns. Coral emerged wearing jungle green, a cap, and hiking boots.

They took Highway 85D north out of the city, a driver and one guard in the Hummer, a Jeep in front, a Jeep behind. Coral leaned on Francisco's arm as he stared angrily out at the night. Upset though he was, he had come.

Halfway there he tried to touch her but she pulled away. Coral meant to test and, if possible, deepen her sway over him. She hadn't really thought about Teotihuacán itself, wasn't prepared for its grandeur in the moonlight.

Like all tourist attractions it had normal opening and closing hours, but for someone like Francisco they didn't apply. An attendant met them at the gate, handed them a map, and let them in. Moments later their little caravan was driving down the Avenue of the Dead that separated the third largest pyramid in the world, the Pyramid of the Sun, from the Pyramid of the Moon. Around them were the shadows of palaces, temples, and the home of a high priest, long gone.

"It is so old no one knows who built it anymore," Francisco said. "They say 200,000 people lived here. In 500 AD it was bigger than Rome."

Coral used a flashlight to read the map. "It had a cult of the planet Venus and they worshipped a 'Great Goddess'. Maybe she was their goddess of love."

"You are the goddess of love," Francisco said. He slapped the front seat. "Por favor."

When the Hummer stopped, he helped her out and led her to a wall, protected by a corrugated roof. He turned on the flashlight and revealed a brilliant stylized image of a crouching jaguar.

"They were mural painters," Francisco said. "They painted their buildings, floors, walls, everything." He looked at his watch. "Let's go, it's getting late."

They got back into the Hummer, proceeded to the Pyramid of

the Sun, and stopped at the sunken plaza in front. When she got out, Francisco pointed up and said, "That is what you wanted. That is where we will go. We have two hundred forty-eight steps to climb."

Coral looked up and didn't care. She felt an incredible sort of energy from the pyramid.

He motioned to his men, "Por favor, amigos."

As they picked up blankets and containers, he took her hand and led her down the steps into the plaza, past a platform at its center on which a building once must have stood. He didn't pause at the pyramid's base, but headed straight up the steep front which ascended in tiers to a top now out of sight. Though she had a dancer's legs, Coral was soon breathless from the climb.

Briefly, he let her rest at the first tier, then grabbed her hand and continued up. She gauged their progress by her gasping lungs and avoided looking down. At the top of each tier he let her rest and she clung to the stone, afraid she'd tumble down and die. Then he'd grab her hand and she'd stumble on, vowing not to risk her own life the next time she tested Francisco.

When they reached the top, Coral staggered to the blankets his men had already spread and lay panting on her back. Francisco seemed barely winded. He lifted her head and poured water in her mouth, dribbled it on her face, and then opened her shirt and cooled her neck and upper chest with it.

A vast expanse of stars and limitless night framed his face.

"Do you feel like a virgin, now?" he asked.

Coral snorted. "That depends. Do you feel like making a sacrifice?"

She rolled over and gazed down the Avenue of the Dead to the Pyramid of the Moon. The view was exhilarating, a moonlit panorama of ruined city and sky. She could imagine a priest feeling so godlike here that he helped himself to people's lives.

"Sing a serenade to me, Francisco," she said. "Sing to me on the heartless pyramid."

She waited, not looking back at him. In Spanish he began to sing, "Yo Soy Mexicano."

"... I'm Mexican
and I am proud of it.
I was born despising
both life and death. ...
I'm Mexican,
I don't trust anybody,
and like Cuauhtémoc
when I am suffering
before climbing down
I resist and laugh. ...
but more than anything
I like to be in love.
I'm Mexican,
very quarrelsome."

She laughed and shook her head. "So romantic."

Coral sat up and wrapped herself in a blanket. Beneath it she began unbuttoning her shirt, unzipping her pants, taking off her hiking boots. Francisco watched at first then he turned to a picnic basket and began to take things out. He uncorked a bottle and poured blood red wine into a glass.

"This is a rare wine from a Mexican vintner, Monte Xanic, in Baja's Valle de Guadalupe. Many talk about it, but few have had the privilege to taste it."

She lay down and uncovered herself, spreading her arms and legs like she imagined the virgins had. "Drink it from my body."

His brows rose. He trickled wine into her navel and lovingly sucked it up, his lips touching her stomach for the first time. He whispered their usual scandalous endearments.

She used her hands to excite him then stopped and wrapped herself in the blanket again.

This time, Francisco looked so enraged she briefly feared she'd become the newest Teotihuacán sacrifice. Angrily, he tossed the precious wine from her glass.

"Why are you behaving like this, Coral? You are like the grave! I am buried in you! What is it?"

She thought Francisco's morbid way of talking was like Mexico itself—full of sacrifice, conquest, dying heroes, and lost gods. "Refill my glass with that rare wine, Francisco. I have something to tell you."

He sighed, poured the wine and sat on the blankets, gazing at the sky like someone doomed. "What am I doing out here in the middle of the night?"

"Luis needs you to do something. It's for the eagles and the people."

He looked cautiously at her. "What? Why didn't he tell me?"

"He said you'd refuse."

"I see. So you are to persuade me."

"Yes," she whispered. "Francisco, I need to know. Is he right in thinking that I can? A putita, a woman like me?"

"Lie down," he ordered.

Coral opened the blanket again and lay down.

"Yes," he breathed. He kissed her mouth. "I will do anything."

"Even a kidnapping?"

He froze.

She kissed him, her tongue darting. When his breath came hard she stopped. "Luis said you don't do them anymore."

"Not for many years." He was taking off his clothes.

"This one's in New York."

He lay on top of her. She knew she'd won when he didn't say *no.*

To seal the deal Coral whispered, "For tonight, Francisco, you can do anything you like with your putita. Even—"

Francisco groaned as she whispered an intimacy withheld.

He rose, opened her mouth, and poured in the blood red wine until she laughed in drunkenness. In punishment for the crime of making him wait, he lay her on a sacrificial altar made of their boxes and blankets and tortured her flesh with his lips.

That night, the sky crowned Teotihuacán in a midnight

procession of clouds, through which stars shone so brightly Coral felt she could touch them if she tried.

Chapter 12

Maggie stood beneath the neon sign at the 131st Street Baptist Church, ushering the homeless and the poor, the downtrodden and the forsaken, into the basement's welcoming warmth of a good hot meal. She'd retreated to her church, spending hours there each day, clad in a simple white dress. Ladies of the church wore white to symbolize faith. In her case, it didn't mean purity. Since that night at The Plaza with Sam, Maggie knew she wasn't pure.

Twice more in that first week she gave in to Sam and together they'd put Sodom & Gomorrah to shame. When she came to her senses, Maggie threw herself into good works, to avoid becoming a slave to the devil through Sam. It hadn't entirely done the trick. She still felt like a Jezebel and a fraud.

Since she was due any day she'd cut back her hours, but felt obliged to be at church for the main meal between 4:00 and 6:00 P.M.

Adamo came to the door in his white apron, waving. "Enough, mia cara, we are full!"

Instead of going back to Italy like she urged, Adamo had stopped drinking then wormed his way into the 131st Street Baptist Church by making an *agnello cacio e ovo*—lamb with cheese and egg—for the minister. In one massive cholesterol overdose, he became the church's cook. Soon they had to keep an eye out for people pretending to be destitute just to taste Adamo's delicious food. Now, after the poor were seated, they let paying diners in.

Sam had given up trying to keep her away from Adamo. She practically lived at the church and Adamo was the cook.

Maggie's grief over Jess had only dulled, not abated. She felt no joy in this pregnancy, only the normal protectiveness toward a child she'd carried so long. She hadn't changed her mind about leaving Sam, or giving up the baby for adoption to someone who didn't have bad memories of its conception. To avoid pointless arguments, Maggie hadn't mentioned this to Sam, but she was sure he had no interest in being a single parent. Sam's mind was on worldly things—his business, his friends at Molly Malone's, the goings-on in the city where he was born, and if she'd allow it, sex. Real love, especially love of God, wasn't on his agenda.

She hung a sign saying, *Kitchen Closed. Come Again Tomorrow* on the basement stairs. She could hear Adamo singing as he worked. Usually it was, "O Sole Mio," a song he never tired of.

Just then a man dressed in rags arrived. She'd seen him several times before.

"Por favor, mother, may I eat?"

He looked incredibly dirty, though Maggie now suspected it might be makeup. His face was almost covered by a beard and long hair that seemed fake. She'd decided he wasn't homeless, just too poor to pay, or too embarrassed to be seen here, eating Adamo's scrumptious meals.

Maggie nodded. "Sí, señor. *Está invitado,*" she replied, using the Spanish Doña Teresita was teaching her.

"Gracias," he said and followed her down through the door marked, *Community Meal Kitchen.*

When food was being served, Sam showed up.

He stood in the doorway scanning the crowd as if he expected Maggie to be attacked. True, they'd had trouble at first from a few zealous people, but word spread about the broken jaw Sam gave a man. It had been a long time since anyone grabbed her, demanding to be prayed for or healed. Things would have settled down, anyway, without Sam's help. This was Harlem, her real home. People respected each other here and kept their mouths shut, just like in Arona, the Italian village where she'd lived with Jess.

As usual, Sam and Adamo glared at each other.

Ignoring them, Maggie picked up her Bible, turned to Matthew 21 and the passages Jess had explained to her in the weeks before his death. She started for the front of the room, but Sam came up to her, whispering, "You need to stop doing this!"

She paused. "Reading my Bible? I'm not ever going to stop that, Sam!"

"You're making them believe crazy things. Maggie, it's dangerous!"

It was true she'd taken on a larger role at church, but everyone seemed happy about it and it was all in the name of God.

"This has been my church since I was fifteen, except when I was in Italy. I'm not afraid."

She continued to the front of the room and, eyeing Sam, said, "Today I'll read about Jesus and the withered fig tree."

Sam stalked off.

> "Now in the morning, as He returned to the city, He was hungry.
>
> "And seeing a fig tree by the road, He came to it and found nothing on it but leaves, and said to it, "Let no fruit grow on you ever again." Immediately the fig tree withered away.
>
> "And when the disciples saw it, they marveled, saying, "How did the fig tree wither away so soon?
>
> "So Jesus answered and said to them, "Assuredly, I say to you, if you have faith and do not doubt, you will not only do what was done to the fig tree, but also if you say to this mountain, 'Be removed and be cast into the sea,' it will be done. And whatever things you ask in prayer, believing, you will receive."

Maggie looked up, hoping the message had sunk in—*ask, believing*. She felt compelled to spread the words Jess had called to her attention. She herself didn't ask for things in prayer, since all she wanted was Jess's return and that was impossible. She just said the, "Our Father," and such. Sometimes homeless people would take her aside, describing miracles after prayer. She envied them. Maggie's belief wasn't simple anymore.

She'd also fallen into lustful yearnings it took focus to control. Her immoral nose caught Sam's smell as he came in and she would have left and gone straight to bed with him if he weren't in league with Satan. She saw him at the doorway, staring at her, and missed believing he really loved her.

A perfect vessel for evil, Sam didn't try to be a part of her world. Rarely did he attend his own church. He just investigated his low cases, hung out in New York, and waited for the birth of his child. He seemed bored, as if he'd rather Maggie try shooting him again.

She began the day's grace. Every week she found a different one.

> "Lord, Bless this food to our bodies and
> our bodies to your service. In Jesus'
> name, Amen."

"Amen, Mother," the diners replied.

She looked up and Sam had gone.

At the front table, Adamo sat beside her. As Jesus advised, they never separated themselves from the others. The Mexican man she'd let in nodded from across the table and Maggie smiled at him, wishing he'd abandon his fake beard and be himself. He smiled back and kept eating the *strozzapreti con tacchino e funghi*, short pasta with turkey and mushrooms, cooked by the only Italian in the church.

"You are very beautiful today, mia cara," Adamo whispered.

"Beautiful?" she whispered back. "With this big stomach?"

"To me you are," he said. "How do you like my dinner?

Maggie tasted it. "Delicious! When we were in Arona, I never knew you could cook like this."

"Nor did you know how I love you."

Maggie put her fork down and turned to him.

"Adamo, don't you see you're doing the same thing you did before? Loving somebody else's wife? In Arona, it was your brother's wife. Now it's me, Sam's wife. You're living in other people's shadows, afraid to have a woman of your own."

"That is not true!" he whispered back.

"Yes it is!"

"No, mia cara, it is not! I have no life without you. It has been like that since we met. I sought you out to talk about my brother's wife only so I could be with you."

"Me, Adamo? The town beauty?"

"You have something more attractive to many men—the fact that you don't know you need us, but you do; your kind heart. I think Jess knew I loved you."

Maggie closed her eyes in pain.

"Oh! I am sorry, Maggie. I did not mean to remind you of Jess here in public."

She breathed deeply.

"Here, here," Adamo said and put some food on a fork. "Don't cry. I am sorry. Have some more strozzapreti con tacchino e funghi."

Chapter 13

At the estate Coral awoke, Francisco sitting beside her on the bed stroking her hair. In the morning quiet she heard her favorite serenade, "Le Feria de las Flores." She loved the plaintive Mexican serenades, the deep chords of the *guitarrone*, the *tricordia's* sweet high notes, the melodious Spanish guitar. She thought that as she drew her last breaths, she'd remember two things: last night on the pyramid with Francisco under the never-ending sky and her one night with Sam, twelve years ago. To Coral, the irony of those twelve years having come full circle—asking Francisco to kidnap Sam Duffy's child—fit the bitter pattern of her life. There had never been a man she could rely on—not her father who died and couldn't protect her from the man her mother married, not Theo who had used her and died, not Sam who might have loved her but who left her, or Francisco who wouldn't marry her. Luis was the only one to offer her security. No question that her loyalty was with him.

As Francisco gazed at her, Coral said, "There's something I didn't tell you."

"What?"

"You have to kidnap a child."

He stopped stroking her hair. "A child? You never said that."

"Yes, in New York. An infant."

"How old?"

"It's not born yet. It's due any day."

"I am a man, not a monster."

She shrugged. "Okay, then, I have to leave and tell Luis."

"No." He held her down then released her. "Coral, what will happen to this infant?"

She sat up and put her arms around his neck. "Nothing. I promise you, Francisco. Nothing. Luis is giving him to someone who will care for him. The child will be completely safe. I promise."

Francisco rose and picked her up, kissing her in a place no longer taboo, holding her to him. "I want to show you something. Let me dress you."

"But—"

"No, I want to."

He carried her to the suite's tub of gorgeous Talavera blue peacock tiles and put her in the water he'd drawn, rolled up his sleeves and began to bathe her. Coral closed her eyes and listened to the music. She imagined she was a child being cared for, though she knew better. He was just a lover who would leave when he tired of her. For now he performed an intimate ritual, dried her body, rubbed on lotion and perfume, brushed her hair, picked out clothes for her to wear, put them on her, slipped sandals on her feet, making her feel safe though she knew she was only being lulled by him and his Mexican serenades.

He took her down to the estate's white tile kitchen trimmed in more Talavera tiles, handmade for grand estates. They sat at the central counter under a massive hood, a cook on the other side frying up eggs and chorizo. Francisco had told her that on many nights, whole families arrived here, hidden in the vans. They came from city slums and countryside, especially Chiapas and Oaxaca. Fed from the estate's four ovens and its walk-in freezer, they were given beds, and trucked off next morning on their journey north. For many, the eggs and orange juice they ate here were the first they'd ever had.

A little boy entered the kitchen as they were leaving. No more than ten, he had hostile eyes. Sullenly he said, "Hola, Francisco."

Francisco nodded seriously to him, "Hola, Miguel."

"Who is he?" Coral whispered.

"They made him a prostitute in Houston. He got away, but his father won't take him back. I feel responsible. Mexica Eterna tries to protect those we take across the border, but sometimes we fail. He lives here, now."

She turned and held out her arms to the boy, "*Ven acá.*"

Francisco lowered her hands. "He doesn't want a hug."

The boy said, "Hola, señora," and moved away from her.

When Francisco and Coral arrived in the courtyard, a single Jeep and an armed guard waited. Francisco said they wouldn't need more where they were going.

"Where is that?" she asked.

"Ciudades perdidas."

"The lost cities?"

"Yes."

On the way, they drove past the most popular city park, also named Chapultepec, as was its castle. To Coral, it echoed the fatalism in the Mexican personality. The last Toltec emperor spent his final days in a cave on the hill there. Mexica made one of its last stands against the Spanish conquistadores there. Benito Juarez lived in the castle before Emperor Maximilian took it as his palace, only to be assassinated on the order of Juarez. At Chapultepec, six young military cadets, the *Niños Héroes*, fought to the death when the USA invaded in 1847. One, Juan Escutia, wrapped himself in the Mexican flag and jumped to his death rather than surrender the flag. That's when Mexico lost half its territory to Uncle Sam—land that Luis's La Reconquista wanted back. "Tell me how you die and I will tell you who you are," their Nobel laureate, Octavo Paz, had said. Because of its dyings, Francisco told her, Chapultepec was a fierce source of national pride.

An hour later when they reached their destination, Coral frowned, confused. "Isn't this a sports stadium?"

"Now it is. Cuidad Deportiva.When Luis and I lived here it was called Borda de Xochiaca, the largest and filthiest landfill in the world. It was in the fair city of Nezahualcóyotl, ravenous coyote, named after a Mexica prince. Until 2006 when Carlos Slim and some others grew a conscience, the entire city was a fierce source of national indifference. We call it Neza for short. It started as a squatter town and became one of the biggest slums in the world, though it wasn't the only one here. Mexico City is ringed by slums with dumps. We call them *barsurero*."

"I can't imagine people living in such a place."

"You don't have to."

Francisco turned on the ignition, drove east then north. Soon she was gaping through the windshield in disbelief, hanging on as the Jeep bumped down unpaved streets littered with trash and rusted cars. A pack of stray dogs parted as they approached. Up ahead she saw a mound of refuse on which scavenging people crawled, many of them children. One stopped and called to his friends who all lined up to watch the strangers. When the Jeep drew nearer they shouted "Francisco! Es Francisco!"

The Jeep reached the top of the hill well ahead of the children. Francisco turned it around and stopped. Before them Coral saw a town of gray, punctuated now and then by spots of red, orange, and blue. It consisted of scrap wood and corrugated metal shanties—color the only resistance to the poverty she could smell as well as see, as if what humans expelled, both physically and mentally, saturated the air. From a shanty boomed a virulent punk rock that Francisco called *La Banda*, saying it was peculiar to this place. She could barely translate the lyrics:

> "... You can't live. You can't think. As long as the government exists. They make you sick. They make you empty. They kill you if you won't die. ..."

Begging children quickly surrounded the the Jeep. They were dirty. Some wore tatters.

"Give us the bag," Francisco said to his hombre in back.

He handed up a bagful of coins.

Trembling from the squalor and the rage in the music, Coral said. "I'll help you pass them out."

Children swarmed close and soon Coral was crying as she handed coins out of the window, the children saying, "*Qué Dios te bendiga, madre,*"—bless you mother—to her. "*No llores,*" don't cry, some said.

"Where are we?' she asked Francisco.

"We are in Chimalhuacán. No one has rescued it yet. The

government would like nothing better than if they all leave here and sneak into the USA. After all, a third of the economy comes from emigrants sending money home. Luis and I are helping them do just that."

"You come here all the time?"

"I was born in Neza when it was just like this. Luis and I escaped by the grace of God."

Coral looked around and tried to imagine Francisco and Luis scrounging in trash heaps for food and begging on the streets, but she couldn't.

"How did you ever get out?"

"His father had a winning streak at the race track when we were young. It was enough to move our family up into the middle class."

"His father helped your family, too?"

He looked confused, then said, "In Mexico, family includes grandparents, uncles, aunts and cousins. We moved to Satellite City where the shopping malls are. Luis went to university, the first in our family. Then came the peso devaluation of 1982. We lost everything. Luis left school. He got a job in a fancy hotel. He met this man, Theomund Brown, and did everything for him. He took Luis to New York. For a time, our whole family was saved and many of our friends. Then came the great earthquake of 1985. It destroyed everything we had."

"Te bendiga, madre; te bendiga, padre," the children shouted as they took the coins.

A tiny girl with large, beautiful, sick eyes reached the door and held out her hand. Overcome, Coral lifted the gold chain and its three-carat diamond from her neck and put it in the girl's hands.

"Coral!" Woefully, Francisco touched her empty cleavage. The girl regarded the stone, eyebrows raised, eyes plaintive, mouth turned down.

"Wrong move," Coral sighed, took the diamond and chain back, dove into her purse, and handed the girl a hundred dollar bill. Smiling, the girl flew away.

When the bag of coins was empty, Francisco's hombre pointed a gun out the window and shot in the air. The children scattered, but Francisco gave him such a threatening glare, Coral doubted the man would shoot around children again.

As they drove away, Coral sat back, overwhelmed. "Why don't they do something about the poverty?"

"More than half the people in greater Mexico City are too poor to avoid dying of pneumonia or diarrhea—the biggest killers—yet the richest man in the world lives here, Carlos Slim, and for years he did little to help. He isn't the only one, though. There are ten or eleven billionaires in Mexico and, not long ago, it had an obscene number of millionaires per capita. Most are the supposedly pure blood descendants of the Spanish and they still act like conquistadores. They take everything and the hell with the likes of us. I used to kidnap them for big ransoms—adults, never a child."

"Why don't the people revolt?"

"For four centuries, the Spanish told us we were worthless because our ancestors engaged in human sacrifice. Unconsciously, we believe them. We are ashamed, silent, like a raped woman who thinks it is her fault she was raped. If we try revolt, our actions are disorganized and hysterical and we are killed, but most don't try. The elites take advantage of the fact that 'life has cured us of fear'." That's what the soldiers sang in the Mexican Revolution. From our ancient cultures we are familiar with death, we play with it, we eat it in cakes on the Days of the Dead. In these slums, we keep the dying up. Sometimes I think the city feeds on it, soaking up our blood, growing richer with each death. I've often dreamed that our last emperor, Cuauhtémoc, will one day rise in our souls. He'll lead us down into Mexico City where we will cut out the living hearts of everyone who lives in a big house."

"That would include you."

"Perhaps I deserve it."

Coral glanced at Francisco. His expression was the same as

the day they'd met—detachment and danger, all on an utterly masculine face. As she thought of the children, his brand of wealth redistribution seemed fair.

"If Carlos Slim helped Neza, surely he'll help this place."

"Eventually, perhaps. Many children will die waiting."

"How many people have you actually gotten out of here, Francisco?"

Francisco's eyes watered. "Out of all the slums? Five thousand seven hundred and eighty-six."

Her mouth dropped open. "That's what? More than twenty a day?"

"I remember them all," he said and gunned the engine.

Francisco drove out of Chimalhuacán as if his screaming tires could destroy it. Eventually he slowed and drove to the center of town and the Paseo de la Reforma, the city's grandest boulevard, modeled after Paris's Champs Elysées. It was a tree-lined parade of art galleries, luxurious hotels, exclusive homes, monuments, and parks. All beautiful. All uniquely Mexican. He pulled up to the Four Seasons Hotel.

"I thought you'd need a break from the barsureros," he said, and escorted her into the hotel's elegant Reforma 500 restaurant. It featured Mediterranean cuisine. They'd once dressed in Mexico's dramatic colors and gone all over town, pretending to be the painters Frida Kahlo and Diego Rivera, icons whose story of art and pain, love and betrayal and death was still part of the city's heartbeat. Once Coral sat on Francisco's lap and, under her long skirt, had sex on a couch here.

Francisco said, "Here it is easy to pretend that the ciudades perdidas don't exist. All is serene in the neighborhoods of the privileged—in Colonia Centro, Chapultepec, the Zona Rosa, and anywhere else tourists and the wealthy go."

"Except when they're kidnapped?" she pointed out.

"Except then. In a way, we are like our forefathers. We know there must be a sacrifice once in a while—a brother, a wife, or even a child."

Coral had read about the murder of fourteen-year old Fernando Marti by his kidnappers. As Francisco studied the wine list, she gazed at him, seeing the luxury around her through different eyes. "Francisco, what would you be doing if you weren't running Mexica Eterna for Luis? Where would you be?"

He didn't look up. "On a ranch in Michoacan breeding Azteca horses—assuming we ever get narcos out of there."

"I didn't know you knew how to breed horses."

"I could learn, just like Luis learned to be a pátron. What would you be doing if you didn't work for him?" He looked up from the menu.

"Dancing or raising a passel of kids."

He looked surprised. "I can't picture that."

Neither can I, she thought.

"Do you want champagne?" he said.

"What really happened to Luis's parents?" Coral asked after they'd ordered, "his brothers and sister?"

Francisco leaned back. "You've seen the statues?"

"Yes, but I don't know the whole story. I only know they taught him not to say ni modo. What does it really mean to him, anyway?"

"*Ya ni modo* or *ya que* is a Mexican phrase trying to minimize injustice. It's a way of accepting that life isn't fair. It means not to get worked up about what can't be changed—lost wallets, corrupt governments. Since Luis believes in change, he does not like me to say it."

"Me either. What about his family?"

He squeezed her hand. "After the earthquake, Luis wanted to bring them all to New York, but there was no quick way to do it legally so he told them to wait. They didn't. They had someone set them up with a coyote who abandoned them in the dessert. We never heard from them again."

Coral gasped. Francisco didn't know the truth? It only took her a second to decide to use this advantage, certain Luis wouldn't mind if it brought results. "That's not true." She put her hand on his arm. "It was Luis who hired the coyote. Don't you see? That's why he's doing this. That's the reason for Mexica Eterna."

Francisco sat back and frowned. "You are sure?"

She nodded.

Francisco choked and looked lost. He rubbed his forehead as if it hurt to have this fact in his mind.

Coral felt guilt, pity, and sorrow—emotions that had never done her much good. But could Francisco refuse Luis, now, knowing this? She leaned on his shoulder. "You'll still do what he asks? You'll kidnap the child?"

Slowly Francisco raised his head. "Of course."

Chapter 14

Coral could see Sam's office even from the sidewalk outside this nineteenth century cast-iron SOHO building. It was behind the third floor window with the painted sign reading, *Duffy Detectives: Confidential Investigations.*

She opened the door and climbed the metal staircase. Coral had purposely avoided early morning and lunchtime, thinking Sam, a detective, would be following people then. She opted for 3:00 P.M., thinking he'd be back lining up new cases, or making notes until the husbands he had to follow got off from work. She'd watched him enter, a morose expression on his face.

Outside his door she paused, fluffing her chestnut hair, pulling down the bodice of the flame red gauzy dress she wore and exposing more cleavage. From her purse she took a small spritzer and refreshed her perfume then examined her red lipstick in her compact. For seduction, no color was better than red.

She opened the door, calling, "Hello?" Hearing, "In here," she walked past the empty receptionist's desk into an inner office and there was Sam, talking on the phone, his feet up on a plain wooden desk, the walls around him unadorned except for a license of some kind. He had the same strong build, the same masculine assurance he'd always had—not unlike Francisco's, except Sam's was all Irish, beer and baseball, where Francisco's was hypnotic Mexican nights.

When he saw her, their eyes met and locked as if no time had elapsed since they first met—as if Sam had since done nothing to apologize for.

"I'll call you back," he said and hung up.

Coral smiled. "I see you're home from Italy."

"I knew it was you before I saw you. What the hell is that perfume you wear? I've never smelled it anywhere else."

"Somebody made it for me. Anybody here, Sam?"

"No, Coral. How did you find me?"

"I stopped by Molly Malone's for old time's sake. They told me."

She tossed her purse onto a chair.

"I'm married now," he said.

She tilted her head to the side. "I'm not."

They surveyed each other, their images alone filling the silence.

Coral began to loosen the belt to her red dress. Last time she did this, Sam told her to stop, but now he leaned back in his chair and clasped his hands behind his head, watching.

"Miss me?" she whispered.

He didn't reply, only watched her reach under her arm, find the red dress's zipper, and pull it down. Slowly she lifted the dress off, revealing a luxurious gold slip. Sam had never seen her in one. She'd worn it to titillate him.

"Shall I keep going?" she asked.

Sam said nothing, his gaze roaming over her.

"Want to know why I'm here?"

He found her eyes, "No, I don't."

She saw a photo of Maggie on the desk and went closer to pick it up. There was no loving couple photo beside it, no adoring husband cradling pregnant spouse.

"So she's your wife?"

Sam nodded.

"You love her?"

"Very much."

Coral stroked her hip. "Maybe I should leave then."

Sam still said nothing, just kept staring in a way Coral couldn't decipher. She started swaying, peeling the slip down with each undulation until it slid to the floor, leaving her naked in her red high heels.

"You're still drop dead gorgeous," Sam said in a low voice. "Did you give up the life after Brown died?"

"Yeah, I did, more or less." She couldn't tell him about Luis.

He pointed behind her. "You'd better lock that door."

Coral turned and bent unnecessarily low to operate the deadbolt then stood, grinning. "Now what?"

"I guess you'd better come over here to me," Sam said, an odd expression on his face.

As soon as Coral rounded the desk, Sam reached up and pulled her into his lap, cradling her as if she were a priceless treasure. He put his hands in her hair, his face in her neck, and sniffed. "What do they call this stuff? An olfactory aphrodisiac?"

Teasing, she whispered, "Wooow, I didn't know you knew the word olfactory, Sam."

He choked as if her perfume were too strong.

"Oh, sorry."

He choked again.

Coral sat still as Sam Duffy tried not to cry into her hair, his shoulders shaking. What was going on? She put her arms around him.

"When I screw up I don't fool around," he murmured.

Of all the reactions she'd had to her naked body, this was a first. Sam held her, murmuring, "Oh God," his face buried in her neck. Then he sat up. " I'm sorry. I've been doing that a lot lately."

This wasn't the Sam she'd known.

"Sorry for what?"

"For everything. For not meeting you sooner, for not loving you harder, for not making you mine, for hurting you like I did." He ran his hands down her shoulders, her legs, but he wasn't making love. He seemed to be apologizing to every inch of her for his transgressions.

"I thought you loved Maggie," she whispered.

"That I do; that I do. The problem is she doesn't love me back. I ask myself why she should. I've hurt her as much as I hurt you."

Coral searched Sam's face, feeling impatient with him. "Make love to me."

"Why?"

"For old time's sake."

"Why did you come here, Coral?"

"For this, Sam. For this."

He sighed, his eyes adoring her. "I can't. I've done enough to you and Maggie."

Filled with desire for this strangely woeful Sam, Coral took his hands and put them on her. "Okay, then just touch me, Sam. That's all."

He groaned and rocked her in his lap, moving his hands over her as if she were a lost possession he'd recovered. He stayed away from the most intimate places, but it didn't matter. Coral knew her response to him would be intense. With Sam and Francisco she'd had the best sex of her life. She put her own hands where he wouldn't and soon was trembling in his arms.

"Oh, God," Sam moaned and gave in, kissing her while he fumbled with his zipper. Then he stopped. "I can't do this."

Coral thought of the five million dollars and reached inside his unzipped pants.

Sam stopped protesting. He stood and carried her to the leather couch, lay on top of her, entered her body with a groan then almost instantly exploded.

As he panted, she said, "Why do I get the impression every time we do this that you haven't had sex for months? Doesn't Maggie give you any?"

"No, that she doesn't. Only three times since the wedding."

Coral chuckled. "Miss Holiness keeps it locked up and let's you walk around horny like this? Her loss."

"Coral, you're a wicked wench."

"I hope so."

"There's something I need to tell you."

"What?"

"If I hadn't met Maggie, it would have been the two of us—if you'd wanted."

"Liar."

He laughed and hugged her and it really was like old times. Sam ordered Chinese, turned the TV on low while they ate, and then resumed making love. Until well after Duffy Detectives was officially closed, Coral savored the kind of ecstasy she wouldn't have felt in almost twelve years if she hadn't met Francisco.

She fell asleep beneath Sam. A dropped shoe woke her. Opening her eyes, Coral found herself alone on the leather couch, the TV on, Sam frantically getting dressed. His eyes fixed on the screen which flashed photographs of Maggie, apparently saying grace to a roomful of homeless people before a meal in the basement of a church.

Coral slipped past Sam and turned the TV up. "This is reportedly the same woman implanted with DNA from the Shroud of Turin more than ten years ago by Dr. Felix Rossi of New York. For weeks, all of Harlem has been abuzz. Is she carrying another clone?"

"Goddamnit, I warned her!" Sam cried as he picked up the dropped shoe. "I warned her!" With the other hand he held the phone to his ear. "Why does she never have her cell phone on? Why doesn't she listen to me?"

Looking at the TV, Coral said, "It probably serves her right."

He whirled and grabbed her. "If you had anything to do with this—"

"What? Why would I, Sam?" Coral tried to look aghast, having accomplished her mission. She'd reconnected with Sam and kept him away from Maggie's church dinner while someone with a hidden camera took photographs—Luis's bait to hook Salati. She wanted to say, *Sam, take her away where no one can find her, or you'll never see your baby again*, but she didn't.

Sam let her go, shouted, "Oh, hell!" and headed out the door.

Chapter 15

The drive should have taken seventeen minutes, twenty tops, Houston to First Avenue then five miles later left on 96th, right on Park Avenue, two more miles then left on 131st, but traffic came to a standstill when Sam crossed Martin Luther King Boulevard, otherwise known as 125th Street.

In the twelve-year-old Range Rover Felix had given to Maggie, he inched through New York streets, screaming into his cell phone at Felix.

"I don't know what happened, Felix! Damn it, I'm not up at that church with her twenty-four hours a day!"

He peered through the windshield as he listened to Felix shout, "Maggie's your wife! She's carrying your child and you don't know what's going on? Why am I not surprised, Sam? Enough is enough! I'm sick of this drama, this mess!"

Sam decided to leave Park Avenue and try Madison. "You're sick of it? You? That's a laugh. I'm the one who told you not to try cloning anybody in the first place, remember? Now you're sick and tired. That's a laugh."

He made the turn, listening to Felix rant and watching dark clouds form in the sky.

"A press conference, Felix? You're going to hold a press conference and tell them there's no new clone of Jesus? Now that should really fucking help! Yeah, they'll believe you, all right—the guy who made the first clone and covered it up so long."

Felix shouted, "Someone has to stop this!"

"You mean someone has to keep them from tearing Maggie apart! That's what's important, Felix! Shut up and make yourself useful. Tell me what they're saying on TV. I'm only six blocks away, but traffic's not moving."

He could hear Felix turn up the TV volume. "They're not

saying anything about what's happening now. They're going over the history—mine, Maggie's and the story of Jess. They're saying if Maggie didn't die eleven years ago, why should they believe Jess died? They're saying I lied."

"Perfect!" Sam growled. "And you want to hold another press conference!"

"I'm not taking my family through a media feeding frenzy again! I'm not going to expose them to kooks! This has got to end!"

"This is what you're going to do, Felix. You're going to help get Maggie out of there."

Turning onto Madison, Sam gave Felix instructions.

"God, Madison is jammed too," Sam growled. He saw a parking space being vacated, pulled head first into it, rolled one wheel up on the curb, dropped it back, then straightened the Rover out—standard procedure if you didn't want your space stolen in New York. "I'm jogging the last four blocks. Take care of it, Felix!" Sam said and clicked off the phone. He looked up at the darkening sky and ran, praying for rain.

When he reached 131st it was clear that Maggie was the source of the traffic jam. Reporters and people with cameras filled the street. Every window was open, every landing, stoop, and step packed with onlookers trying to get a glimpse of the woman carrying the second clone of Christ.

Sam had to force, and sometimes fight, his way down the street. When he reached the converted stone townhouse that was the 131st Street Baptist Church, he saw that the doors and windows had been locked. Only a single police car was there and its two occupants seemed to have given up. Either that, or they were complying with international standards for crowd control to the max—using no force to disperse non-violent unlawful assemblies. Sam made his way to the police car and rapped on the glass. When the window rolled down he said, "I need to get in there. Will you help me?"

"Come back another day, bud. The place is closed."

Sam looked up at the sky from which not a drop of rain had

fallen. If it did, it would disperse the crowd. "My wife's the one on the news. She's pregnant. I've got to get her out so these lunatics don't hurt her. Give me a break and help me get in there."

The policemen looked at each other, "If we put up blockades, this crowd is going to overrun them and mob your wife before we get her in the car. We can't shoot and club people just because they think it's the Second Coming. The mayor wouldn't like it."

"All right, can you just get me in there?"

They left the police car, nightsticks and bullhorn in hand, "Get behind us," one of them told Sam.

"People!" yelled the officer with the bullhorn. "Get off the church steps!"

Startled, the crowd surged away from the doors but with nowhere to go on the full street, surged right back.

"People! Get off the steps!"

Somewhere a TV camera's floodlight came on. The police pushed forward, making a moving barricade with their nightsticks, Sam behind them.

People! Get off the steps!"

Some pressed against the guardrails, others jumped into the sidewalk crowd, trying to make space for the police and Sam.

At the door, Sam asked to use the bullhorn. "Maggie!" he called. "It's me! Open the door!" Cameras flashed.

The door opened only slightly against the crush. The minister's arm reached out and pulled Sam inside.

Maggie lay on the leather couch in the minister's office, her hand over her eyes, wishing she could shut the world out. She had a pain in her back and Adamo was sitting beside her in a chair.

She heard Sam's voice. "Let go of my wife!"

Only then did she realize Adamo had been holding her hand.

She opened her eyes and sat up as Adamo stood. Sam crossed to him and pushed him in the chest. "What are you doing with your hands on my wife?"

Adamo, who was shorter and slighter than Sam, nevertheless

had his fists clenched at his sides. "*Desiderate combattere?*" Adamo said. You want to fight?

"Leave, Adamo. Just leave," Maggie said.

"*Vaffanculo,*" Sam replied in shockingly vulgar Italian, especially given that they were in church.

"Adamo, I asked you to leave!" Maggie cried as Sam circled him. She'd seen what Sam did to Felix years ago when he first learned about the cloning.

Adamo went to the door, jabbing his finger at Sam for emphasis. "I leave only because you ask me to, mia cara!"

Sam yelled. "I'll show you mia cara!"

As Maggie shot from the couch to grab Sam's arm, Adamo swiftly left and closed the door.

Sam turned on her. "Why the hell is he always hanging around you? Why don't you ever have your damn phone on?"

Ruefully she smiled, grateful to see him. She turned and peeped out between the shutters. "How are we going to get out of here, Sam?"

He sighed. "What have you done to us, Maggie?" Leaning over her stomach, he cupped her face in his hands. "What's to become of us now?"

"You can have the baby," Maggie said.

He frowned.

"You made me carry it, but I can't raise it, Sam. I just can't. I should have told you. I want a divorce after it's born."

He looked astounded. "You don't want your own baby?"

Maggie exhaled and breathed in a woman's scent, vaguely familiar. As she sniffed, her nostrils filled with the musky odor of sex. Then she remembered exactly where she'd smelled that perfume before. Maggie flew toward the rack holding the minister's magazines and, one by one, starting hurling them at Sam.

"You've been with her!" she shouted.

Sam raised his arms to block the magazines. "Uh, no, I haven't!"

"You have! You've just had sex with Coral!" Maggie yelled.

"No, I haven't … uh, well you won't sleep with me, so … now and then I have to do it myself."

"Wearing perfume?" She flung more magazines at him.

"Wait! You just told me you want a divorce!"

Sam's cell phone rang. He turned away to answer as magazines pummeled his shoulders. "Okay, we're ready. It's 131st Street."

He made his way through the magazine bombardment and grabbed Maggie. "It's Felix. He's getting us out of here. Let's save this for later."

"I'm not going anywhere with you!" Maggie cried.

"Yes you are!"

"You've betrayed me again! How many times do you plan to betray me, Sam?"

Sam pulled her to him. "Only a couple more than you!"

"What?"

"You abandoned our marriage bed. You hid in this church and left me to myself. You're spending time with another man. Worst of all, Maggie, you've endangered our child. Now it turns out that you don't even want it!"

Maggie glared at Sam, her nostrils full of Coral's perfume. She knew Sam was right, but she wouldn't admit it.

Gazing around the room from which she'd emerged to marry Sam, she whispered, "What are we going to do?"

He ran his hand down her shoulder. "We never had a chance once Jess died, did we, Maggie? Forgiving me felt like betraying him, didn't it?"

Maggie said nothing.

"Let's get out of here."

He opened the door, his arm around her. There kneeling on the floor were Sharmina, the minister, his wife, the head deaconess, and a couple of regulars from the Community Meal Kitchen. Adamo wasn't kneeling, just glowering.

"We were praying for you," the minister said.

"While listening at the door, I see," Maggie said.

"I guess this could be my fault," Sharmina added, pointing to the door and the crowd beyond it

"Sharmina, my lass, I have a feeling that's true," Sam said.

"No, Shar," Maggie said, rubbing her back.

"How do we get to the roof?" Sam asked the minister.

Leading the way to the top floor, the minister lowered a flight of collapsing stairs. Sam helped Maggie climb it and they were on the roof.

He scoured the sky. "Lucky for us there are so many private helipads in this city that helicopters know how to land on any roof if the building's sturdy and you've got enough money."

"Where will we go, Sam? The press probably know where we live."

"Wait! That's it!" Sam said. "Money. Enough money is all we need." He took out his cell phone and pushed a button. "Felix, it's Sam again. Listen, the only way this is going to be over is if Maggie and I disappear. We need to get out of the country right now. Today! All you have to do is pay for it. We'll disappear, just like she did before. Then you and your family can relax."

Below her the streets were full of people, hoping for a glimpse of something tangible to believe in. She'd seen it happening, had allowed the church people to believe, rather than dash their hopes. It reminded her of when Jess was alive. Belief was real for her then because she could embrace the Son of God, feed him dinner, put him to bed, tell him stories about the wonderful lost world he'd save one day.

She saw a helicopter approaching in the distance.

"What?" Sam shouted. "What do you mean you're not getting involved? She didn't do it deliberately, Felix. I know you want to put your family first, but—"

Sam listened.

"For God's sake, it's because of you that—"

Felix interrupted, shouting so loudly Maggie heard him, too. "The boy I cloned is dead. It's outrageous, just outrageous that the two of you have stirred this up again. If you think I'm going to pay for you to disappear and leave me and my family here for the press to feed on, you're wrong. The two of you did this. The two of you fix it. In fact, the hell with you, Sam."

"Well, the hell with you, too!"

"Sam, I have money," Maggie said.

He hung up the cell phone. "Don't worry. Somehow I'll—"

Maggie felt a twinge radiate from her back to her stomach.

"I do, Sam. I saved all the money Felix paid me over the years."

"You did? Well, it should help a little."

He started waving his arms because the helicopter was starting to descend.

She bent sideways to relieve the twinge. "Sam, I had the bank invest it. My savings grew. I think by now it's over two million dollars."

The people on the street must have seen the chopper, too, because Maggie saw them pointing up. Sam stopped waving at the helicopter and turned to her. "You have two million dollars?"

"I think so." Maggie grimaced. "Sam I—"

He glared at her. "You must have got a big laugh out of Duffy Detectives then."

"Money's not something I think about. I'm used to living off a normal household budget. It's been piling up for years and I just didn't think about it."

"You had to think about the money when you were buying those clothes in Milan. I thought you were spending your last dime. You had to think about it when I was buying you that discount wedding gown."

Maggie hung her head, ashamed. He was right.

"Holy Mother! Bless us Mother!" called people from the street.

"I'll give you that divorce as soon as we're out of here, Holy Mother," Sam announced.

The helicopter was landing. Sam turned to wave it down.

Maggie groaned. "Sam, I might be having a contraction."

Sam snorted in disgust. "Sure, right" he shouted. "What's this? Act IV of Maggie hates Sam? 'Sam, I'm so glad to have your baby,' *let me drink this tea to kill it.* 'Sam, I love you,' *but I'm murdering you on our wedding night.* 'Sam bust your balls to take care of me,' *so I don't have to spend my two million dollars?* 'Sam, I'll have your baby,' *you can keep it, and I want a divorce?* Another lie to jerk stupid Sam around?"

She shook her head in regret as the wind from the helicopter blew their clothes and hair.

Sam turned to help the pilot maneuver the tail rotor between an air-conditioning unit and a chimney. When he turned back, Maggie was gasping.

He cursed, helped her get into the chopper then said to the pilot, "Can you get us close to the Yerbería Guadalupe on Luis Múñoz Marin Boulevard near Third Avenue?"

"Not very," he said.

"What about 127th and Madison? That's where my car is."

The pilot gave a thumbs up. "Sure!"

Sam buckled Maggie in. "Or does all of Harlem know you're giving birth at the yerbería?"

"No, Sam! Just Sharmina."

Sam groaned.

Maggie quickly forgot her backache and her argument with Sam because of the chopper's ascent and flight. It began promisingly enough, lifting off into a hover, sitting on a cushion of air. As the rotors sped up, the chopper turned into the wind and she felt a powerful upthrust, like a giant bird had taken wing. Suddenly, gravity no longer applied. The helicopter bounced, heaved, swayed, and pitched—an eggbeater trying to stay in the air—not unlike her life, she thought, speeding out of control in a direction she couldn't guess. As she fought nausea, one of the dials caught her eye. Labeled *altimeter*, it drifted all over the place. Was the pilot noticing, too? He could have been listening to music in his headphones, for all she knew, his hands gliding lazily on the controls. With a shock she realized they'd actually headed south and now, praise the Lord, were approaching their destination. If she could keep from getting sick and get her feet on solid ground, Maggie knew what she would do.

When the helicopter landed they made their way from the

roof to the building's lobby. Sam searched for the ladies room and took Maggie there.

Outside the door, he said, "Can you manage not to talk to anyone for a few moments and announce you're the Virgin Mary?"

She hung her head, "Sam—"

"Stay in a stall while I get the car, okay? I'll come back and knock. Then you can come out."

Sam sprinted around the corner to the car. Blaring his horn, he bulldozed through traffic using the aggressive, fender-first, *I'm taking the space that doesn't exist in front of you,* mode of progress favored by New York drivers.

He gave a startled newsstand owner a hundred dollars to sit behind the Rover's wheel for five minutes while he went to get Maggie. Otherwise, it could fall victim to the ravenous tow trucks that scoured the streets looking for double-parked cars.

Back inside the building, he banged on the ladies' room door and waited. No answer. Maggie didn't come out. He banged again and then went in. Maggie wasn't in the stalls. Frantic, Sam ran back into the lobby, searching for her but she wasn't there. He went outside, ran up and down the street, calling her name with no response.

Maggie left the ladies' room as soon as Sam was gone. On the street, holding her stomach, she'd flagged the sole cab whizzing by. The cab had slammed on its brakes and backed up. The driver hopped out and opened the door, took her arm to help her in.

"Which hospital, lady?" the cabbie asked.

"Not a hospital," she replied, settling in the seat. Her back pain was no worse, so she thought she had time. She asked if he knew the TV station broadcasting the story about Harlem's Black Madonna.

"I was just listening to it," he said.

"Would you take me there?"

She saw him gaze in the rearview mirror, probably realizing who she was, but New York cabbies were their own special breed—cursing stoics who'd driven everyone to everywhere in pursuit of everything on earth.

"You got it, lady," he said and pulled into traffic.

She pictured Sam finding her gone, and asked God to keep him from running around and shooting someone. She regretted not having told him her plan, but there was no help for that. He would have stopped her.

In the chopper, she'd made up her mind to undo what she'd done. Felix was right. There was only one way out—tell the truth.

Chapter 16

At the penthouse Luis sat cross-legged on his bed and, two feet away, Coral lay propped on one arm, a bowl of hot popcorn between them. Nearby, Mexican beer cooled on the silver cart Luis's man had rolled in so they could serve themselves while they watched TV.

Coral hadn't been in this bedroom since before Theomund died. Luis had kept the basic furniture—table, salon chairs, three-door wardrobe. The two-tier mahogany platform bed in the middle of the room gave the impression you were about to sleep on a throne. Luis had added a brilliantly colored textile that resembled the Teotihuacán paintings she'd seen with Francisco—pre-Columbian Mexico meets the Victorian era. Mariachi art hung on a wall, a nearly life-size lone musician in a black Spanish suit, long black waves falling on his white ruffled shirt. Evocative, it drew the eye, like Luis would if he'd focus on something other than La Reconquista.

"Turn it up, Luis."

He picked up the remote. "I can't believe she's going to talk."

Coral grabbed a fistful of popcorn. "Me neither."

They watched as an announcer introduced the segment, calling it the interview of the century.

In a news studio, Maggie sat in a chair that emphasized her pregnant stomach. She wore a white maternity dress and sensible white shoes. She looked like a pregnant nurse.

Luis asked, "That's her?"

"Yeah, I'm pretty sure."

Somehow she seemed both regal and pained, determined and scared.

"Have you met her?" Luis asked.

Coral remembered their only face-to-face encounter at Molly

Malone's when Maggie was pregnant the first time. Sam had tried to hide it, but Coral had suspected he was involved with this plain black woman. She'd seen Sam's smitten face when he danced with Maggie.

"Only briefly," Coral said.

"Me too," Luis replied. "I only saw her once at the elevator."

The interviewer was no less than the network's evening news anchor. "Mrs. Duffy," he said. "Thanks for granting us an interview. I understand it's your first."

She said, "Uh-huh, it is. I need to set the record straight."

Coral remembered watching Felix's famous press conference ten years ago with Theo in the library here. Excerpts still appeared on the news whenever the rumored Christ clone story came up. Felix had confessed the cloning, but he'd lied and told the world Maggie and the clone were dead.

"Well, it's a pleasure to be able to talk with you," the anchor said, all seriousness and sympathy. "Why the long silence?"

"It's pretty obvious, don't you think, given who my son was?"

"You mean a clone of Jesus of Nazareth?"

Maggie looked nonplussed. "Well, technically, Jess was a clone of somebody's cells that Felix Rossi found on the Shroud of Turin. I guess nobody can prove who they originally belonged to."

"Jess, that's his name?"

"Yes."

"Eleven years ago, Felix Rossi said you and Jess died."

Maggie blinked. "He had to say that to protect us!"

"But it was a lie."

A long pause.

"It was a lie."

"Dios mio!" Luis murmured. "She's really going to tell the truth? That could complicate things."

"I guess Salati is watching this?" Coral asked.

"I alerted him, but I am starting to wish I hadn't."

The news anchor continued, "In other words, you're saying a potential clone of Christ survived? That would make him ten, eleven years old now."

"Yes, I mean no," Maggie said. "He died eight and a half months ago." The camera did a close-up on her eyes, full of tears.

"Ah!" the interviewer said, disbelief on his face. "He died about a year ago?"

"Yes."

"In Italy?"

"Yes, that's right."

"May I ask how he died?"

"A man threw stones at my son, then he vanished."

"Your son vanished? I see. Mrs. Duffy, do you believe that happened because your son was a clone of Christ?"

Silence.

Luis and Coral both grabbed for popcorn.

"Yes. Yes, I believe that's who he was."

"Why? Did he perform miracles?"

"Only one for sure."

"What was it?"

"He saved my life."

"Tell us about it."

"I … I was sick. Well, I took poison and died. He brought me back."

The camera lingered dramatically on Maggie's face.

"You tried to commit suicide? Why?"

She didn't answer.

"Probably when Sam raped her," Coral said.

"Let's talk about something else, then," the interviewer continued, "You were Felix Rossi's maid?"

"Yes, I was."

"Why did you agree to be the surrogate mother of Dr. Rossi's clone?"

"I … I was a virgin at the time and I'd always felt God was … saving me for some reason. I'd always wanted a child. I prayed and prayed about it and it felt like I was supposed to be the mother."

"Interesting. Your name was Maggie Johnson then but it's Maggie Duffy now, is that right?"

"Yes, that's true."

"What does she think she's doing?" Coral said, shifting her position on the bed to lean on Luis, who patted her shoulder.

"Your husband, Sam Duffy, used to be the doorman at the building where you worked—at Felix Rossi's building."

"Yes, that's right."

"The two of you have lived in Harlem for several months."

"Yes ... more or less."

"You're not sure?"

"I've been in mourning is what I mean."

"You mean since the Shroud clone died."

"Since my son died."

The interviewer leaned forward. "Before then, when your son was alive, Felix Rossi saw him regularly, cared for him I assume?"

"Yes, medically and he supported us, too. He took responsibility for my boy."

"Yet both you and Dr. Rossi kept his existence secret all those years."

"We had to for his sake."

Coral said, "That reporter's about to go in for the kill."

"Sssshhh," Luis replied.

"Mrs. Duffy, can you explain why there is a rumor in Harlem that you are carrying another Christ clone?"

Maggie shifted in the chair and to Coral she seemed in real pain. "That's why I came here. I asked for this interview to set the record straight. Those rumors are just that. Rumors. They aren't fact. There is no second clone that I know about. If there is, I'm sure not carrying it." She touched her stomach. "I'm carrying my husband Sam Duffy's child."

"And if you weren't, would you tell us?"

Maggie's face seemed to lose its muscle tone as awareness of her predicament obviously dawned. "What do you mean?"

"If Dr. Rossi had implanted a second clone in you, Maggie Duffy, would you tell us or would you deny it like Dr. Rossi did before?"

Maggie blinked. Her fist balled in her lap as she spoke. "Are you calling me a liar? I'm telling you there is no second clone. As far as I know, he used all the DNA the first time."

"Do you have evidence of this?"

Maggie searched the air. "Well, no."

"When are you due?" the interviewer asked.

Maggie rubbed her stomach. "Any time."

"Mrs. Duffy, isn't it true that if you were carrying a second clone, you'd deny it just like you are right now?"

The camera zoomed to Maggie's face. She spluttered. "If I was, I wouldn't be talking to you, that's for sure! I'm only here because it isn't true!"

"But your secret's out already, isn't it? Someone else revealed it, not you. Aren't you simply trying to hide it again?"

"No, no!" Maggie said.

The picture dissolved on her panicked face as she pulled the mike from her blouse and stood up, ending the interview. The station's logo aired, followed by comments from people who attended or lived near Maggie's church, all convinced Jesus was returning through her.

"OhmiGod!" Coral breathed and flopped back on the popcorn-littered bed. "Anybody who saw that is absolutely sure there's a clone."

The phone rang. Luis waited until his servant appeared. "It is Padre Salati."

Luis picked up the extension. "You saw it, Your Eminence?"

Coral sat up, smiling, thinking of how she'd be secure now with five million dollars.

"It is only a matter of days," Luis said.

He hung up and hugged Coral. "It's working, hermosa! In exchange for Maggie Johnson's child, Salati will order American Catholic Churches to give sanctuary to those my eagles fly across the border!"

Luis let go of her, stepped down from the platform bed, and paced. "Let me think. I don't want to overlook anything."

Coral stared at the fabulous painted musician, thinking of Francisco. She didn't want to linger on how Sam and Maggie would feel when their baby was gone. It would be perfectly safe. It would have the most pampered upbringing in the world. She didn't want to think about her fantastic afternoon with Sam or compare it to her soul-searing nights with Francisco.

Luis stopped. "Wait. Sam Duffy might not go back to his office, now that the press knows who he is. He and Maggie surely won't go back to their house. How will you reach him, hermosa?"

Coral tapped her forehead, "I have his cell phone number safe right here."

In front of the TV station, Sam sat in the Range Rover, his head on the steering wheel in despair. Felix had called, irate about Maggie's TV interview. That's how Sam learned about it. He wished this was all a dream from which he'd awake with his child safe. How he'd protect his baby, now, he didn't know. Maggie had just delivered it into a lifetime of scrutiny and pursuit, much of it hostile and fanatic. He should have realized long ago that her grief over Jess had dangerously impaired her judgment. Now she'd destroyed their baby's chance for a normal life—a baby she'd just told him she didn't want.

His cell phone rang and he numbly answered it, saying, "Duffy here."

It was someone from the TV station, calling to say his wife asked if he could pick her up. They gave him directions to the private entrance. Good thing because press from other TV, radio, and news outlets swarmed the sidewalk, waiting for Maggie.

"Yeah, I'll pick her up," he said. "I'm right out front."

He turned on the ignition, pulled around the corner and into the TV station's underground garage where a guard let him through. After a few moments, Maggie appeared. Sam got out to open her door, not speaking to her because what was there to say? He helped her into the car and didn't look at her. He got behind the wheel, staring ahead.

"Well, where to, madam?" he said. "We can't go home, that's for sure."

"The Yerbería Guadalupe, Sam. I really am in labor."

He turned and saw her stomach move. "And you came here knowing that? You took that risk?"

"I caught a cab here. I told the TV people who I was. If push came to shove, I knew they'd watch out for me."

"And maybe televise the birth!"

"I had to try," she said. "I had to try to end this."

"You failed."

Sam pulled the seat belt around her and buckled it. In silence they drove out of the garage.

Chapter 17

Incense drifted through the birthing room of the Yerbería Guadalupe. At Maggie's request, recorded gospel music played. Early on she'd asked Teresita to play God's music during her labor, in case she was really carrying the devil's child. Once again she heard the Lord's Prayer, this time in a recording by The Five Blind Boys, *Thy kingdom come...thy will be done.*

All around the room candles burned and, in the center, Maggie relaxed in a birthing tub full of warm water.

Just as Doña Teresita had promised, this was nothing like a conventional birth. Maggie entered the pool when she was dilated to 5 cm, which happened quickly enough after they arrived. As soon as she was in the water, her pain ended. Warmth surrounded her. The water supported her. She felt in control of her body and at one with the process unfolding inside.

An hour and a half later and she was dilated to 9 cm. One more and she'd start pushing, but this time she had no fear. Doña Teresita's water birth was like a ballet, conducted from within Maggie, and nothing interfered. In the water, Maggie sensed and responded to her body's urgings, slipped easily into positions that felt best—sometimes on her side or kneeling, sometimes on her back Christ-like, arms spread.

There was no straining. She connected to the power of birth and in the loving warmth of the candle-lit room, helped her baby descend.

Sam, nervous, came in and out. He massaged her body when she asked, left her alone when she asked. Once his cell phone rang and it was Felix. As Sam left the room, Maggie could hear Felix shout that his home phone was ringing off the hook because of her.

Yet nothing existed for Maggie except the drama within. She often forgot Sam and Doña Teresita were there until they came to the tub with herbal tea and lotions. Teresita kept the water warm, and checked Maggie's progress without making her get out of the tub.

Lulled by the water, Maggie thought of her new secret—one not even Sam knew. It was something she'd overlooked in her fog of grief, only realizing it when she got into this tub. She remembered what Jess said after Carlo Morelli threw stones at him, making him fall, mortally wounded, onto their lake house deck.

> Jess's eyes had opened and he said to her, "You are crying."
>
> "Oh, that horrible, horrible man!" she replied.
>
> "No, Mamma," Jess whispered. "My death will bring Signor Morelli to God."
>
> Violently she'd shook her head and raised him to her, put his head on her shoulder and rocked him like she'd done all through his growing years.
>
> She heard barking and looked up. All the swans had come.
>
> "No, no, no!" she'd cried as his favorite, King Silent, took position below the deck and swam in regal figure eights as if on watch.
>
> Maggie had looked down on Jess. "Don't! Don't! Please, my sweet darling. Make one more miracle for your poor Mama. Stay here with me!"
>
> He closed his eyes.
>
> Maggie looked up to the sky and prayed, "Oh, Father! I still need him. Don't take him back! Please don't!"
>
> She'd felt Jess touch her face. When she looked down, his eyes shone like the dawn.
>
> "Mother, I am your sorrow and your laughter. I am the tears you shed. You will not be alone. I am with you always. I am the father; I am the mother; I am the child."
>
> "No, no!"
>
> He'd touched her stomach and said. "Another one will come."
>
> "Oh, Jess!" she cried. "You are my only one!"

Shortly after that, Jess made her turn away and when Maggie looked back, his body had vanished. Jess Johnson, savior of the world, had gone.

In the yerbería, Maggie smiled in gladness. No one else had seen Jess touch her stomach. No one else heard him say, *Another one will come.* She'd assumed he knew she was pregnant with Sam's child. Only now did she realize it could have meant something else entirely. Jess might have performed a miracle and caused her pregnancy. She might be carrying a child more sacred than any cloning could achieve.

Thinking of this, Maggie now gloried in the spontaneous rhythms of her body, Doña Teresita watching nearby. She felt strong, joyful, blissfully at one with the universe, as her precious baby turned and descended inside her. The urge to push rose spontaneously as an empowerment of her womanhood, rather than a descent into pain. Jess couldn't have created—wouldn't have called her attention to—a devil child.

She must have moaned because Sam and Doña Teresita came to her. Sam put on trunks, got in the tub as they'd rehearsed, and supported her back. The pushing was intense, consuming, unavoidable, astounding—power surging through her. After each contraction, she reached down to see if she could feel her baby's head and when she did, Maggie cried, "He's coming! He's almost here."

When the head crowned, Maggie entered what women call the "ring of fire." As her skin stretched to let the baby's head pass, she pushed her hardest and screamed in triumph, feeling life emerge, Sam holding her.

"The head is out," Doña Teresita said.

"My God," Sam said. "Maggie, Maggie you did it."

She rested, reached for strength, and with a final cry pushed her baby's shoulders and body out.

"It *is* a boy," Sam said. "How did you know, Maggie?"

She barely heard him. Maggie lay against Sam, exhausted but at peace. As she gave birth she'd been with God. Doña Teresita kept the baby in the water until his umbilical cord pulsated less, then she lifted him and laid him on Maggie's breast.

"Hello, Peter, hello, son," Sam said, using the name Maggie had picked.

Maggie looked into her baby's eyes, touched his tiny hands and feet, smoothed his hair. No, this was no devil child. "Hello, Jess," she said.

She felt Sam get out of the tub. She heard whispering, but all Maggie could see were the tiny eyes she'd seen before. "Hello, Jess. Hello, Darling. I knew you would come."

Twenty minutes later when Sam had cut the umbilical cord and the placenta had been delivered, Maggie lay in bed in Doña Teresita's guest room, in her apartment behind the store. Sam came and went as did Doña Teresita, but Maggie didn't care. She lay back and at long last nursed the son she'd lost.

Sam entered Doña Teresita's yerbería from the back hall. Watching the street, he stared through the hand lettering on the glass display windows, *Sexopronto, Aguas Espirituales, Libros Místicos.* Parked in back, his car was ready for an escape if anyone found them. The young girl who helped Teresita in the store slipped away when Sam bent over in despair, tears spilling from his eyes. Sam couldn't remember crying even once as an adult before meeting Maggie. He was a faucet now. If he had a soul, she'd touched it. No, she'd ripped it apart. He was crying because she'd left him no choice.

Wiping his eyes, he clicked on his cell phone, stared at it, and then dialed.

"Hello?" a woman answered.

"Hi, Coral, it's Sam."

He thought she drew in her breath. "Sam? Where are you? What happened?" She sounded genuinely concerned.

He cleared his throat. "Everything. Did you see the news?"

"It was hard to miss."

"Listen, I'm in trouble. I need some help."

"I know you're in trouble, Sam. What can I do?"

"I need a place to stay for a while, a place where people won't look for me. And I could use some money, too."

"You've got it. I'll find a place," she said. "In fact, you can have anything you want from me, you know."

He laughed wearily. "Yeah, that's nice to know. Coral, listen, I'm leaving Maggie."

Silence.

After a while Coral murmured, "I've actually dreamed of those words. You mean it?"

"Yeah, I mean it." He took a deep breath. "I need a place to hide with my son, Peter, until I can figure out what to do. Maggie's not well. Mentally, I mean. She doesn't want Peter or me, either, for that matter; and her interview makes it unsafe for Peter to be with her. The press and half the world are looking for her."

He heard Coral gasp and felt like slime. No doubt any woman would react to a man kidnapping a newborn from its mother.

"You mean she's had the baby?"

"Yes."

"You can … you can stay at my place, Sam."

He let out his breath. "Thanks. That's great. Nobody will look for Peter there."

"I'll get a crib in."

"Great. That'll help. By the way, what's the address?"

In his pocket notebook, Sam wrote down the address to a luxury residential building, seeing the *no sex* note from his first case—the rich tattooed daughter and the Korean chauffeur. They'd eloped. No Alps. No money. Disinherited. Plenty of sex.

Coral lived at the Park Hudson. He'd never been there. When Maggie made him apologize to Coral, he'd contacted Brown's lawyers who informed him she was on Brown's yacht. He'd never learned where Coral lived.

"Okay, thanks," he said. "When can I come?"

"Anytime between ... twenty minutes from now and forever, Sam."

"I appreciate it, Coral. I really do."

"See you soon."

Sam clicked off the phone and wiped his face. He realized Doña Teresita was behind him.

She held out herbs in a plastic bag. He'd had the first herbs she gave him analyzed and it was green tea, like she said.

"These herbs are in case the child does not nurse. If so, it will not be immunized from her breast milk. Make a tea and mix it with Peter's formula. It will protect him, and so will this." She gave Sam a silver pendant necklace with a raised image of the Virgin of Guadalupe.

Sam felt grateful. He kissed her cheek. "Thank you, Doña Teresita. You've been good to us."

He put the bag and necklace in his pocket, took out his wallet and put money in her hand. "Thanks for everything."

"The press will find her, Señor Duffy—tonight, tomorrow. They will find her. I will help her, though. Goodnight," she said and left the room.

Had Teresita read his mind? Sam went back to the guest room where Maggie and Peter slept. He looked down on his wife, hating that she'd always thought herself ugly. Even now—especially now—he found every inch of the sleeping Maggie Clarissa Johnson Duffy beautiful. She didn't love him, though, or his son. Sam had to face that.

More importantly, half the world recognized her, now, and would speedily make Peter's life a living hell. He was glad Maggie had Teresita and two million dollars to take care of herself. As for Peter, Sam needed to protect him.

Quietly, he reached down and lifted Peter from beside her. He reminded himself Maggie had shown no interest in Peter until he was born and she thought he was Jess. He draped Teresita's necklace around his son's ankle, wrapped him tightly in the woven Mexican blanket she'd given them and walked out of the Yerbería Guadalupe.

Coral hung up her cell phone and turned to Luis who'd listened avidly.

"Quit whispering when I'm talking on the phone, Luis. I said I'd work for you, but I didn't throw my apartment into the bargain. I've never done business there. That's *my* place. It's where I live."

"But he's bringing the baby right to you!"

Coral couldn't believe Sam's call. "I shouldn't have let him do that."

"How could you say, no? Besides, who knows where he might have gone with the child? Maybe somewhere out of reach." He called down to The Barracks for a limo to be ready take Coral home.

"Okay, now we've got to think." She rose from the platform bed and sat in one of the Victorian salon chairs, tapping her toes on the carpet, remembering how Sam said he was leaving Maggie. She couldn't think about that.

"Wait a minute. Nothing has to change," she said.

Luis sat up. "You are right, hermosa. Call Francisco and tell him it's time. Tell him to come. Then don't return here once Sam is at your place. If necessary, we'll talk on the phone, but don't email or text unless it's vital. That makes a record."

Coral picked up her cell phone to make the call they'd planned for months, knowing Francisco was now entirely under her spell.

Coral, I'm leaving Maggie, Sam had said.

Francisco didn't answer his cell phone. Coral had to call the house where the phone rang a long time. Finally a maid answered. She summoned Francisco.

"Buenos dias, Coral," she heard in the same warm voice.

Coral swallowed, thinking of Sam.

"Qué dice mi chico?" she purred.

Chapter 18

Holding Peter carefully, Sam watched the building's valet drive the Range Rover toward the underground parking garage of The Park Hudson apartments. He should have guessed Coral would opt for a stylish West Side address. She said she was freelancing, now that Brown was dead. The East Side across the park was where the old money was—most of her actual or potential clients. The more diverse West Side had entertainers, theater people, and such—though many a Wall Street millionaire lived here on the Hudson River, in walking distance of Lincoln Center and Central Park. Here on the West Side, Coral probably felt more like she was away from her work.

He said to the doorman, "I'm ready now."

"Miss Anders said to send you up."

Sam entered and took the elevator, Peter sleeping peacefully as if being born, then spirited from his mother moments later, were ordinary events. Sam allowed himself to wonder if Maggie was awake, yet, and had discovered Peter was gone. His cell phone's silence could only mean she was still asleep, or overjoyed to have them both gone.

It was 1:30 A.M.

He had delayed almost an hour before coming here. He walked down the hall and stood outside of Coral's door, thinking. Though Maggie rejected Peter, he doubted she'd be thrilled to know her baby was at Coral's. Sam didn't have another option right now. Pat, the bartender at Molly Malone's, might have asked his wife to let them stay but not at one o'clock on a Monday morning, Pat's only night off. A hotel was out. Sam couldn't check in with a newborn and not raise unwanted questions. Besides, the room wouldn't have much that Peter needed, unlike a woman's apartment.

Outside Coral's door, he stroked Peter's hand, amazed at how fragile a new baby felt. He whispered, "Shall we go in, Peter, m'boy?" His eyes closed, Peter stirred, took hold of Sam's little finger, and went back to sleep.

Sam knocked. The door opened. Coral stood there barefoot, wearing black tights and a loose white shirt, her hair tousled.

"Well, I guess you two had better come in," she said, sounding like the idea didn't appeal to her.

"Coral, if this is an imposition—" He stopped. He had nowhere else to go.

"No, no. Come in. I invited you, remember?"

Sam stepped into her foyer. His gaze landed on a stunning painting of two ballet dancers.

"Fonteyn and Nureyev, if you must know," she said. "Come in."

He followed her into the apartment, whistling. "Whoa, what an elegant place."

He started to sit on an upholstered maroon chair when Coral called, "Come in here, Sam."

Following her voice he entered the sumptuous master bedroom suite, which featured a bath and walk-in-closet. A portrait of a dancer in yellow, black, and white dominated the wall.

"Margot Fonteyn as Aurora in Sleeping Beauty," she said.

This was the home of a diva of the theater—or someone who'd wanted to be. Sam felt like an intruder.

"Bring him here, Sam."

Coral had managed a crib, all right—a bassinet with a hood, covered in tiers of white lace. A white rocking chair and white dresser with a changing table stood beside it.

"The concierge got it from someone in the building. I had him cancel my maid service. You don't need extra eyes."

"What's this place run you?"

"About six grand a month." Coral reached out for Peter and Sam let her take him. She folded back the Mexican blanket and said, "Oooohhh! Now aren't you a looker? Just like your dad.

Hardly at all like your mom, which is just as well."

Irritated, Sam said, "Don't talk like that around him, Coral!"

She sniffed. "He needs changing, Sam. Did you bring diapers?"

"Uh, no. Is there an all-night pharmacy around here?"

"Over on West End."

He looked toward the door, then back at Peter.

"That's okay. I'll get some delivered. Meanwhile we'll improvise."

She lay Peter on the changing table, went around the corner, and came back with a small yellow towel. "I don't suppose you thought to bring formula?"

"I didn't. He's just been sleeping."

"All right. For now I can water down some soymilk and put a few drops of molasses in it. A baby bottle kit and blankets came with the dresser."

Sam knew he and Coral were going through the motions—not focusing on what their actions meant. He was trying not to wonder when Maggie would wake and what she'd think when she did. He knew he'd done the right thing, but that didn't make it feel good.

He sat on the stool at Coral's dressing table. "Guess I didn't know child care was this innate."

She glanced over her shoulder, "I babysat when I was young, Sam."

He tried to smile.

"There. All nice and clean," she said, lifting Peter. "Come on, papa, kiss him goodnight."

Sam went over and kissed his son. Peter was already asleep when she wrapped him tightly and lay him in the crib.

She said, "He'll feel safe, wrapped tight like this, like he's in the womb."

They looked away from each other.

Coral opened the dresser drawer and removed bottles. Sam thought she was trying not to think about Maggie, too.

"We'd better get some formula made. He'll be hungry when he wakes."

Following her to the kitchen past the gallery of dancers, Sam gave Coral the herbs. "Maggie's midwife said to add a tea of this while he's not nursing."

They looked at the herbs, but didn't speak.

Sam's cell phone rang. He took it out and checked the number. The call was from the Yerbería Guadalupe. Did Maggie want Peter after all? He felt angry that she'd put him in this position.

"Maggie?" Coral asked.

"Yeah."

"You going to answer it?"

For a while he just held the ringing cell phone. "No, I'm not."

Coral put water on for Peter's tea. Before it boiled, Sam's cell rang three times more. It rang five more times while Coral diluted the soymilk, added a bit of molasses and the warm tea. He didn't look at the messages while Coral filled the bottles. She dropped one and had to re-sterilize it as they listened to the ringing phone. She put the bottles away and leaned her forehead against the refrigerator door, trembling.

"Remind me again why you did this, Sam?"

Angrily, he said, "I dunno. Let's pick: attempted abortion, attempted murder, sexual rejection, child endangerment—the whole world knows about Peter now and thinks he's Christ, for God's sake. To top that off, today she told me she doesn't want Peter, only a divorce. I can have him. Guess what else? I've been busting my ass for months and—big secret—she's fucking rich. Has been all along."

Coral sighed.

Sam hung his head. "Peter isn't safe with her after that interview."

She took out a red wine that was already open, filled two glasses, and handed one to him. Leaning against the refrigerator as he leaned against the wall, they both drank.

"Are you sleepy?" he asked, seeing the Yerbería Guadalupe in his mind.

"Not me, but you've had quite a day, haven't you? A romp

with me at your office, then off to rescue Maggie in time for her TV interview, then you became a father and now ... well, now you're a fugitive."

Sam stared. "If she reports me, that is."

"Do you think she will?"

"She knows I've got Peter. She knows I won't hurt him. Why would she complain? She doesn't want him, anyway." He knew he looked unconvinced.

"Well, if I were you, I'd be pooped."

"Are you?"

"No."

Sam realized she looked beautiful in her tights. "This is a great apartment, you know. Show me around."

Coral gazed down at her feet, took a breath, then folded her arms and looked back up at him. "Well, aren't I lucky that you approve? I could show you my underwear drawer, my toothbrush? Let's see, what else?"

Sam straightened. "I didn't mean ... Coral, what's the matter?"

"Nobody's been here before, Sam! Not Theo, not any of the men."

"Yeah, I figured." He didn't know what else to say.

She poured more wine then set the bottle down hard, "I'll show you what I do when I'm alone at night."

She left the kitchen and went back toward the bedroom. Peeping in on Peter first, Coral opened another door, went in, and switched on the lights.

"Take off your shoes"

Sam did.

The room was no more than twelve by fifteen feet, but both of the longer walls were mirrored from ceiling to floor. Handrails ran the length of them. A small stereo unit sat on a stand with space for CDs below. She'd turned the apartment's second bedroom into a dancer's studio. The wood floor felt resilient.

"Sit down, if you like."

Sam did.

"I had this floor installed. It's maple tongue and groove. There's a subfloor with hard rubber cushions at each joint. Regular floors give dancers shin splints or worse."

She opened a closet that had racks full of dancing shoes. Coral removed a pair of red toe slippers, put them on, and laced them above her ankles.

She went to one of the railings, said, "This is called the barre," and began to do exercises.

Fascinated, Sam watched. Theomund Brown had found her in a musical's chorus line and turned her into a stylish whore. Yet the original Coral was still here in Lincoln Park, where so many well-off theater people lived—the Met, the American Ballet Theater, and more in walking distance, Broadway only a short hop away.

"I guess you go to the theater a lot," he said.

"Yes, alone." She used the bar to limber up, doing movements he couldn't name.

"You made a hobby out of a former career. That's good."

She humphed. "A hobby? I guess I never thought of it that way. Yes, I guess it's a hobby, but I'm damned good at it, Sam. I can do the greatest thing Margot Fonteyn ever did."

Sam wished he could take back the hobby part. "What was that?"

She paused, getting her breath, hands on her hips. "The Rose Adagio."

"The rose what?"

"Reach in the CDs to the Ts and take out Tchaikovsky's Sleeping Beauty."

He found it, saying, "You know you can download these online now."

She snorted. "Look in the closet. You'll find four silk roses."

Sam found them. "Now what?"

"She did this in October of 1949 in Act I of Sleeping Beauty. The Princess Aurora is having her eighteenth birthday party. Four suitors come and give her red roses."

Coral got into position, her arms out. "Okay, start the music."

He did and heard harps.

Coral's body began interpreting the music.

She lifted her arms over her head like they were flower petals opening. Effortlessly she twirled. She rose to her toes, bent from the waist her arms flowing, did it again and again, and then glided across the floor like a swan. She looked like the princess of any man's dreams as her red shoes flew.

"Now come here, Mr. Duffy. Stand in for the princes courting me. I'm Princess Aurora. Hold your hand out. I'll lean on you. I'm going to do a second arabesque on point."

From the stereo trumpets blared and drums rolled. Then the full orchestra played majestic music.

Coral rose and balanced on the tip of her left toe, right leg arced behind her in the air, one hand resting lightly on Sam's. He couldn't believe it.

"Turn me," she said.

He did, fearing she'd fall, but Coral turned like a top.

"Hand me a rose."

He did and she let go and took the rose, balancing without help on her left toe. She didn't tip, but stayed erect. It looked impossible.

She took his hand. From the stereo, cymbals crashed.

"Do it again."

Three times they repeated the process —turning, letting go, balancing only on the left toe. Each time, drums rolling, she took another rose.

Finally, Coral lifted both arms triumphantly over her head and stayed on point for what seemed like forever, all four red roses in her hand. Then she pirouetted away and made a bow.

He couldn't believe it. He wanted to dig up Brown's grave and re-kill him for Coral's sake. Amazed, Sam applauded, shouting bravas.

Coral twirled into his arms, kissed his cheek, and said, "Thank you, prince."

As the music stopped they heard Peter cry.

It took a while for Coral to get Peter back to sleep. Sam watched anxiously from the side of her yellow bed to see if Peter would take the bottle and keep the homemade formula down. He did. As she put Peter in the crib, she saw Sam dial in for his messages, listen briefly, then swiftly hang up, taking a big swig from his wine glass.

"A little late for that," she heard him murmur to the phone. He looked at her. "Maggie's upset, but I can't take Peter back. At least one person at her church—a very kind blabbermouth—knows where she is. Reporters could find her any time now. What am I going to do?"

"Well, you can't do much of anything until the morning. Let's get you out of these clothes."

She took his glass and slipped his shoes and socks off, raising her eyebrows at the smell to make him laugh. "Give me those pants," she said, and he took them off. His shirt followed. Saying, "Thanks, Coral," Sam slid under her yellow comforter and was immediately asleep.

His clothes in her arms, Coral glanced from Sam to Peter. So far so good. Sam suspected nothing. He was a big blob of sleeping putty for her to shape.

Theoretically she could pick Peter up and take him over to Luis's right now, but Coral had no intention of starting her new life with the police after her.

She wondered when Francisco would arrive, scope out nearby locations, choose one, and make a plan.

Folding Sam's shirt, she thought of the last time she saw Francisco sleeping, the day before she left Mexico City. He'd lain on his right side, like Sam. He'd slept quickly, like Sam—a troubled sleep, eyes moving under closed lids, no doubt dreaming of kidnapping a child. Sam's eyes moved, too—seeing a woman weep, probably. Maggie may not have wanted Peter before, but that may have changed. From a client whose wife worked for an adoption agency, Coral knew how hard it is to coax newborns from birth mothers, even though they'd already signed papers giving them up.

She put down the clothes and reached for Sam's cell phone. He might not be interested in Maggie's messages, but Coral was. If there was a chance Maggie could interfere, Luis needed to know. Slowly she slid the phone off the black end table, watching Sam's eyes move rapidly in sleep. She tiptoed into her bathroom—black tile floor, yellow shower curtain, a wall of mirrors, globe-shaped vanity lights.

Knowing Sam's passcode from watching him use his cell, she sat on the commode and called the last number dialed. At the prompt, she entered Sam's code.

Maggie's first message was short and angry, "Sam, bring Peter back right now!"

The next was less sharp and a little longer, "Sam, we can talk about why you did this, but first you need to bring Peter back." The next was desperate. "Sam, are you getting my messages? Why aren't you answering?" The next was full of tears, "Where are you? Why did you do this? Is Peter all right? Call me back. Please, call me back."

The next one surprised Coral. "Sam, all right then. You need to know the truth! There's a chance Peter isn't your child! There's a chance you have no right to him at all. None, do you hear me? When you bring him back, I'll explain."

Coral smiled. *Good try, Maggie.*

The last message shook Coral.

"Sam, you bring my baby back to me! Sam, bring my baby. He needs me; he needs me. I didn't mean it when I said I didn't want him. I didn't mean it! He's just a little thing. You can't do this! Bring him back to me, Sam, you *bring* my baby, bring my *baby*, *bring my baby*! He needs to nurse! Don't you understand a little baby needs to nurse! What's the matter with you? Do you want me to die? All I've ever wanted was to be a mother. That's all. Just a mother. I know I said some bad things, but I didn't *mean* them Sam. *Bring Peter back to me!* Bring my baby, *Sam*. You've got to bring him back, please … won't you, please? Don't kill me, Sam. Don't kill me."

The cell dropped from Coral's hand onto the bathroom carpet. Woman to woman, she understood. All Maggie ever wanted was to be a mother. Coral had wanted that, too, before she became a prostitute.

Then all she'd wanted was to dance.

Maybe some people wouldn't think dancing was as important as motherhood, but she'd tried everything to do it. She'd gone to plastic surgeons and asked for breast reductions, hip reductions, asked them to cut off every curve that barred her from her dream. They wouldn't do it. They said it would deform her, risk her life.

Woman to woman, how could she end Maggie's dream? Coral bent over, feeling Maggie's pain as if Peter had been snatched from her own womb. A memory came rushing back. The man her mother married and how at night when her mother was asleep he'd taken everything Coral had—her innocence, trust, and belief in life. Her mother should have protected her, woman to woman, but Coral was left to be his eight-year-old plaything. Too young she'd learned about the big bad world.

Peter would be all right. Salati wouldn't hurt him. Maggie could have another baby if she hurried up. Coral would never get to dance the Rose Adagio for anyone but Sam.

Wiping damp eyes, she straightened up, tiptoed out, and put the phone back. She checked on Peter then knelt beside his bassinet, whispering, "Your mother loves you, little boy. Your mother absolutely loves you."

Feeling angst, she delayed then finally got her own cell phone. Whispering to Peter, "I'm so sorry, sweetheart," she snapped his photo. Behind her, she heard a gasp.

Sam sat up in bed, perspiring. Had he seen what she'd done? She palmed the cell.

"It's all right, Sam. You just had a nightmare." She went to him and stroked his arm, letting the cell drop on the carpet. "It's Coral. Here, go back to sleep."

"I know what to do, Coral! I know how to fix this. Really fix it!"

Coral tensed. "How?"

"A DNA test! All I have to do is get a DNA test. It will prove to the world that Peter is my son. It will prove it to Maggie, too.

She said crazy things when he was born, and she's letting people at her church believe sheer nonsense."

Coral kept a straight face. "A DNA test?" For her, it would ruin everything. Salati would know Peter wasn't a clone. Her mind raced. "A DNA test? Oh, what a good idea! How long do they take?"

"I don't know, but I'll find out. I think all they have to do is swab my mouth, Maggie's, and Peter's but I'm not sure how long the analysis takes in the lab. Felix could take the samples. No, not him. We need an independent source, but that's the answer. Why didn't I think of it before?"

"Well, you've thought of it now. Go back to sleep."

Sam yawned. "Yeah, I can sleep now. Thanks, Coral. Thanks for everything."

Sam lay down and Coral sat on the bed until he was asleep. She'd once loved him and perhaps still did. He didn't love her, though. She could tell.

She changed into yellow silk pajamas and went into her living room. She broke protocol and emailed Luis about the DNA test, attaching Peter's photo.

Chapter 19

When Maggie first woke in the darkened Yerbería Guadalupe and realized that Peter and Sam were gone, she didn't worry. He was probably in the hall rocking Peter in his arms, like a good father.

She lay in the dark, feeling safe in spite of what still awaited them in the outside world. Gradually she made out the contents of Teresita's extra room. A nightstand with medicines was beside the bed—not that she would need anything after that wonderful water birth. On the other side was a small rose-covered altar to the Virgin of Guadalupe. About a month ago, Teresita had explained why the rose was the virgin's flower.

She said ten years after Cortés conquered the Aztecs, a poor man named Juan Diego was on a hill called Tepeyac. Some say he was on his way to church in Mexico City and others say he was about to worship the Aztec goddess Tonantzin, whose temple was once atop the same hill. In either case, Juan Diego heard the beautiful singing of birds and climbed the hill to see them. Instead of birds, he saw a wonderful lady, her garments shining like the sun. The earth around her sparkled with all the colors of the rainbow and the plants glittered like jewels. He fell to his knees and she greeted him. "Juanito, the most humble of my sons, where are you going?" Juan Diego told her and the lady asked him to take a message to the bishop of Mexico City. Would he build a church where she could comfort the sorrowing Mexican people? Juan did, but the bishop didn't believe the story.

When Juan came back, the lady agreed to the bishop's request for a sign. She told Juan to climb to the top of the hill and gather flowers. It wasn't the season for them, so Juan was surprised to find the craggy hilltop covered with fragrant roses. The lady asked him to fill his cloak, called a *tilma* or *manta,* with the flowers and take them to the bishop, who was amazed when Juan opened his cloak. All the roses spilled out and revealed an image of the Lady of Tepeyac, the Holy Mother, inside Juan Diego's tilma. The bishop built the requested church. Every year since, a celebration has occurred at Tepeyac, Teresita said. Like Juan Diego, pilgrims walk the stone street to the Virgin's Basilica on their knees, calling her Mystical Rose.

Maggie thought she could still catch a whiff of scent from Doña Teresita's dried roses. She listened for Sam's footsteps in the hall and, not hearing them, rose to see where he'd gone—probably to the bathroom or to Teresita's kitchen. The hall was empty, only a faint glimmer from a night light at the end.

Ignoring her discomfort, she tiptoed to the bathroom. The door was ajar and he wasn't there. "Sam?" Maggie called. She went to Teresita's kitchen and the birthing room and found them empty. She tiptoed up to the yerbería. He wasn't there. She stared at Teresita's covered front windows, confused. Then Maggie remembered the whispering between Sam and Teresita. She couldn't recall what they'd said, only her joy at Peter's birth. Barefoot she padded back into Teresita's hall, opening doors. Sam wasn't there. Perhaps he couldn't sleep and went for a walk, leaving Peter with Teresita.

Hating to wake her, Maggie rapped softly on her door.

"*Adelante,*" Teresita replied.

"It's me, Maggie. Sorry to wake you. I'll take Peter back. Do you know where Sam went?"

Teresita sat up in her ruffled nightgown, long black hair trailing onto her white pillowcase.

"Señor Duffy is not here, *mi hija*. He has taken Peter away."

Before Maggie could react, they heard muffled voices from the street. Relieved, she started toward the front, but Teresita caught her hand. "Reporters, mija. They have been calling. I turned off the phone and lowered the security shutter. They will think no one is here."

Sharmina must have blabbed after all.

"Your husband and baby are gone."

That's what Maggie thought she's said, but it made no sense. She rushed back to her room and rummaged in her purse for the cell phone she never turned on. Sam was always fussing at her about it. Tomorrow she'd worry about reporters; right now she had to find Peter. Maybe Sam tried to call, or left a message to keep from waking them. Fortunately, her phone was still charged, but there were no messages. She dialed Sam's number, got no answer, but left a stern message for him to bring Peter back.

While she waited for Sam's call, Maggie went to the little altar and picked up one of Teresita's dried roses. She carried it back to the bed and sat down, smelling its faint scent. She wondered if her message had been clear enough and called Sam again, picking a dried petal from the rose. He didn't answer. She left another message, then another and another, pacing the floor in the darkened room, wearing the plain linen gown Teresita gave her, and pulling dried petals from the rose.

He didn't answer; he didn't call. By her last message, Maggie was on her knees sobbing, beating the bed with the wilted rose until the petals were gone and its thorns scratched her hand. "You've got to bring him back, please … won't you, please? Don't kill me, Sam. Don't kill me."

Maggie hung up, hid her face in the bedclothes, and wept inconsolably, realizing at last what she'd done. She'd blamed Sam for things that weren't really his fault. He'd been in a coma, brain-damaged. It was never his fault. Then she rejected him sexually and, oh yes, she did shoot him on their wedding night. Maggie had forgotten about that. She'd also allowed Jess's death to obscure Peter's welfare. She'd said she didn't want Sam, or his son. How could she have said that? Then she went on TV and convinced the world Peter was divine.

Seeing for the first time how wrong she'd been, and how seriously she'd endangered Peter, Maggie staggered to the bathroom and threw up. Soon Teresita's cool hands were on her forehead.

"Ssshhh, mija, ssshhh."

Teresita wiped her face with a wet cloth and helped her back to bed, Maggie sobbing and begging for her baby.

"Ssshhh, sshhh, drink this."

Teresita put a cup to her lips.

"Drink this, mija."

Eagerly Maggie drank, hoping it was a magic potion from Teresita's shop that would swiftly return lost babies.

She lay on the bed, gasping, and in no time was asleep.

What awakened Maggie was the temperature in the room. Warm before, the air was suddenly cold. She reached for the covers, but must have kicked them off. She turned on the nightstand lamp, looking for them on the floor. She saw feet. Small ones. One toe had a familiar scar.

Frantically, Maggie rubbed her eyes and looked again. The feet were there, attached to slim bronzed legs. Their owner bent and gazed into her eyes.

"Mother, can you see me?"

It was Jess!

Maggie shrieked and jumped back on the bed, pinching herself to wake up from this dream. When she didn't wake, she covered her mouth with the pillow and screamed in joy, staring into Jess's eyes.

"Mother, don't be afraid."

Her heart pounded as if it would break through her chest.

"Don't be afraid. Ti voglio bene, Mamma," he said.

Maggie lowered the pillow. It was Jess.

"Are you real?"

"Yes, Mamma. I was real even when you couldn't see me."

"Oh, Jess. You've come back! Oh, my darling. Will you stay?"

"I never left. I have been here all along."

Maggie settled on the bed. "You have?"

"Yes, Mamma. The place of death is not so far away. It is near. It exists between the moments you call time."

"It does?" She wiped her eyes. "Imagine that."

Maggie got out of bed and walked nearer to the ghost of Jess. He wore a shirt over his bathing trunks, just like he'd done in their endless hours on Lake Maggiore's shore. He was taller, though.

"Oh, how you've grown!"

"I am eleven, now."

"Eleven? How?"

"I did not die. I continue."

Maggie reached for him. "Is it all right if I touch you?"

Jess grinned. "I have missed that a lot."

Maggie reached out into the electric air and watched her hand approach his sausage curls, sure it would pass through them. It didn't. Jess's hair was in her hand. She was ruffling his curls. At this great gift, she closed her eyes, full of happiness. She wouldn't offend God by asking for more. Just this—this touch, was enough.

"Ti voglio bene, Jess," she said.

After a moment, he replied, "Aren't you going to hug me?"

Laughing, Maggie stooped and wrapped him in her arms. They clung to each other in the dark of Teresita's room and stroked each other's face and hair.

"Oh, how I've missed you, my little sweetheart. Your death turned the light out in my life. For so long I was in darkness. I even think I was in hell for a little while. Yet here you are, here you are. I can feel you in my arms. I can smell you. I can hold you. Must you leave me again, Jess? Must you go?"

"I think so, in the way you mean."

"When will you leave?" she asked.

"I'm not sure, Mother, but I think I can help you while I'm here."

Jess said he'd only been born to help her, make her happy, Felix, too, not save the world. It caused Maggie great guilt. Who was *she*? Lovingly she scrutinized his face. "You have helped me already. You just don't know how much."

He smiled, moved away, and made a windmill of his arms as he used to, moving about the room in his carefree way as if neither time nor death were real.

"Something tells me you would like to see Peter," he said.

"You know about him?"

"Oh, yes. He and I are great friends."

"I would definitely like to see Peter."

Jess laughed and instantly Teresita's walls disappeared. She and Jess stood next to a frilly white bassinet, watching Peter sleep.

"See? He is safe," Jess said.

"Yes, but where is he?" Maggie cried. "I need him back!" She reached for him, but her arms held nothing. They were within Teresita's walls again.

"Thank you, Jess. I won't be ungrateful. Thank you for that. I suppose there are more important things on this earth for God's son to worry about than my and Peter's troubles."

"No, there are not. I can show you one thing more," Jess said.

Maggie noticed he was shining like the Lady of Guadalupe on Juan Diego's mountain. Once more, Teresita's walls vanished. Maggie heard a clock strike nine times and she gathered it was 9:00 A.M. by the sunlight. In the next moment, they were in Central Park.

"Jess, do you know you were born here?"

"Yes, I know."

Maggie pointed. "Not too far from here, in fact. Right down that path, over a bridge and down beside the waterfall."

"I think it was farther north, Mamma. We are only on 65th Street."

"Oh. Well, we were hiding from some very bad men when you were born."

"Yes, I talked with one of them recently. Look," Jess said.

Maggie saw a couple walking a baby in a pram. A woman on a park bench stared at them. Then the man left to buy a newspaper and the woman left the bench. Four men swiftly approached the pram from different directions and the baby was gone.

"Ti voglio bene, Mamma," Jess said.

"Are you going? Don't go, Jess."

Angels appeared in the electric air, smiling at her. She could tell what they were by their sweet expressions.

Jess skipped toward a large bronze bust of someone in the park, the angels following.

"Every day I come into your thoughts and tell you that I love you, Mamma. Every time you cry I hold your hand. I am with you always. Remember, remember," Jess said.

In Teresita's room, Maggie opened her eyes. She lay in bed, a newly cut flower beside her.

"The flower is my love," she heard.

Maggie rubbed her eyes, sure she'd dreamed but not remembering exactly what. She sat up, wondering why, in the middle of the night, Teresita had brought her a fresh red rose.

Chapter 20

On his terrace the next morning Luis paced, fingering his Mexica dagger in its ornate pouch and wondering if his plan would fall apart. Sam Duffy wanted a DNA test. Luis had thought of everything but that.

When Luis was Theomund Brown's butler, he might have been fired for not anticipating such a game-changing possibility. His job had never been in danger because he'd never overlooked anything key. Luis was a detail-oriented perfectionist, someone to be counted on. Brown hired him for that. How, in a far more important matter, had Luis not thought of the obvious when he'd had years to assess all involved?

Coral would act on self-interest, ruthlessly using her great beauty. Francisco would risk all for a great passion, if he ever found one. Sam liked to avoid trouble, but he was smart. Only the best could outwit him. At kidnapping, Francisco was the best.

Luis had overlooked that Sam—a ladies man full of Irish blarney—turned into a knight of the round table if anyone he cared for was in danger. Maggie was just a friend of Sam's when Felix Rossi began his cloning project. In the process of protecting her, Sam fell in love. Tonight Sam realized the world was a threat to his wife, his wife a threat to his son, and now he was going to fix it all with a DNA test.

Luis had to prevent that. Instead of unfolding like a choreographed dance, the kidnapping's elements were colliding. After Maggie's interview, Cardinal Salati promptly boarded a plane to cross the Atlantic and come here. Francisco would arrive any minute.

Luis had planned that they never meet.

Meanwhile Coral, who was supposed to greet Salati, was trying to delay Sam's DNA test. Luis hadn't meant that she be anywhere near Sam when the child was snatched.

Luis went to the salon and unlocked it. He flicked switches, made lights come on, and let the haunting sound of a Mesoamerican wind instrument fill the room, followed by the beat of drums.

As his people's ancient music played, he walked over to the statue of his mother, Aileen-Reynoso, his father, Juan Pablo, and touched their hands.

"Amá, Apá, soy yo su hijo, Luis."

He longed for their frozen lips to reply. He went to his sister, Cyntia Cualli, his elder brother, Eduardo Itzli, his young brother, Roberto Mazatl. His father had given them names from a dead past, but Mexica Eterna would make the past live again.

He noticed someone outside the door—his cousin and servant. However hard Luis tried to change him, this cousin behaved in the old way: Luis was el pátron to be served unquestioningly.

"Francisco comes," the cousin said and disappeared.

Luis went to a monitor trained on his private garage. He saw Francisco get out of a limo with the three cómplices who had once been in Los Jinetes with him.

The Military Riding School where Luis's father got Francisco a job made him remain a stable hand because of the Mexica ancestry he wouldn't disavow and his Neza origins. Francisco wouldn't have become a kidnapper if they'd let him ride.

On the monitor, Luis watched them enter his elevator. Then he went to the lobby. Even when Francisco became a criminal, he and Luis had remained close. Now, Francisco was a power broker and the ideal head of Mexica Eterna.

The elevator doors opened and there was Francisco, his favorite cousin, dark eyes and black hair set off against pale skin. In the old days he would have been considered white or *castizo*—a white Mexican of mixed parentage—instead of mestizo, like Luis, who was a shade darker. Even Luis could have passed for white if he chose, but fierce loyalty to their Aztec heritage, instilled by their parents, prevented them from identifying themselves in that way. His father counseled it would be like killing Moctezuma and Cuauhtémoc all over again.

Francisco's men would be housed downstairs in The Barracks, the rooms used by the building's guards. Whatever happened, authorities would not come searching for kidnappers here. Luis had already dined with the governor, the police chief, and the mayor, and made it clear he would faithfully continue Brown's generosities to the state, the city, to their political parties, and campaigns. In reality, the USA and Mexico weren't so different when it came to bribery. Here, at the highest levels, it just had legal names like *speaking fee* and *campaign contribution*, *bonus* and *investment*.

"*Qué tal*, Francisco. Thanks for coming. We have a few hours before the Cardinal arrives."

"*Quiubo*, Luis," Francisco replied.

Luis knew Francisco didn't want to kidnap anyone, not anymore. Their Neza past was long gone—scrounging through heaps of refuse, begging on the streets, stealing something to eat from street vendors when the proprietors' backs were turned. When they moved out of Neza, his parents suddenly comparatively rich, he and Francisco had gone back to those same street vendors and stuffed themselves—paying this time. It took months for them to believe food wouldn't disappear. Then the peso devaluation came.

They exchanged an abrazo and Francisco stepped back, looking past Luis into the apartment. "¿Dónde está Coral?"

Luis had been afraid of this. He had to lie. "*Paciencia*. It isn't safe for her to be here until this is over."

Francisco folded his arms. "*¿Por qué dices eso?*"

"She's with the man who has the child and her leaving might raise suspicion."

"The man thinks she's going to kidnap his child?"

"Of course not, but—"

"Then I want to see her."

"You will, you will!" Luis put his arm around Francisco's shoulder. "Come. Have something to eat. *¡Come algo!* Let's catch up and then make plans."

Francisco removed Luis's arm. "*Mira.* Let me tell you something, Luis. Ordinarily I would do anything for you, since you are my cousin, but not this. I would not kidnap a baby for you. In fact, I would not kidnap a baby for land and liberty, for the eagles, for La Reconquista, or for all of Mexico. I'm doing this because Coral asked me to." He gave Luis a threatening look. "Don't use her like that again. Do you understand?"

Luis nodded. "You have my promise, but this was important."

"So you say. Right now, I don't want to eat and I don't want to catch up. I want to see her. *¡Ahorita mismo, entiendes!* Otherwise, Los Jinetes will return to Mexico."

Luis felt sorry to have involved Francisco in kidnapping again, but this time the cause was an unselfish one. He laughed. "Mexico City must long for the days when Los Jinetes was around. Kidnappings are not only way up, hostages are twice as likely to die, I hear."

"That's the work of the drug cartels and Calderon's ineffective war against them. To make extra money, the drug gangs kidnap illegal immigrants, now, and hold them for ransom. They demand payment from anyone illegally crossing the border. Anyone but Mexica Eterna, that is."

"They are afraid of you!" Luis declared in admiration.

Uncharacteristically, Francisco looked worried. "Yes, for now. If Mexico and the USA don't get serious, though, soon the cartels won't be afraid of anyone. They already do mass killings. Do you know they are also threatening, even assassinating, U.S. diplomats along the border? So far, most victims are Latino, but that will change. They will get bolder. One day, they will shoot gringo mayors and sheriffs in the USA itself, like they already do in Mexico. The USA will pay a high price for its marijuana and cocaine addictions."

"That makes Mexica Eterna all the more important. Our emigrants need an alternative to this brutality. Who will protect those going north for work, if we do not? You are doing important work, *primo.*"

Francisco's gaze turned fierce. "Why is Coral with this man? Who is he to her?"

"We all used to work for Theomund Brown."

Francisco glared at him. "I want to see Coral. *Deseo verla.*"

"You are really so attracted to a gringa, that you cannot take care of business first?"

Luis turned in disgust and led the way to the terrace where Francisco took a gulp of the sangrita they were served, a traditional Mexican aperitif of tomato, lime, and orange juices, hotly spiced and chilled. They usually sipped it alternately with tequila, but they needed clear heads now.

"Do not call her a gringa," Francisco said. "Not that I care anything for this country. It has no soul. It is full of arrogant people who think they are better than us and it has an arrogant government that shows no respect. Not only did they take half of Mexico away, they try to tell us what to do with what's left. The U.S. only wants our oil and cheap laborers who return to Mexico when they're told."

Luis nodded. "Maybe so, but I have come to like the U.S. It's organized here. The country has ideals. In a way, it is still innocent, like a spoiled baby. It is just beginning to see that when it throws its weight around, it might also hurt itself. Besides, when La Reconquista happens—"

Francisco downed the rest of his sangrita. "Luis, you are my cousin. I love and respect you, primo. That's why I am willing to give you one hour to get Coral here, or I am gone."

Coral lay beneath her yellow quilt, Sam taking a nap beside her. When he first woke, she pretended to be waiting for a call scheduling his DNA tests. Meanwhile, she'd kept him occupied with feeding Peter while she cooked a slow breakfast, then followed it with the kind of sex neither Sam, nor any man she'd been with, could resist. Awed, Sam nicknamed it her *snapping pussy*. She always produced a blush when a man mentioned it, but she knew it was true. Sam said he'd learned the term from black guys, and thought it a myth until he met her. Add her sensuality and he was a goner, Sam said. She expected he would be out for another hour, at least.

Her cell phone buzzed and she wondered if Francisco had arrived. She eased out of bed, went into her studio, and closed the door. "Hello?"

"Coral it's Luis, I—" Abruptly he stopped talking.

"Buenos dias, Coral."

"Francisco?"

"Come to me."

Coral picked up her red ballet shoes that were still on the floor from last night. She had to make this sound good. "Francisco, I can't. I have to—"

"Come to me!"

"Francisco, please—"

"Come to me now, preciosa, or I will leave." He hung up.

Coral clicked off the phone, thinking that when it came to sex she could count on Francisco being impatient, impetuous, domineering, insatiable, and insane. Then she remembered it was partly her own fault. She went into the bedroom and, looking at the clock, scribbled a note for Sam: *Had to leave. I've arranged the DNA test for tomorrow afternoon. They'll come here and do the swabs then go wherever Maggie is, if you want. Don't leave. Back soon.*

It was a lie. By tomorrow afternoon, Francisco would have done his thing and Peter would be on a plane to Rome where, in the secrecy of the Vatican, he would be crowned the new Christ.

Quickly Coral showered, rummaged through her closet, found something lovely Francisco hadn't seen, doused herself in perfume, slipped on sandals, and left. Chris, her doorman, flagged a taxi to take her across the park to Luis's place. When she arrived, Luis's doorman uncle sent her up in the elevator. Francisco was there, blocking her way when the doors opened.

"Where have you been?" he demanded. He came into the elevator and backed her into a corner.

She heard Luis's voice, "Francisco, the three of us should talk," but from his eyes she saw Francisco wasn't interested in words. He pushed the button to close the elevator doors. Then he flipped the switch so they wouldn't reopen.

Coral reached up and touched his face, full of anger and desire for her. "Here I am," she whispered, "Your putita. Here I am."

"Where were you?" he said. Without asking, he pulled the lovely dress over her head.

"Where do you think? I was off being the whore you say I am." She was unbuttoning his shirt.

"Was he good? Was he better than me?"

"He was good."

She saw Francisco swallow. She almost thought he had to fight tears as he caressed her, his warm hands making her breath come hard.

Here they were in Luis's elevator, only hours from a kidnapping that could ruin them all if it went wrong, or if it went well make Maggie and Sam cry their eyes out for years. Yet Francisco wanted sex.

They watched each other's moving hands. She decided that if you were going to sell your soul for money, a person might as well have sex.

They tongue kissed like teenagers, and in her mind Coral heard her favorite Mexican serenade, "Le Feria de las Flores." In a way, it reminded her of the Rose Adagio from Sleeping Beauty. She wondered what it would feel like to be a princess courted with flowers or, as in the serenade, a prized flower a man would fight to transplant to his garden.

"When this is over," he whispered, his body pressing hers, "Come to Mexico and live with me." He put his aparato inside her and it felt wonderful. She heard his familiar sigh of bliss.

"Why?"

"Because I love you."

Together they did a lot of moaning as Francisco pushed against her, his pants down around his ankles.

"Marry me," she said though she hadn't meant to.

He paused. "I love you, isn't that enough?"

Coral shook her head.

If she weren't a putita, a gringa whore, she'd be ashamed of having sex with a man so soon after having had it with another.

Instead, Coral felt a kind of victory when Francisco stopped moving, paralyzed by ecstasy, crying out that he loved her. Sam had just done the same, shouting lustful lies. Neither knew they were in a battle for survival, but Coral did.

She was about to have five million dollars. Two weeks ago she'd stopped using birth control. Then last night, as Sam watched her dance the Rose Adagio, she'd made this plan, knowing she could have loved Sam as easily as Francisco.

She wanted the best man to win.

She wanted Francisco's kamikazes to fight Sam's. She wanted their sperm to fight in her womb, like God had designed sperm to.

She planned to stop being a putita. Coral intended to buy a nice house with flowers, trees, and a lawn, and, if she got pregnant, raise the victor's child.

Chapter 21

Refusing to rest like Doña Teresita had advised, Maggie retraced her steps in the Yerbería Guadalupe, waiting for Adamo Morelli to knock on the back door. She had phoned him, not knowing what else to do. To keep reporters away, Teresita hadn't raised the front security shutter.

Maggie had to sit down in the rocking chair Teresita brought to her, but going back to bed with her baby missing was out of the question. If she passed out on the street, Adamo would help her, but Maggie didn't expect to. The water birth had been quick and easy and she was no wimp, in any case.

She stared at the hypnotic eyes on the portrait of Teresita, the folk saint. Doña Teresita had been named after her. The original Teresita was said to have magic powers and be able to see things others couldn't. Maggie wished she knew her secret because, all morning, Maggie had the feeling she had seen something, too. She just couldn't remember what.

She heard, "O Sole Mio," coming from the back alley and knew it was Adamo. Unable to contain his inner happiness, he let it out of his mouth. He knocked on the Yerbería Guadalupe's back door and Teresita let him in.

"Mia cara!" He held out his arms. "You are a mother! Congratulations! But shouldn't you be in bed?"

Maggie burst into tears.

He rushed to her. "What is the matter? Why do you cry?"

"Sam ran off with my baby, Adamo!"

Adamo balled his fists. "What? I will kill him!" He put his arms around her. "Do not worry, mia cara. I am here. We will find your baby. Come, tell me, was it a boy or a girl?"

She leaned against him. "A boy, a beautiful boy. I named him Peter."

"Peter. Yes, he must be beautiful with such a fine name. I saw your TV interview. You were wonderful, mia cara. How could those stupid people think Peter is the Son of God? He's just a baby."

"It's all my fault," she wailed.

"No. You are wonderful. Where is the phone? We will call the police."

She grabbed his hand. "We can't. There'd be publicity and there's already been too much. I've got to find Peter myself and then I've got to hide him." She sat down.

"Yes, of course." Adamo kneeled next to the rocking chair, patting her hand and ruffling his black hair in thought. In silence they stared at each other. "Yes, of course," he repeated. "Mia cara, where will we look?"

"I don't know! I don't know! I've been trying to think where Sam would take him."

"Does he have friends or family here?"

"No. Wait, yes!" Maggie cried. "Yes, he does! He has friends all over New York. He sees them every week at this bar called Molly Malone's."

Maggie's heart sank at the idea of going there. To Sam's cronies at Molly Malone's she'd look like a crazy nurse in her newly loose white maternity dress and white shoes, not like a sister of the church. She pictured their faces as they saw her. Would they feel any sympathy? Or would they just stick up for Sam, their friend?

Adamo stood. "I will go there immediately!"

Maggie decided. "I'm going, too."

Adamo lifted a warning finger. "You will rest, my Maggie. That is final. Leave this to me."

They heard Teresita's chiding voice. "I have tried to make her go back to bed."

Adamo kissed Maggie's cheek and left the yerbería. When he turned to look back, Maggie was following.

Waiting for Coral to come back from her appointment, Sam spent time discovering his son. He wouldn't have thought of it as *discovering* before Peter's birth, but to Sam these hours were just that. He felt like a new man, venturing onto an unsuspected landscape that contained nothing but love.

Sissy stuff, he would have called it less than forty-eight hours ago. What man fell head over heels in love with something that couldn't hold up its head? He hadn't seen it coming, didn't know he was capable of it.

Since Coral left, a sun had risen in Sam's heart, a floodlight had turned on in his mind. The source was Peter, his son.

First of all, he was perfect.

His proportioned face had cute baby cheeks, a button of a nose, a chubby but promisingly square chin, and startling eyes, like his mother's, except hers were green, the baby's ocean blue and so huge they made you go *aaawww*, when he opened them. He already had plenty of blond hair like Sam did when he was a baby. He and Maggie were both responsible for his skin color, his mom's womb a Riviera in which Peter tanned. His ears weren't funny looking like Sam's had been, so there'd be no teasing on that account when Peter went to school.

Though he was only twenty-one inches, all parts were present and working as far as Sam could attest, not least from the vigorous streams Peter lofted into the air when undiapered.

Eight pounds at birth, Sam suspected Peter had lost weight and started to panic. He turned on Coral's computer and found it password-protected—strange since she said no one came here. He used a guest account to go online to a baby website. They obviously didn't expect men to log on because everything was pink, but he persevered and learned newborns lose weight until their tenth day. Their stomachs can't hold enough for weight gain until then.

But to Sam the coolest thing about Peter was what Sam felt when his baby woke and gazed at his dad. Peter seemed to know who Sam was. *Amazing.* Experimenting, Sam learned that Peter could see his face when it was about ten inches away. If Sam got closer, Peter's eyes crossed. But stay at the right distance and Sam would see recognition in his son's eyes. He'd settle down. He'd smile with delight. He'd reward Sam with a look of perfect trust, as if saying, *Hi, Dad. Thanks for being here. I know I'm safe when you're around.*

The first time Sam saw it, he was sunk. What could beat that? Nothing. Not money, not sex. In that moment, with Peter smiling, Sam vowed to be there for the rest of this kid's life. Even when Peter next wrinkled his brow and made a giant poop into his diaper, Sam shouted, "Good boy!" and, head over heels in love, went to get a fresh one.

For two or three hours Sam discovered his son, jingling keys, making sounds, talking, carrying him around, feeding and bathing him, engrossed in seeing Peter react to the world he'd been born into. Only at length did it strike Sam that Maggie was missing this. He wondered if she'd come to her senses when she found Peter gone. If she was herself again and wanted her son, he wouldn't keep them apart. When the DNA tests were done, she could have Peter back.

He heard keys in the door and Coral coming in.

Her return reminded him of his other dilemma. When Maggie and Peter were safe, when he'd made sure the world had lost interest in them, would he give Coral up?

"Hi, Sam," she said in a voice so sultry it sent shivers through him. "How did my two boys make out while I was gone?"

The wind had tossed her hair and most of her lipstick had worn off, but Coral still seemed like womanhood itself. It didn't seem fair that God had put her on the same earth with other females. All Coral had to do was crook her little finger and even well-intentioned men would forget their girlfriends and wives.

Sam had certainly forgotten his and he wouldn't make excuses for it. If Maggie wanted him back and if she asked, he'd tell what he'd done. The truth was their only chance. But that was for tomorrow. It was for after the DNA test when he, Maggie and Peter could return to their lives.

For now, Aphrodite herself stood a few feet from him and Sam had given up pretending he didn't want Coral as much as he wanted Maggie, except Coral wasn't the mother of his son.

"We did fine," he said. "By the way, did you know this baby is a prince?"

"Guess so," she said and kicked off her shoes. "His dad's royalty."

Sam grinned. "Back in a sec," he said and took Peter to his crib for a nap.

When he returned, Coral stood next to Fred Astaire and Ginger Rogers, her dress on the deep burgundy carpet.

"Do you know it's been almost five hours since we made love?" she purred, making him wonder how she did that.

"Has it now?"

"Mmm-hmm. I'm going to the bathroom to freshen up. Hope you're out of those clothes when I get back."

Sam was. He found a blanket and spread it on the floor in the dance studio and had Tchaikovsky's Sleeping Beauty cued and ready to play.

"No, not on the floor," she said.

Naked, Coral sat on the blanket and put her red toe shoes on, letting him enjoy the view as she laced them up. By the time she finished, he couldn't talk. He watched as she rose and went to the railing she called the *barre*, limbering up, her hair wet from the shower. To Sam the movements of her body gave a whole new dimension to ballet.

"Put the music on," she said and he did.

Facing the mirror, with one leg up on the railing, Coral crooked her little finger as the music soared. For what Sam sensed was the last time, he crossed the floor and embraced the other woman in his life.

Luis decided that if Francisco asked him one more time who Sam Duffy was to Coral, he'd scream. They were in the library, Luis's feet up on Theomund Brown's American chestnut desk, working out the logistics of tomorrow morning, Francisco and his cómplices sprawled on sofas and chairs, beers in their hands.

Francisco and his men had already visited The Park Hudson

where Coral lived, and explored the neighborhood. Now they were finalizing their movements, drawing lines and crosses on a big map of Manhattan on the wall.

For the third time Francisco said, "Excuse me," to his men. "Luis, I need to see you outside."

Again, Luis rose and followed Francisco to the terrace.

"If this Sam Duffy is just a man who used to work for your Señor Brown, if he is just a friend of Coral's, why is he sleeping at her apartment, again?"

Luis sighed. "I told you, Francisco. He's afraid for his son. He brought him there because he had nowhere else to go."

Francisco strode across the terra cotta tiles, gesturing with his beer. "Nowhere else? Nowhere else? This man has no mother? No father?"

"No, they're both dead. Anyway, Francisco, this has nothing to do with our plan, either way."

Francisco paused. "Maybe nothing for you. I will decide what has something to do with me. Why can't she just let him use her place? Why must she stay there all night?"

To hide his irritation, Luis flipped the Aztec knife pouch he carried. He'd become a bit obsessed by it, he knew, because it symbolized the glorious past he hoped, in part, to restore. Alone at night, he often imagined he was Moctezuma—not dying at the Spaniards hands, but defeating them so his people could survive.

"Luis, did you hear me?" Francisco said.

"Who leaves their own home when someone asks if they can spend the night?" Luis replied. He'd never intended for Francisco to know of Coral's connection with Sam.

Francisco finished his beer, put it down and walked up to Luis. He took the knife pouch from him, withdrew the knife and ran the back along the palm of his hand.

"I think you are lying to me, Luis."

It had been years since they'd fought. Luis was sixteen, Francisco fourteen, but big for his age. He was still big for his age.

"Why would I lie to you?"

Francisco put the knife back and handed the pouch to Luis. "You tell me."

Instead of returning to the library and the planning, Francisco walked down to the salon. "Why keep statues of them here? Why? You should wait until Los Días de los Muertos, the Days of the Dead like everyone else! It's not good to have the spirits of your family always around."

Luis grunted. "That is my business."

Francisco turned. "And Coral is mine."

Luis rolled his eyes. "I don't know what you want me to do."

"Perhaps, Luis, you do not understand a man's feeling for a woman. Perhaps you don't have normal protective instincts." He gestured angrily toward the statues, "or Cyntia, your sweet sister, might be alive!"

Only Coral could have told him. What a fool he'd been to like and trust her.

Enraged, Luis charged Francisco and slammed him into the wall. Bigger, stronger, Francisco shoved Luis, who fell to the floor beside Cyntia's frozen statue. Seeing her face, Luis's woe exploded. He grabbed the Aztec knife and sailed it within inches of Francisco's head. In Neza, he'd learned how to handle knives to keep from being pushed around.

Francisco roared and started toward his cousin. Then he stopped, groaned, and hung his head. In despair he patted the statues. "Don't blame Coral, Luis. She told me only to convince me to help you."

Luis said nothing, but he intended to repay Coral's betrayal.

"I apologize," Francisco said and bowed his head, "*Por favor, perdóname no debi haber hecho ese comentario.*"

Those were the words Coral had used to apologize that first night. Luis had listened outside the door and heard her. Francisco told her no apology was needed because she was just a gringa whore. How had Francisco forgotten that? How had Luis forgotten that? How had they let a gringa whore come between them?

Francisco put his hand on Luis's shoulder and rejoined his gente in the library.

On the subway, halfway to Molly Malone's, Maggie almost fainted. Seeing her condition, Adamo took her off the train and when she refused to return to the Yerbería Guadalupe, hailed a cab. It took them the rest of the way.

Maggie felt anxious when she stood on the sidewalk beneath the sign with the green shamrock.

"Are you ready, mia cara?" Adamo asked.

She nodded and followed him in.

Pat, the bartender, looked surprised at first. Then she saw recognition dawn. "Is it Maggie, then? Come in, lass, come in. Are you looking for Sam?"

In relief, she said, "Yes, Pat. Do you know where he is?"

"Acting up, is he? I'll break his head for you when I see him, Maggie girl, but he hasn't been here for days."

Charlie, Sam's best man, said the same. So Maggie and Adamo waited, questioning everyone who came in, her hopes dwindling. They hadn't seen Sam. They didn't know where he was.

Finally, Maggie did.

Coral's perfume had been on Sam when he came to her church yesterday. That's where he'd gone—back to Coral. He'd stolen her baby and taken him to his beautiful whore. They'd probably been screwing each other for months.

Maggie refused to picture Peter in Coral's arms. If she did she knew she'd go crazy, want to get another gun and shoot that *bitch* like she deserved—a word Maggie hadn't used before meeting Coral. How could Maggie have ever told Sam she didn't want Peter? God was punishing her terrible thoughts. She had to repent but, for now, all she wanted was to find Peter.

Unfortunately, Maggie had no idea where Coral lived and there was no one to ask. Coral didn't work for Theomund Brown anymore because he was dead—praise the Lord for a little less evil in the world. Even if he were alive, Maggie knew Brown wouldn't tell her a single thing about his prize prostitute. No point in trying the phonebook. Even if Coral were listed, Maggie didn't know her last name.

Until yesterday, she'd thought Coral was in their past, but no. Her rival had everything Maggie longed for—her baby and her man.

In Molly Malone's dart room Maggie wept, Adamo trying to console her. She had the feeling there was something she should remember. Not recalling upset her more.

"It is late," Adamo whispered. "Come back to my room with me, mia cara. No reporters will be there." He caressed her back a little too tenderly.

Maggie raised her head. "Is this what life is, Adamo? Is this it? No one's faithful to anyone? Nothing's precious? We just play musical chairs in each other's beds and then one day we die?"

"I love you, Maggie," Adamo said.

She frowned at him. "Why? I tried to kill my husband on our wedding night! For months I hated my own son!"

Adamo frowned, too. "Sam must have provoked you. I won't. I love you."

"But why do you love me, Adamo? I'm not beautiful."

"You are mistaken, mia cara," Adamo said.

Maggie rose. She had decided. She would return to the Yerbería Guadalupe and sneak in by the back door, because she still needed Doña Teresita's care. Then she'd think of a way to find her baby. Whatever happened, never again would Maggie believe a man's vow of love.

Chapter 22

Coral woke at seven in the morning and slipped out of bed. They'd fed Peter twice in the night and hadn't gotten much sleep. In the living room she stared in fear through her glass front walls at the Hudson River, shrouded in a thicker than usual haze. She whispered, "Oh, God, don't let it rain!" The kidnapping couldn't happen if it did. "Please don't rain!"

"What's the matter, Coral?"

Sam stood at the bedroom, wearing nothing but the jeans her father wore when he died of a heart attack, running to the hospital when she was born. She'd sent Sam's clothes to the concierge to be cleaned. They'd be returned before nine.

"I was just telling the sky not to rain. The DNA people are due here at two o'clock and it might delay them."

"Oh."

"You've got to call Maggie, you know," she went on, needing to keep up the lie, "and find out where she is so they can test her. You can't keep putting it off."

Sam nodded. "Yeah, I know. She's going to chew my ass off, though."

"Maybe not. If you had my kid, I'd be calm as hell when you called. At least till I got him back. Is Peter awake?"

Sam yawned, "Yeah."

"Let me fix him a bottle and us some breakfast."

"Okay," Sam said. He brought Peter from the bedroom and stretched out on the couch with him, the TV remote in hand.

Coral listened to the morning news while she cooked, surprised to hear nothing more about Maggie's baby being a Christ clone. Bored with the lack of developments, the news had moved on. As far as Luis was concerned, that was fine, Coral knew. His Eminence Evaristo Cardinal Salati must have arrived by now and would be waiting at Luis's penthouse. The story had done its job. She couldn't go there to see Salati, but it didn't matter any more. The die was as cast as die could possibly be.

"You want bacon, eggs?" she called.

"Yeah, thanks. Scrambled."

She heard Peter fretting, took his bottle from its warm pan of water and tested the formula on her wrist. She took it out to Sam, who began feeding his baby. It made an odd sight: Zeus tenderly feeding his child instead of swallowing it alive. Of all the men she knew, Sam was the last she expected fatherhood to domesticate. Even Francisco was more natural father material compared to rough and tumble ladies man Sam.

"How do you feel, being a father?"

Sam looked up. "I dunno. Weird, I guess, like this is all that matters."

Coral blinked. "When are you going to call Maggie?"

"After breakfast."

She went back to the frying bacon, taking deep breaths, refusing to think any thoughts that might interfere with having five million dollars. If she could count on Sam, like Peter could count on Sam, maybe things would be different, but they weren't. She could screw Sam's brains out, dance the Rose Adagio all day, and she'd never see that sappy look of adoration he had on his face as he fed his son.

He was burping Peter when she took breakfast in.

"Too bad we don't have one of those little chair things for him to sit in," he said. He lay Peter on a towel on her sofa and put cushions around him.

The doorbell rang.

Sam looked ready to pounce.

"It's just the valet with your clothes."

He followed her to the foyer and stood behind her on the black tiles as she answered the door. It was the valet with the clothes.

Sam tipped the man and when he left, grinned at Coral. "You want to shower together?"

"Nah," she said. "You go. I'll watch Peter. I brought you a razor and such. Look in the cabinet."

"Thanks." Sam grimaced. "Okay, I'm calling Maggie now. I've got to face her." He took out his cell phone and she went back into the kitchen to listen.

"Maggie, it's me. Be calm. I'm sorry I didn't call you back before. Are you okay?"

Pause. Coral didn't have to peep in to know the reason for the pause.

"You're right, Maggie. I'm sorry. Just listen for a minute. I figured it out. All we need is a DNA test. That will prove who Peter is and then it will be safe to bring him back, if you want him."

Coral peeped around the corner and saw Sam holding the phone away from his ear as Maggie screamed. So much for calm.

"Well, that's not what you told me. You said you didn't want him. Besides, I couldn't leave him there. The press might have found you. And you were calling him Jess."

Pause.

"I can't say where I am because you'll come here. Just tell me where you'll be at three o'clock and I'll send the DNA test people over. All they have to do is swab your mouth. Then, when we get the results back, you'll know and I'll know the truth. We'll call the TV stations and then we can go home and figure things out."

Pause.

"Peter's fine. Don't worry. … No, really. He's fine. … Okay, so you hate me, but I still love you, Maggie. I'm sorry. … I do, too, love you. Bye."

Coral couldn't resist. She stood in the kitchen door. "Remember a couple days ago in your office when you were telling me all that baloney about you and me?"

Sam came and caressed her. "Coral, I meant it."

"Yeah, right. Get in the shower, Mr. Duffy, before I tell you what I think." She gave him a fake smile.

He returned it and left.

He came back clean-shaven with freshly blow-dried hair. "Your turn. I tried not to wet the floor."

Again the doorbell rang.

This time, Coral went to him and kissed his mouth, whispering, "I thought you and Peter deserved a surprise."

"A surprise?" Warily Sam followed her to the foyer.

A deliveryman stood there when she opened the door. "Coral Anders?"

"That's me."

She signed his clipboard and he rolled in three boxes, one large and rectangular, another flat and rectangular, and a square one.

"What's all this?" Sam asked, when the deliveryman left.

"Open them, Sam."

He took out a pocketknife with a scrimshaw handle, got on his knees, and went to work on the boxes, Coral holding her breath because this was it.

"What in the world?" He pulled out blankets from the flat box and tiny jumpers, booties, shirts, a whole wardrobe for Peter.

"Coral, you didn't have to do this."

"I wanted to."

From the square box came the kind of baby seat he'd just been talking about.

"It's a combination baby carrier and car seat," she said.

"Thanks, I guess I should have thought of all this myself."

"Don't be silly, Sam. You're a man."

He opened the large box and removed something wrapped in plastic. Cutting through it, he found a dark blue pram.

"It needs a little assembly," she said, "but it's one of those English prams. I figured Peter, here, should have the best, shouldn't you darling?" She made cooing sounds in his direction.

Packing materials and baby things covered the deep burgundy carpet. "Coral, I'm going to pay you back."

"If you insist."

"If I don't, Maggie will have my head, assuming she ever speaks to me again."

Coral glanced out through the glass wall. The sun had melted the morning fog and the sky was clear, thank goodness.

She made her way around the carpet debris. "Set the pram up while I'm showering then get Peter dressed. We'll take him for a walk in Central Park." She said it nonchalantly.

Before she reached the bathroom she heard, "That's not a good idea."

She turned to Sam, putting innocent confusion on her face. "Why not? It's only two blocks away." She looked through the glass walls. "The weather's fine."

"What if somebody recognizes me? That's all we need is a bunch of press here."

She laughed. "Sam, your mug looks like every other Irish one in New York. Besides, it's Maggie's picture they have. If they've got one of you, it's twelve years old by now. Peter's been cooped up in here too long. He needs sunshine and fresh air, don't you darling," she said, walking to Peter and stroking his nose, as he kicked his baby feet, "and I'm getting cabin fever."

"I guess you're right."

"Of course I'm right. Rush hour will be over when we leave and everyone will be at work. We'll have the park to ourselves."

Sam nodded and started picking things up from the carpet. In the bathroom Coral showered, dropping soap from her nervous hands, sweating after applying antiperspirant. She looked in her closet, wishing she had dress shields. What would Mata Hari wear?

She emerged in a leather pantsuit. The pram was assembled. Peter was dressed in a blue jumpsuit.

Sam patted the carriage's white tires. "How'd I do?"

"It looks like we're about to take the prince for a walk."

"Yeah, it does."

She picked Peter up and lay him in the pram, covered him with the blankets, put a cap on his head.

"One more thing," Sam said. He went to the bedroom and returned, tucking a gun inside his jacket.

Coral's heart almost leapt out of her chest.

"Sam, I didn't know you had a gun."

"Sorry. I hid it."

She thought of Francisco and his cómplices who had kidnapped for years without using a gun or hurting a soul.

"I'm not comfortable with your having a gun around the baby."

Sam laughed and patted her bottom. "With all those lunatics out there?"

He pushed the pram to the foyer, took a last look at Fonteyn and Nureyev, opened and held the door.

"Come, milady," he said.

They left the building at 8:58 A.M., two minutes ahead of schedule.

After Sam's call, Maggie fell into a troubled sleep in the Yerbería Guadalupe. Now she woke, crying. Frantically she reached for the phone and dialed Sam. No answer. His cell must be turned off. She left a message. "Call me, Sam; it's urgent."

She dialed Felix and was astonished to find his home phone not working. She frowned. Felix's number that he'd had his whole life couldn't be disconnected. She redialed. It was. Remembering part of the number for The Barracks where the guards at Felix's building were, she dialed different combinations, getting hang-ups, until she reached them. *The Rossi family moved yesterday and left no forwarding address.* It dawned on Maggie why. Her TV interview had wreaked havoc in his life. True, the NYPD didn't allow paparazzi to turn the Upper East Side into utter hell for its rich residents, just the purgatory of wondering what tree a photographer hid behind; what car would follow and create hell somewhere else. She rose, grabbed a dress, and struggling to get it on, woke Teresita. Could she borrow the yerbería's car or be driven to Midtown Manhattan?

Maggie had remembered dreaming about Jess and a pram in Central Park then waking beside a fresh red rose.

Chapter 23

For Luis's tastes, there were far too many complications, all of which he hid from Salati who sat nearby calmly swirling an Italian Illy Caffé Luis had ordered for him.

"What do you see down there?" Salati asked.

"Nothing, Your Eminence."

Over the terrace wall, Luis was actually watching Francisco and his men leave in separate cars, rented with fake IDs. They and Evaristo had narrowly missed each other, one coming up from the garage, the other leaving through the front door.

What shocked Luis was Coral's effect on Francisco. Could the seduction games Coral played have worked this well? Could sexual tantalization really be so strong? For now he had to contain his anger at her betrayal, but their friendship was over.

"You must call me Evaristo, Luis."

"Yes, Evaristo." Luis left the terrace wall and looked at his watch. "There isn't much time."

Salati put down his cup. "I would enjoy spending the day here talking with you, but, yes, business first." He stood and placed his hand on Luis's back—a friendly gesture from which Luis recoiled.

"Your limo is ready downstairs," Luis said, easing away from Salati's hand. "Here are the baby's papers."

Luis handed him a passport with a photo Coral secretly took of the baby. The name on the passport read: Vincenzo Salati. Peter had become Salati's nephew, traveling with his mother, an Italian woman waiting in the limo in Luis's garage.

"It is amazing to think he may indeed be a clone of the Christ," Salati said. "Even if not, a child born of Shroud DNA belongs to the Catholic Church. We have protected many sacred secrets. This boy will be another. We will study him, understand him, make the best of him."

"Catholicism's answer to the Dalai Lama," Luis said with derision then cleared his throat. He had to hide being scandalized on behalf of the Virgen de Guadalupe. How could a priest be deluded about a simple black woman's child?

"I believe you are right," Luis said. He walked Salati to the elevator. "Wait in the limousine. Another car will enter and park beside you. The baby will be handed out."

"As soon as that happens, I will make a phone call," Salati said. "Then the head of Mexica Eterna may visit any American Catholic Church, especially those with a shrine to the Virgin of Guadalupe. He will obtain assistance for the ones your eagles fly across the border."

"Thank you, Your Eminence."

Italian style, Salati stepped forward and kissed Luis's cheeks.

If you wanted to have New York's Lincoln Center all to yourself, there was no better time than 9:00 A.M. on a workday morning, Coral knew. She and Sam took a detour through the fifteen-acre site, which, among other things, housed the ballet, two opera companies, the philharmonic, Juilliard, and the chamber music society. Coral looked for inquisitive strollers whose presence might alarm Sam, make him want to take Peter back before they reached Central Park West. Thankfully, Central Plaza was empty, but for stragglers late for work. Only two bums shared their view of the Met's reflecting fountain and its six famous arched windows, behind which everyone with a voice had sung.

Already the day was glorious, not a rain cloud in sight.

Coral listened to the pram's white wheels roll across the plaza's blue and white tiles. She should stop this. She should pretend to faint, sending Sam and his gun back to her apartment. She should take another route where Francisco couldn't find them. She would have already if every revolution of the white wheels wasn't taking her closer to five million dollars.

"Have you ever hated yourself, Sam?"

She'd never seen him so happy, just pushing the carriage. "Yeah, Coral, that I do. I owe you an apology. I said I was leaving Maggie, but now that all the problems are going to be solved, I can't keep a mother from her child."

"Oh, I see."

"I know, I know." He stopped on a blue section of pavement and faced the fountain to gaze at her. "I guess you're wondering why I don't take Peter back and then stay with you?"

Coral searched his face. "Why don't you?"

He looked down at the pram. "I can't leave him."

"Oh, I see."

They resumed walking. The pram's white wheels rolled. They reached 65th and Columbus Avenue. On the far left corner sat the neo-Gothic Hotel des Artistes. In spite of its name it was never a hotel, but studio lofts. Gargoyles on the outside represented the arts. Norman Rockwell once lived there.

One block to go to Central Park West. With each step, Coral's feet felt harder to move, her breath harder to draw.

"Sam?"

"Yeah, babe."

"I guess we'll never see each other again."

"Yeah it feels like that." He didn't stop. "It feels like this is the end. Are you okay?"

"I hate it."

"Yeah, so do I. I really do. I love you, you know." He didn't stop walking.

"Cut the crap, Sam. You're the type of guy who forgets his obligations until right after he's been screwed."

"I hope not, but maybe I am. For what it's worth, you're an amazing woman. I'll never forget the past two days."

They walked in silence. A warm wind blew under the bright sky. They passed a newsstand on the street. The pram's wheels rolled onto Central Park West.

There was Francisco.

Coral saw him right away, sitting in a rented car, his shoulder against the side window, his arm on the wheel, looking determined, like he was about to step on the gas and run down God. She looked at Sam and wondered if she was pregnant and, if so, whose kamikazes had won, his or Francisco's.

"Let's go to the playground," she said.

"Sounds good."

They crossed the street. She saw Francisco's cómplices waiting in other cars.

"Don't you just love this place?" Sam said.

They entered the park. The pram wheels rolled past the steps to The Tavern on the Green where many a newlywed had their wedding reception—the restaurant's crystal pavilion sparkling, two smoke stacks rising above its rustic French-style roof.

They entered the park at 67th and had two options for playgrounds. The under five set had a small one filled with colorful climbing pipes, sandbox, swings, and such. Older kids had an adventure playground with stone fortress, a tree house, a water feature, trees and bushes and flowers everywhere. Just ahead, she saw the huge bronze bust of the Italian patriot, Giuseppe Mazzini, a gift to the city from Italian-Americans. Francisco would look for them at the benches nearby.

"Sam," Coral said, her jaw tight to keep her chin from quivering. "I meant to get a paper to read while we're sitting here."

"A paper?"

"Yeah, there's a stand right up on the street. We passed it."

"Oh, right."

"I hate to send you back, but pretty please?" She blinked. She wanted to warn him, but she didn't.

He kissed her cheek. "Okay, I'll be right back." He touched Peter's chin. "Now don't you two go anywhere."

He hustled off in the direction of Central Park West, his fatal flaw at work. He had talked to her about it. Sam was a human golden retriever, primed to deliver, eager to fetch. It was a strength. It was his downfall. But for that trait, he would have stayed in Italy with Maggie, and Jess would be alive. But for that trait, Peter wouldn't be here alone with her.

She saw Francisco no more than twenty yards away. He wore a jacket loose enough to hide a baby. Then Coral glimpsed a woman sitting on a bench, shredding Kleenex in her hands.

Maggie?

They saw each other at the same moment. *Oh no. Oh God!*

"Give me my baby!"

No lioness had ever roared louder. Her cry shattered Coral's heart. Time imploded. Coral wanted to reach for Peter and give him to Maggie before all was lost, but Francisco was there, looking in the carriage, too, his sicarios all around.

Maggie screamed.

She ran toward the pram.

Newspaper forgotten, there was Sam, drawn by Maggie's cries, gun outstretched, his true strength revealed—he would kill, he would die, to protect those he loved. Why had she done this?

"Get down!" Sam shouted. "Maggie, Coral, get down!"

Gunfire.

Not from Sam, but from Francisco, who looked toward Sam, enraged. *Oh God!*

Nannies in the park with their children screamed.

Coral picked Peter up and, cradling him, hit the ground.

Maggie was there, crawling to Coral.

Shots rang over their heads. A stray bullet ricocheted onto the pram's wheels and the white rubber exploded into the air.

"Bitch, give me my baby!" Maggie demanded, taking him.

"Yeah, I'm a bitch, but we need to get the hell out of here."

Looking terrified, Maggie nodded.

Crouching, they rushed back toward 67th, Coral glancing frantically back through the stream of fleeing mothers and nannies and children.

"Run ahead," Coral said when they reached the street, depositing her keys in Maggie's hand. She said her address. "Tell the doorman I said to let you in or I'll tell it was him who stole the Porsche. Quote me. Wait there."

Coral turned to intercept one of Francisco's men who ran out of the park.

"*¿Qué chingada madre?*" she said innocently, which means, "what the hell?" in Mexico.

The shot that hit Sam drove him to the ground. The thought of Peter brought him up. He lunged behind a tree, scattering startled squirrels that now scurried to the treetops.

Who had shot him? How did Maggie get here? What in holy crap was going on?

"*Atrápalos, güey,*" one of them said. Trap them, dude. The big, tall one said it—the one who had the gun.

What the hell? Sam aimed at the man and got off a shot. It struck a branch, which crashed to the ground, scattering the men. *How many were there? At least three. If he could hold them off five minutes, New York's finest would be here to help kick their asses.*

Inching closer to the next tree, Sam searched for the tall man. A blaze of gunfire came from a tree near the Mazzini statue. He ducked even before he heard the sound. His knees like springs, he rose, and got off a two-handed shot toward the tall man as he peeked from behind his tree. *Who the hell was he*?

"*¡Atrápalos!*" the man called to the others.

Sam whispered, "What the fuck? A Mexican kidnapping ring in New York?"

"*¡Quitenle al bebé!*"

Snatch the baby?

Sam scanned for movement and got off two shots at others trying to leave their hiding places. No one on this earth was snatching his son. He ducked and waited for return fire, which didn't come. Only the tall man must be armed. Good thing, because—Sam looked down—blood was pumping from his leg. If he didn't stop it, he'd be a corpse.

"Hey, you, big guy behind that tree," Sam called, tearing off a piece of shirt. "What do you want with my son?" He wrapped the cloth around his thigh beneath the gunshot, and with his teeth pulled tight.

"What do you want with my woman?" The voice was deep,

heavily accented, contemptuous.

His woman? Oh, crap! Coral?

Sam shouted, "She sucked me off for a couple of days. I'm done with her."

Sam crouched and scurried, squirrel-like, to the next tree and the next as the man, outraged, let off a blizzard of deadly shots where Sam no longer was. Now he had a better view and didn't think he'd been seen. The man looked Mexican to Sam—tall, dark, dangerous—just the kind of bloke Coral might not ignore. In fact, but for the man's dark hair and olive skin, Sam could have been fighting himself behind that tree. *Life is paying you back, Duffy, for wanting whores all these years.*

The man replied, "A fool would value only her mouth, señor!"

Sam agreed, but he valued something else more. He aimed for the tall man's chest, whispering, *this ones for you, Peter.*

As if he'd heard, the man turned and aimed for Sam.

Sam fired at the Mexican's heart and was shot a second time, blood spraying from his chest, as he got the bullet off.

Coral was alone on Central Park West when the gunfire stopped because his cómplices had run back to Francisco. It took only an instant for her feet to move, but she thought the silence would never end.

She ran, wiping at tears threatening to blind her—back to the park and the statue and the playground and the trees.

Francisco lay on the ground, his men kneeling over him.

Sam lay yards away.

Motionless

Neither one victorious.

Blood everywhere.

"*¿Por qué trajiste un arma?*" she cried to Francisco. "Why did you have a gun? You never kidnapped with a gun."

"*¡Por tí!*" Because of you, cried his cómplice.

Police sirens wailed.

Helplessly she gazed at the two men she loved and thought

she would die from the sight. She remembered Maggie and Peter and said "*¡Váyanse de aqui! Dígale a Luis qué me llame.*" Get away from here. Tell Luis to call me.

Seeing only darkness, Coral ran from the park toward the Metropolitan Opera House.

Chapter 24

As soon as Maggie reached Coral's apartment she kissed Peter over and over, whispering, "Oh, my sweet baby, I found you. I thought I'd die when you were gone." Peter's little hands pushed against her, his mouth open, seeking her breast.

"You know you're back with your mama, don't you? It's all right, now. It's all right." Maggie unbuttoned her dress enough to nurse him.

Not wanting to think about what was happening in the park, she reminded herself that Peter was only getting colostrum from her this early, not milk, but it had vital antibodies and the exact nourishment he needed at this stage. She sat down on the elegant sofa, aware of nothing but her baby and this connection she'd longed for. She felt her uterus contract as he fed and, instead of thinking about Sam, marveled at the perfect baby-making system God had put in women. A loved man's touch made the uterus contract, causing her to desire him. Nine months later, the baby's nursing made the uterus contract until it resumed its normal size, readying the woman for the man's seed again.

She heard a knock at the door and jumped to her feet to look through the peephole, carrying Peter. It was Coral. Maggie opened the door and Coral burst into the foyer, throwing off her jacket so fast that she knocked over a vase of yellow tulips, spilling water. Coral flushed when she saw Maggie and Peter, no doubt with shame, Maggie thought, for helping Sam keep them apart.

Where's Sam?" Maggie asked, returning to the sofa and trying to control her fear.

Coral sat down, heaving in air, and held her head in both hands. "Oh God! Oh God!"

"Where's Sam?"

Coral looked up. "He was hit."

Maggie held Peter closer, trying to breath. "Is Sam all right?"

Coral stood. "I don't know." She went into the kitchen, pulled the cork from an open bottle of wine and swigged from it. She brought it into the living room and leaned against the wall beside Fred Astaire and Ginger Rogers, shaking her head, breathing hard.

"He's my husband, Coral. I need to know if he's all right."

Coral spoke firmly. "All you need is to stay put. We'll hear. I'll call, or someone will call us. Bad news never waits. You saw for yourself they're after Peter."

"I know," Maggie said, woefully. "Nobody would have bothered to try to kidnap Peter if I hadn't gone on TV."

Coral looked at her strangely. "If you say so."

As Peter nursed, Maggie glanced around the room, taking in the posters and portraits of dancers and trying not to think about Sam. *Was he living? Had he died?*

"You were a dancer?"

"Yes."

Peter began to fret. She lifted him and patted his back, closing her dress.

"Here, I have a place you can lay him down," Coral said.

Maggie followed her to the bedroom. The bed wasn't made. It smelled musty like sex. Against the wall was the white lace bassinet Jess had shown her in a dream, just before she found the red rose.

Looking guilty, Coral pulled her bed's yellow comforter in place, as Maggie put Peter to sleep.

They left the bedroom, saying nothing. In the living room, Maggie kept her gaze on the burgundy carpet so as not to see Coral and all the baby things.

"Here, take this." Coral handed her a glass of wine.

"I can't while I'm nursing."

"Oh, right."

"I just want to know about Sam."

"Wait, it might be on TV!" Coral picked up the remote. She flew through channels until she glimpsed the words, "Live" and "Gunfight in Central Park." They saw a view into the park from a helicopter and medics working over a man. They almost put their faces into the TV screen.

"Can you tell who it is?"

"No," Coral said.

The station reported they hadn't learned the men's condition or what had caused the gunfight.

Coral flicked on her cell phone and dialed. "It's Coral. Have you heard the news?"

Pause. A wary frown.

"I'll explain later. Just find out, find out! Call me when you know." She hung up, looking quizzically at the phone.

"Who were you talking to?"

"Uh, just a reporter friend who knows Sam and me," Coral said.

Maggie thumbed through the baby clothes piled on the sofa and touched the combination car seat and baby carrier. "Sam was going to leave me, wasn't he? He was going to stay with you."

Coral sighed then came and kneeled in front of Maggie, taking her hands. "Look at me instead of the carpet, okay? You're wrong. He wasn't going to do that. Just before I saw you, he told me this was the end."

Maggie stared into Coral's hazel eyes, unable to believe her. What man would leave a woman who looked like that? Maggie extricated her hands, rose and walked toward Peter's crib, and saw another door ajar. It looked like a dance studio. She pushed the door open and looked inside.

Red toe shoes were on the floor, a blanket, wine glasses almost empty but not quite. She walked in. Coral came behind her. In the mirrors they scrutinized at each other, two completely different women in love with the same man.

"You danced for him, didn't you?" Maggie said, looking at the slippers. "You drank wine and made love in here."

Coral looked away. "Yes, we did."

Maggie reached out and pushed Coral to the floor. She pounced, screaming in fury, and grabbed clumps of Coral's chestnut hair. Pulling, she shouted, "You bitch! Why can't you leave my man alone?"

Coral didn't fight, she just yelled, "Ow!" tried to protect her hair and cried. It made Maggie loosen her grip and sink down. They wept together, soon rocked each other. To Maggie it felt ancient—the sobs of women whose men were dying for them, for country, clan, or God.

"You saved Peter," Maggie murmured. "If Sam loves you, it's not right for you to part. I didn't give him what he needed. You did."

Coral straightened, shaking her head.

"Would you stop being miserable for a minute and listen to me? He doesn't love me! Yeah, I love him but the feeling's not mutual. He married you! Hell, he told me you tried to kill him and he even stayed after that."

The phone rang. Coral ran for it. She listened, wild-eyed, and said, "Oh, my God, Sam's alive!"

"You thought he wasn't?" Maggie cried.

Coral called the concierge and arranged a babysitter for Peter—not here, but at a sitter's in the building, just in case they'd been followed.

She and Maggie went out and asked the doorman to flag a taxi, which took them to St. Vincent's in Greenwich Village. It had a world class Trauma Center.

At the desk they were met by a man they both knew, Dr. Chuck Lewiston—the one who'd killed Theomund Brown.

Dr. Lewiston hadn't confessed. No one who knew had told. Lewiston had cared for Sam the ten years he was in a coma, imprisoned the two of them in Brown's penthouse. As far as Maggie was concerned, Lewiston had snapped and done the world a favor by killing Brown.

He took them into a consultation room and closed the door.

"How is Sam, Dr. Lewiston?" Maggie asked.

He put his hand on her shoulder. "Not good. You're going to have to be brave."

All day Sam was in surgery and recovery. The hours weighed on Maggie. How long had she foolishly hated him, refused him in bed? Twice she took a taxi back to the sitter to nurse Peter. In the cabs she listened to traffic, yearning for the laughter, the joy, she'd silenced in Sam. Woefully she remembered a line from a Thomas Hardy poem Sam liked—"Nor God nor demon can undo the done."

That evening, Chuck Lewiston came to fetch them from the waiting room. They followed him through the halls. He stopped outside a room. There was Sam, IVs and oxygen in his nose. Monitors beeped beside his bed.

Lewiston, who knew their history, said, "I'll leave you alone."

When they entered, Sam opened his eyes.

His pale color frightened Maggie. He looked exhausted. They sat on either side of the bed, opposite poles of a battery, Maggie holding one hand, Coral the other—as if together their energy could revitalize Sam, make him stand, sweep them off their feet, and break their hearts again.

After two attempts he spoke. "They didn't get Peter?"

"No," Maggie said.

"Good." He sighed. "They shot the hell out of me, though."

"I had no idea this would happen, Sam, I didn't," Coral said.

Sam nodded. "Not the shooting part, anyway. I know you, Coral."

"You were wonderful," Maggie said, glancing at Coral in confusion, "so wonderful."

Sam groaned and closed his eyes. For a while he didn't move as they held his hands in theirs, stared at his strong face, at his neck scarred from brawls, at the hair they'd both run their fingers through.

When he opened his eyes and smiled, Coral winked at Maggie and put on a sultry voice.

"All right, Sam. We've got you cornered now. Confess. Who do you really love? Just nod at the one."

Sam managed a chuckle. "I'm on my deathbed, Coral." He interrupted when they started to protest. "I know I'm not getting up. Besides, neither one of you wants the truth."

Maggie squeezed his hand, "Of course we do, Sam. This is the time for it."

He looked at them with such tenderness Maggie wanted to weep. Jess was gone. Now Sam was leaving, too? Why did God keep taking those she needed most?

"I love you both."

Coral rolled her eyes up. "Even now you give us Irish blarney, Sam?"

Weakly, he smiled, coughed, dug for strength. Ignoring their efforts to quiet him, he began talking non-stop. "That's the trouble with you women. If you don't like what you hear, it's a lie. If men hand you a bunch of bullshit—oh, now—that's got to be true."

"But how can you love two women?" Maggie asked, though she didn't care. He could love the whole planet, as far as she was concerned, if he just wouldn't die.

"I love half the universe," Sam said, as if reading her mind. "Old people, babies, dogs, cats. I even love teenagers—"

"Nobody loves teenagers," Coral joked.

"Sam," Maggie said, "Don't try to talk so much."

He grinned. "I won't have another chance." He paused then went on. "Peter had me with his first smile. I sure as heck love grown women knocking my eyes out as they walk down the street! I'd run after most of them, if it wouldn't get me in trouble. God, I sure tried."

"Sam," Maggie whispered, "Don't blaspheme. God is listening."

Sam coughed and Maggie could see how much it hurt him. "Yeah, I hope to have a long talk with that dude." He grew hoarse. "First question? Why make a man like me, then put him in a place where if he acts like himself, he'll go to jail?"

Coral smiled and pinched his cheek, "You're just an incurable dog, is all."

"You both know I ain't headed upstairs."

Coral said, "If you're talking about what you did when you had amnesia—"

Maggie interrupted, "We've long forgiven you, Sam."

He chuckled. "I thought we were going to tell the truth. Here, help me sit up some," he asked, and they did, adjusting his pillows, fluffing them, asking if he wanted to sip water from a straw, pulling his sheets straight, tucking him in, trying to keep out the night.

He turned toward Maggie. "Take care of Peter, my girl."

"I will, Sam, oh I will!"

He looked at Coral. "Here's the truth. I've loved no one like the two of you." He turned to Maggie. "No one. How could I give you up, either one? Maggie, you're all goodness, at least you were until you stabbed me—no you shot me; gee, I hate being shot—and, Coral, you're all heart. What's more—" he paused to take breaths. "What's more both of you are blazing hot. Coral you're honest about it; Maggie you're not. You could learn from each other. You two loved the hell out of me. You want the God's truth? I'd die for either of you." Sam coughed and closed his eyes. "And I guess I am."

His head sank so slowly back onto the pillow that it took a while for Maggie to comprehend. She didn't move until Coral screamed. Maggie pushed the call button and bolted out to get the nurse, who signaled a code blue. Instantly the room filled with hospital staff. Minutes later, or was it hours, a doctor pronounced Sam dead.

The staff pulled off their gloves and left to prepare for the next code blue.

Maggie and Coral rushed to Sam, weeping. They kissed his hands, his immobile face.

Maggie sobbed, "Oh, Coral. He's not here anymore! He's not here."

A decent interval later and a nurse ushered Maggie and Coral gently but firmly out. They found themselves on 11th Street in Greenwich Village, standing in front of the hospital's brown facade, their hearts split open, holding hands in the dark.

At first they didn't talk.

They strolled, watching the sidewalk and the buildings go by. A few blocks and Coral told Maggie about her mother's husband and how he'd made her his lover when she was eight years old. She confessed the kidnap plot, everything about Luis and Francisco. Aghast, Maggie shook her head, shedding tears. Then Coral told her about the five million dollars. She didn't ask forgiveness. Maggie didn't offer it, but she was through with hating people. *Love your enemies,* Jesus said, and Maggie would. Her grief and hate had caused this, just as much as Coral's greed.

Still they walked, pausing for Maggie to phone and check on Peter and for Coral to call Luis, who said he didn't know where Francisco was and couldn't inquire because, if he was alive, he was under arrest. Luis said he was trying to pull strings. Coral frowned at the phone.

"Do you know where Peter is?" Maggie heard the man on the phone ask. Coral told Luis she didn't. "When will you come to the penthouse?" he asked. "Tomorrow," Coral said.

They passed a food cart that steamed in the misty night. Its owner nodded to them and touched the brim of his Spiderman baseball cap. They reached a café on a corner, came to a salsa club open late, and went slowly by, listening to the music as the people danced.

Now and then they said, "You okay?" and the other answered, "Yeah, you?"

All the while they held onto each other.

They walked blocks and blocks together, and it crossed Maggie's mind that this was the first time she'd been so close to another human being, understood another person so well. They were like sisters, thinking about Sam, what he said before he died, and how they'd loved him. As long as Maggie held Coral, and Coral held her, they were in a world occupied by Sam.

So they walked, holding on, waving away taxis that—seeing them alone in the dark—stopped to offer them safety. They declined, not wanting to let go, open the taxi door, and start living in a world without Sam.

In that world, loving one another could be the second most important thing, the third, or the fourth, not the first—the only—thing, like it was for Sam.

At length it seemed to Maggie that she and Coral weren't

separate. They seemed to breathe together, sigh together, and she felt deep comfort in the closeness of another person with whom she'd shared such important things. Her thoughts lingered on this feeling, now arm-in-arm, now hand-in-hand, clasping each other's waists, their heads dropping to the other's shoulder, and not wanting to let go, though this was her rival, the woman she'd hated, the woman who'd tried to kidnap her baby, the woman who'd made her feel insecure.

It dawned on her that Coral was feeling this, too.

They didn't speak about it, but Maggie knew they were thinking the same things as they walked—how they once disliked each other but didn't anymore, and how they wanted to hold on. She knew their feelings fit this hour of their lives.

They walked themselves out of Greenwich Village and into Chelsea, Maggie more and more aware of Coral next to her. She could feel Coral in all her senses. She wondered if they would always be in each other's lives. One thing was sure; she wouldn't hurt Coral in any way now.

At last Coral spoke. "Are you trying to seduce me?"

"I don't think so," Maggie gasped, laughing. "Are you?"

"I'm not sure. Nah, you'd need a beard."

They faced each other, threw their arms around each other, and held on.

"Sam's dead," Maggie wailed.

"Oh, God," Coral moaned.

Slowly, they stepped back and let go.

Chapter 25

Luis knew exactly where Francisco was. It had cost him a half million dollars to quietly get the charges against Francisco dropped, get police removed from his hospital door, get his part in the attempted kidnapping erased, while the best doctors in New York tried to save his life. The gringa whore, Coral Anders, would never know. Francisco said she'd helped the child escape. Adios to her five million dollars.

Luis had begged Francisco not to hurt her. He wouldn't yet. He would reassure Coral, make her believe he'd lost interest in the child then use her to find it. What he'd do next, he wasn't sure. Perhaps sell her to a coyote with teeth, make her feel what his family did.

Someone knocked on Luis's bedroom door. He said, "Sí?" and the door opened.

It was Evaristo Salati who had waited in vain in the limo to receive the baby. Luis already told him there'd be a delay, perhaps a long one, but Evaristo had decided to wait.

Sitting in one of the Victorian salon chairs, Luis had drunk copious amounts of beer, anxiously flipping TV channels and silently praying to the Virgin for Francisco. In the two hours it took to find him, Luis's defenses had disappeared.

Salati had been consoling.

Luis looked away in shame as Evaristo Salati sat in the other Victorian chair.

"Is there any more news from the hospital?" Evaristo asked.

Luis tried not to sob, but Evaristo was suddenly there. Luis found himself being held by this priest who would dishonor his religious vows and shame both their manhoods.

They didn't kiss and they hadn't. There had been so sex. They just clung to each other arm in arm, chest to chest, Luis tragically repeating *ya que, ya ni modo,* in penance for rejecting that life isn't fair, and begging God that Francisco not die.

"I lied to you before," Evaristo said.

Luis didn't move. "About what?"

"I noticed you all along. In those years I visited Theomund on business, did you never suspect I was sometimes only coming to see you?"

Luis closed his eyes. "No, no, no."

Evaristo rose and strolled to the windows, looking like Rudolph Valentino.

"Have you heard this song? It was originally a poem by Walt Whitman." Salati opened his mouth and sang like a matinee idol:

> "O YOU whom I often and silently come where you are, that I may be with you;
> As I walk by your side, or sit near, or remain in the same room with you,
> Little you know the subtle electric fire that for your sake is playing within me."

It was the most gentle, touching melody Luis ever heard. It made him forget he was el pátron. If God meant for men only to love women, and for women only to love men, why put such feelings in his heart?

Evaristo whispered, "Luis, I would leave the priesthood for you. I would."

Luis forced himself not to tremble, to be like steel inside. "Come with me," he said and got up.

He took Evaristo into the salon. He showed him the statues of Aileen, Juan, Cyntia, Eduardo, and Roberto, ringed by marigolds. He played the haunting music that always brought them back into his heart.

"This is my family. They died in the desert, but they aren't the only ones. It will not stop. The immigration will not stop. No matter what laws are passed, no matter how many soldiers guard the border, or how cruel the coyotes. It cannot stop. The border is too long and my people are too poor. So many Aileens and Juans will die if we don't help them. The drug cartels and coyotes will feed on them, destroy them. So many Cyntias and Eduardos and Robertos. Surely they are worthy of life."

"So for you it's not really La Reconquista," Evaristo said, "it's the people."

"It is the people."

Evaristo made the sign of the cross before Luis's statue of the virgin and kneeled down in the marigolds.

In her foyer, beneath the painting of Fonteyn and Nureyev, Coral and Maggie hugged a final time.

"I hope you hear good news about your friend, Francisco. Even though he was after my baby, I don't want him to die."

"Haven't heard a peep, which means something's wrong, but that's my worry, not yours."

Maggie stepped back.

"When you leave," Coral said. "It's like Sam's going to die again."

"Don't I know it."

"All right. If you're determined to do this by yourself—"

"I had this baby myself; I'm going to save him by myself."

"You know where to find me if you need me."

Maggie opened the door and stepped out, Peter in the combination car seat and baby carrier. "Thank you, Coral. I guess if my husband had to be with another woman, I'm glad it was you."

Coral winked. "And if a man I loved had to marry somebody else, I'm glad it was you."

Maggie couldn't help saying, "Unlike you, Coral, I've never loved anybody else."

Coral chuckled. "Not even this fellow, Adamo, you told me about last night?"

Their temporary closeness was disappearing and they knew it.

"Thanks again, Coral. Let's leave it at that."

They were too different. Under normal circumstances they'd slap each other's faces, report each other to the police, get restraining orders, call each other a thousand bitches—the usual things women with a passionate rivalry did.

Maggie couldn't go back to hating Coral, though. She knew she'd never been in Coral's shoes.

She took the elevator down to the lobby. The Range Rover sat in the driveway, keys in the ignition, obligingly retrieved by the Porsche-stealing doorman, Chris.

Maggie opened the back door and, lying Peter down, secured the car seat then strapped him in. She got behind the wheel, being careful not to snag the soft hooded white dress Coral had let her wear. Other than her wedding dress and morning clothes, it was the most elegant thing she'd ever had on—tainted by Coral having sold her body to get it, but Maggie had nothing else to wear.

She drove to the street, Sam's unopened DNA test results in her purse. Before he died, Sam had the hospital swab his mouth so she and Peter could get on with their lives. Maggie had an appointment for them at a clinic near her church.

She would take the Hudson Parkway to the 96th Street transverse, then go left on Park Avenue to Harlem. It was on the Parkway on the night of Jess's birth that she, Sam, Felix, and Frances made their harrowing escape from Brown's men.

Her route would take her the same way: onto the 96th Street Transverse, except Maggie was coming from the south and Felix's Cliffs Landing cottage was north. She wondered if that's where Felix and his family were.

That night, Sam had almost died protecting her from Theomund Brown's men. Yesterday he'd done it again—at the cost of his life, this time. She wanted to see the Hudson River because Sam had loved it so.

At a stoplight she dialed her church.

"Ciao," Adamo answered.

For a moment Maggie wondered what the world was coming to, Italians answering phones in black churches and black women giving birth in Mexican yerberías. Maybe this was God's plan.

"Ciao, Adamo."

"Maggie? Where are you, my Maggie? Why haven't you called me? I heard that Sam died. I am so sorry for you. You must be very upset. Perhaps heartbroken. I would understand that. Did you find Peter?"

"Yes, Adamo, I did."

"Oh, this is wonderful. Mia cara, I wish you to forget that I said I would kill your husband. That was terrible of me. Imagine, killing a baby's father."

"Don't worry about it, Adamo. I'm just taking Peter to get a DNA test at the clinic near the church and—"

"Ah! I will meet you. I will go there now and be there when you arrive."

Maggie smiled. "You are a good friend, Adamo."

"I will not remind you that I love you, mia cara, because your husband has just died. It is too soon."

Maggie's voice shook, "Yes, Adamo, it's way too soon."

She hung up, having reached the 96th Street Transverse. She turned onto it and stopped at the first red light. She could almost feel Sam in the back of the car, ready to protect them. She gazed back at Peter, asleep, and lingered on the feeling that Sam was somehow near. She saw a pedestrian weaving between the stopped cars. Two of them. No, three.

Oh, no! Oh, Sam!

It was the sicarios, as Coral had called Francisco's men in contempt—the ones who'd tried to kidnap Peter.

They rushed the Range Rover and reached for her doors. Had she locked them? Frantically, Maggie operated the global door lock. Undeterred, one of the men smashed the right rear window in broad daylight and reached inside.

Peter woke, crying.

One car from the intersection and safety, Maggie shrieked and stepped on the gas. The car in front of her rocked as she bumped it. The light changed. The car moved.

Maggie sped off, but the sicario was on the mud rails. He

reached for Peter, who screamed in terror.

"Help! Help!" Maggie shouted. No one heard, she was sure. A TV show could be filming, for all anyone knew.

Sam! Sam! What do I do?

Holding the wheel, she reached back for Peter, but the man pushed her hand away.

Sam! Sam!

Wildly she stepped on the gas and by instinct veered toward a traffic light. She let the four-wheel drive take the Rover up on the curb, smashing the man between the car and the pole. He fell off, howling in agony.

Begging God's forgiveness, Maggie sped through the streets, her body shaking, her senses alert. They weren't going to stop. They were coming after her baby and they wouldn't stop until they had him. Would they even believe the DNA tests?

And what if the DNA tests proved Peter wasn't Sam's? Had Jess, with a touch, fertilized her womb, creating another miracle child? Should she even risk proving that with a test?

She couldn't live like this anymore.

As if Sam were in the car, guiding her, Maggie decided what to do. She called Adamo and when he answered, said, "I'm not coming."

"Why? What is the matter? Where are you going?"

"I'm going back."

"Where is back?"

"I'm going back to the building where I used to work." Maggie couldn't believe she'd said that. She should be going in the opposite direction, but it felt like Sam was turning the wheel.

"No!"

"You can't stop me."

"Mia cara, no!"

Maggie hung up and drove into Central Park where Peter had almost been kidnapped, where she'd given birth to Jess as Brown's men shot Sam, where she and Felix walked during the days he was extracting DNA from the Shroud of Turin. She drove near a remaining marker for the old Boston Road. Logic said she should be escaping, like the slaves once did. What was leading her back to Fifth Avenue? Maggie parked at the curb in front of Felix's building. When the doorman rushed up, objecting, she told him she was here to see Luis.

He opened the car door for her then. She unbuckled Peter and took him in her arms. On the red carpet, beneath the green awning, the doorman preceded her to the heavy glass door and opened it by its brass handle. Maggie descended the marble stairs into the building where she'd worked for Felix. It felt empty, now. She could tell from the air that the Rossi's were gone, that Sam Duffy wasn't here—good-hearted, wise, a rascal to the death, but loving, so loving.

Maggie gazed at herself and Peter in the floor-to-ceiling mirrors, knowing the building guards were looking back, alerting the penthouse occupant that she was here. Was she a Black Madonna holding a sacred child, or was Peter just a baby and she just a maid who'd once rented her womb to a mad scientist?

In her soft, hooded white dress, she felt like a glamorous Joan of Arc—ready for the bonfire, and to Maggie that was okay. Twelve years ago, she'd gazed in this mirror, proud of her brand new Graham Smith hat. She'd gazed in this mirror in her black veil when Jess died. It felt okay to be looking in this mirror, at what could be the end of her life.

Peter, nestled in her arms, kicked his chubby baby feet, trying to grab a big button on the front of her dress. When he couldn't reach it, he fretted and Maggie rocked him, humming, "O Sole Mio," Adamo's song.

She saw the *L* light up above the elevator.

"Mia cara," someone said.

She turned and there was Adamo, his warm smile and carefree manner replaced by a look of horror. How had he gotten here so fast?

"Come from here, my Maggie! I beg you!"

"No Adamo."

Her heart was throbbing like thunder, her eyes were weeping like the rain. "Jess is with me. Sam is with me. God is with me. Yea though I walk through the valley of the shadow of death."

The elevator came. She stepped inside.

Adamo entered behind her. "I am with you, too."

They held hands as the elevator ascended.

When the doors opened, Luis Moctezuma stood there, gems and jewels and crystals shining from backlit cubicles on the foyer wall. He had boots on his feet, a fancy sash at his waist, a silver knife in his hand.

"If you make a move, señor, I will slice her face," Luis said.

Peter fretted.

"Let go of her hand!" Luis ordered.

Adamo didn't.

"Step out, Maggie Duffy. You, señor, stay there, unless you want to see her die." He pointed the knife between Maggie's eyes.

Adamo let go. Maggie stepped out.

Holding the knife on Maggie, Luis leaned inside the elevator and pushed the lobby button.

The doors closed. Adamo was gone.

Luis gazed wide-eyed at Peter. "*¡Gracias a Dios! Aquí está el niño.*"

Terrified, Maggie cried, "Speak English!"

Luis scowled at her. "Yes, that is the cry of the gringos, 'Speak English! Bow down to us!' What if we said to you, 'Speak Spanish, Señora Duffy'?"

"What?" she said in disbelief. "At a time like this, you're complaining to me about a language I didn't pick, any more than you picked Spanish?"

"My blood is mixed!"

"Huh? Well, so is mine!"

Luis sniffed. "I see why there is conflict between Mexican-Americans and African-Americans."

"There is?" Maggie said. "Nobody told me about it. People are people. Come to think of it, whatever problem you've got about Mexico, I might have a similar one about Africa." She tried to smile. "Maybe we can talk about it."

"*¡Mujer estúpida!* Give me the child," Luis said, his silver knife aimed at her heart as if he were about to cut it out.

Maggie held Peter closer.

"Give me the child!"

"Why?" she screamed. "Why, why, why?"

He gave a wry smile. "It's for La Reconquista, if you must know. Hand me the child!"

"The recon what? You used to be the butler here. What is going on?"

Luis trembled, mumbled words she didn't understand. Swiftly he stepped closer, put his hand under Peter, and struck her with the handle of the knife. She felt the side of her head explode in pain, saw white light, but she didn't fall. Maggie only staggered and gripped Peter, who wailed in fear.

Luis put the knife to her throat. "Give him to me or I'll take your life! I will not let one person stop me from saving my people!"

"Saving your people?" Maggie said, gasping. "Go ahead, then. Do it. I can't take no more of this. God didn't mean for me to be a mother, that's plain as day. I'm not arguing with God anymore and I'm not running from you anymore!"

Luis raised his eyebrows and pointed the knife at Peter's throat.

Sobbing, Maggie cried, "When you kill him, kill me, too. I can't survive losing a child again. I can't survive it. Kill us both at the same time. Go ahead and do it!"

"You dare to think you are the Madonna?" Luis shouted. "You are not! You are just another whore!"

He reached out and tore at Maggie's soft white gown, pulling it from her body. She held onto Peter as Luis ripped the dress away, until she stood in her white slip, which was over her white, firm-control brassiere and white panties that came up to the waist.

Luis backed up and burst out laughing, holding the knife.

Was he evil or crazy? Desperate, Maggie looked up to Luis's ceiling and began to pray. "God, it's me, Maggie. Are you listening?"

Luis laughed louder.

"Hear me in my hour of need. It's your servant, Maggie Duffy, and I need your help. I am asking. …"

"Shut up!" Luis yelled.

"I am seeking. …"

"Quiet, I said!"

"I am knocking on your door. I am asking you to save Peter, my son. Whether or not he's another Jesus, he's just a little boy."

"Are you going to shut up or not?"

"I believe in you. I have always believed. Even at this moment, I feel you in my heart."

Luis sneered. "I can tell you what you are, Señora Duffy. You are a stuuu-pid woman! You wear silly underwear! And, Señora, you are ugly, very ugly, did you know that? Probably no one tells you to keep from hurting your feelings."

"God, it's Maggie Duffy. I am asking, I am seeking, I am begging! Move a mountain for me, now!"

Luis chuckled, "You are perhaps the most stupid woman I have ever known. You brought this on yourself. How dare you claim to be what you are not? Your son is just one boy among millions who have no chance to stay alive, much less play hoaxes on the public. My people need your son. You will give him to me."

"Move a mountain. Please!"

Maggie wasn't sure what happened next, but it seemed to her that the air filled with the scent of roses. She looked around the room to find the source of the scent, feeling like Juan Diego on the Tepeyac mountain when the Lady of Guadalupe created roses for him.

She knew Luis gasped. Then the room somehow filled with light. She knew Luis dropped his knife and fell to his knees, tears suddenly streaming down his face. Then he spoke in Spanish again.

"*Nuestra Señora de Guadalupe!*" he cried.

The next part was even weirder. He said, "Lady, I am Luis, your humble servant. You have blessed me by appearing."

His eyes looked so strange, Maggie waved her hand in front of them, but he didn't react. Whatever he was seeing, wasn't her.

Then to her shock, Luis bent low and kissed her feet.

Maggie stared at him, eyes wide, and decided this was a good time to leave.

She moved toward the elevator, but Luis followed on his knees like the pilgrims Teresita had described, his expression blissful, no bitterness or danger in his eyes. She pushed the elevator button, Luis still on his knees—moving as if he weighed nothing, as if he knelt on air instead of the hard floor of Brown's foyer, carrying on a conversation with whomever he thought she was. It was in Spanish so she couldn't make it out.

He clasped his hands in prayer then touched them to her feet.

Thankfully the elevator came quicker than usual and Maggie got on. Luis tried to come, too, but she decided that wasn't a good idea. In what she hoped was a scary voice, Maggie shouted, "No!" and held up her palm.

Luis backed up and put his face on the floor like a man whose soul had been saved. As the elevator doors closed, he rose and spread his arms wide, saying, "Gracias, gracias, gracias Señora!" Maggie wanted to weep at his devotion, but she didn't. She needed to see.

Instead, she said, "Thank you, thank you, thank you, God," all the way down.

Adamo was there when she reached the lobby and so were the police. He'd called them. They'd said they weren't about to burst into Luis Moctezuma's home for no reason. Did Adamo have proof that a woman and baby were being held against their will? Furthermore, was it an American citizen reporting this alleged crime? Where were Adamo's visa, passport or immigration papers?

That's when Maggie came.

They saw her and respectfully asked if she was all right.

She said, "I'm fine."

They didn't stop her when she took Adamo's arm. With Peter in her other arm, Maggie went outside and on the building's red carpet breathed New York's air.

She noticed that passerby gawked, no doubt wondering if this would end up on the evening news. They weren't used to seeing a woman standing on this part of Fifth Avenue in just a white slip.

"Wait here," the doorman said and went to fetch the Range Rover from the tenants parking garage where he'd put it.

All the while, Adamo kept watch on anyone who approached. Soon the car pulled up.

Maggie touched Adamo's beautiful mustache. "I'm glad you came for us."

He said, "I love you, mia cara. I will wait for the day when you love me, too."

Peter cooed and Maggie kissed him.

The kings of her heart were dead; long live the kings.

Epilogue

Three years later at a ranch in Michoacan, Francisco walked his newest Azteca mare. He'd bred her with a prize stallion from another ranch and now she was in the first stage of labor.

"It's all right, Sleeping Beauty. It's all right," he murmured to the horse.

From the main house came a Mexican serenade, "Le Feria de las Flores," The Flower Fair. A pregnant woman came out and called to him, her hand on her back. She was the flower he had transplanted to the garden of his house.

"Francisco, it's your mother on the phone."

His mother hadn't come to their wedding. According to family whispers, he'd married a mujer putita, a gringa whore.

The woman called, "She says she wants to be here when her first grandson is born. What shall I tell her?"

Francisco smiled at Coral. "It is up to you."

She stood for a moment in thought and then decided not to hold a grudge. "Let her come."

Francisco nodded.

On the porch behind Coral, their red-haired daughter played. "Mommy, Daddy when is my brother going to come?"

"Soon, preciosa," he called.

Francisco watched Coral pick up the child. No one had to do a DNA test to know who her father was. When she was born, Francisco refused to see or speak to Coral for three days. Then he returned and signed the birth certificate. He told his family that until they accepted his wife and daughter, they weren't welcome at the Michoacan ranch.

He watched Coral kiss the red-haired girl they'd named Samantha Miguel in honor of both her fathers.

The Vatican was dismayed at the loss of Evaristo Cardinal Salati, whom many considered its prince. Shortly after he left, a great philanthropic organization, Milagro de la Virgen, Miracle of the Madonna, was formed, though no one knew the identity of the owners. At each of its many USA locations, it offered free English classes to Latino immigrants and expensive Spanish classes to gringos with sense enough to take them.

In Mexico, guarded by a band of Francisco's gente, Milagro de la Virgen pursued ambitious long-term goals, the first of which was persuading rich and poor alike that the dying could end and the living could start. It sought to thwart the systemic corruption that held up the drug cartels and weighed down the economy. It promoted growth, so Mexicans didn't have to steal across the border to stay alive.

Milagro de la Virgen encouraged Mexico to think of tomorrow while honoring the past, confront the negative self-images the conquistadors left, and at last take the government's boot off the peoples' neck.

It took three months for the press to lose interest in the Yerbería Guadalupe. Teresita didn't mind because a man on a bike delivered a large envelope with no note or return address, but stuffed with cash.

Maggie Clarissa Johnson Duffy Morelli never had a DNA test done. She, Adamo, and Peter disappeared. Some say they live in a different villa on the shore of another of Italy's vast and beautiful northern lakes.

— THE END —

About the Author

J R Lankford is the author of the scientific-religious thriller *The Jesus Thief*, which BOOKLIST called "great stuff" in a starred review. Published in 2003, it was nominated for awards, translated into multiple languages, optioned for film, and used in college courses such as "Genetics in Literature" at Copenhagen University. Next in the series was *The Secret Madonna* in 2008. Lankford lives in Texas where she continues work on the next book.

IN MEMORY OF my brother, John Porter Rhines, operatic tenor, lifelong friend, and confidante, who helped with all my books because he was the soul of kindness and so smart. Save a seat for me in the choir, John.

Much gratitude to my invaluable first readers, Frank Lankford and Chuck Schwager, who comment on initial drafts of *The Jesus Thief* series chapters as I write them. José Rodea and Becky Soria gave wonderful feedback and corrected my Spanish mistakes. Any remaining errors concerning the language or culture of Mexico are entirely mine. Special appreciation as always to the incomparable members of NovelPro, the online workshop I founded. Critiques from these talented authors help me shape subsequent drafts.

I would not be a writer were it not for my late parents — Jacinto Aneille Rhines, Sr. whose spirit has been with me since he left this earth when I was four, his first novel unfinished; and poet Julia Watson Barbour, who filled our home with books, my mind with ideas, and my heart with love until she died in 2006.

Frank Lankford picked up where they left off, faithfully supporting me with the latest computers and supplies, with research trips abroad and reference materials, long before I'd published a single line. Forever isn't long enough to thank you, Frank.

JRL/2012

www.ingramcontent.com/pod-product-compliance
Lightning Source LLC
LaVergne TN
LVHW091048080826
845145LV00002B/668